DEATH OF A MAMA'S BOY

A LYDIA BARNWELL MYSTERY

JAMES H LEWIS

DEATH OF A MAMA'S BOY

by James H Lewis

CHAPTER ONE

MARTY SULLIVAN WAITED weeks for someone to die. Not just anyone. Someone important, either revered or feared. When Alberta Allen's heart attacked her, he saw his chance. Bert, as she was known, had served as principal of the middle school for over two decades. He'd attended there, and his mother had taught history. Everyone knew her. The whole town would turn out for her service and, more significant to the young man's plan, her viewing.

Marty arrived at the funeral home at seven wearing his one suit, which he'd bought for his graduation. In the ensuing years as a roofer and handyman, he'd put on muscle. He felt trapped inside the jacket and would be glad when he'd accomplished his mission and could return it to his closet.

First, however, were the obligatory expressions of regret. He took his place among the mourners as they inched their way through the receiving line. While he recognized many of those around him, none seemed to recall him, which was just fine. When he reached the family, he muttered a few words to Bert's two sons, who he knew, and her daughter, whom he did not. None gave any sign of recognition. "So sorry for your loss," he said to each of them, an endless mantra repeated at the reception for his own mother five months before.

Others passed by the casket, peering at the waxen face of the woman they'd known, but he backed away. It seemed a pagan ritual. Whoever had inhabited that body was gone. Did they need to gape at her shell? What were they thinking? Were they grateful they weren't inside the box?

"How're you doing?" Jerry Mullins, one of his high school friends, blocked his way as he tried to leave the room. They'd served together on the track team before Marty had quit, but hadn't seen each other in years.

"Fine," he said. "I'm good."

"I was sorry you lost your own mom not too long ago."

"Yes," he said. Marty wasn't sure how to react. Should he thank the man? All he wanted to do was get out of here undetected.

"Is Dora here?" Jerry asked.

Marty gave him a blank look. "I don't know. I haven't seen her."

"Well," Jerry said, looking past him for a way to escape, "take care."

"You, too." Marty waited until he'd moved on. He looked around him, but no one seemed to notice the man with the ascetic features and the head of thin brown hair, growing sparse at the crown.

He retreated along the hallway, peering into darkened parlors, putting on a show of curiosity in case anyone noticed him. Pushing open the double doors beneath the exit sign at the end of the corridor, he found himself alongside an elevator leading to the rooms in the lower level where bodies were embalmed, their hair arranged and makeup applied to make them look better than they had in life. He crept down the flight of stairs, which doubled back halfway down.

The preparation rooms were to his right, but Marty's interest lay elsewhere. With his phone's flashlight illuminating the hallway, he passed two restrooms until he found what looked like a utility closet. Opening the door, he trained his beam on a furnace and air conditioning unit and, against a back wall, the breaker box and control panel for the alarm system. He knew it was an older model, having examined the building permits at the town office.

Marty switched on the overhead light, draping his jacket across the doorsill to prevent a shaft betraying his presence. He pried open the panel and studied the wiring, satisfied it was identical to the schematic he'd found online. Taking a narrow plastic case from the coat's breast pocket— he'd worn the hated suit only to conceal his tools—he fitted one of the small drivers to an aluminum handle, then donned a pair of thin rubber gloves.

After disabling the power to the console, he unscrewed the system's back plate and disconnected the wires to both the main and backup batteries. Finally, he reassembled the unit, examining it to ensure he'd left no sign of tempering. His task finished, he turned off the light and listened at the door before stepping into the hallway.

Marty crept upstairs to join the stragglers who milled around the reception area, as though waiting for something to happen. Bert Adams' children chatted with those they knew. If their experience was like his own months before, they wished everyone would leave.

No one paid him any attention. He left the room and turned toward the entrance. A few people were leaving, and he held the door for them, allowing his eyes to fall to the lock. As they departed, he examined it from the other side. A smirk tugged at his mouth. It would present no problem. He'd opened doors far more complex.

Whoever tried to arm the system tonight would be unable to do so. They'd call the security company in the morning, but would be told it would be at least two days before they could send someone out to diagnose the issue. One of his customers had just gone through this.

Tomorrow night, he'd make his move. Bert Allen's funeral at All Saints would be over, her body lowered at St. Mary's, and the mortuary would be closed. He would return to exact his revenge.

ALLEGHENY COUNTY POLICE detective Lydia Barnwell took a deep breath as the prosecutor finished eliciting her testimony and turned her over to the defense counsel. Damien Goddard was a tall, wiry Black man with a full head of hair and trimmed goatee, a dark blue suit gathered at the waist in the newest style, and a reputation for eviscerating white police officers testifying against minority defendants, which was the case here.

"Ms. Barnwell," he said, acknowledging her without using her title, also part of his act. He turned and faced the jury with a smile that conveyed the message, "Watch this!"

"You testified that when the Wilkinsburg police force arrested three young men on charges of stealing an automobile, they brought you in to investigate. Why did they find that necessary?"

Lydia, dressed in gray slacks, a dark brown blazer, and a white blouse, open only at the collar, did not hesitate. "The county is charged with investigating all major crimes, including armed robbery, grand theft auto, homicides, and—"

"But the local police made the arrests. Why did they need you?"

"Three men fled the car," she said. "They called us in to determine who was driving."

"And so they chose you," Goddard said.

"I was assigned to the case."

"How long have you been a county detective?"

"For five months, but prior to that—"

"Five months as a detective," he said. "And during that time, in how many automobile thefts have you been the lead investigator?"

"This is my first, but I've worked—"

"A brand new detective," Goddard said, angling his body toward the jury box, "working her first investigation of this type."

"Objection," the assistant DA said. "Detective Barnwell has—"

"Overruled," the judge broke in. "You'll have your chance on redirect."

The lawyer smirked, a reaction meant for the seven men and five women on the panel, half of whom were Black. "Three young people were in that car. Wilkinsburg police claim they caught them after they fled. Is that not correct?"

"It is." Barnwell knew from experience to keep her responses brief and to the point. She'd tried to clarify three answers so far and been shut down on two of them. The jury must not see her as argumentative.

"When you questioned the three boys, they denied having anything to do with the theft. Is that not correct?"

She longed to correct the impression he was creating that the thieves were mere teenagers, out for a joyride. If they hadn't reached eighteen years of age, they would have been in juvenile court. "It is," she said.

"How long did you question them?"

"Initially, for an hour each."

"But after that. You spoke to two of the boys for over two hours, didn't you?"

"My partner and I did." Detective Lyle Jeffrey had also been present during the interviews, but had not been called to testify.

"And then what happened?"

"Two admitted their involvement."

"And they pointed to my client as the ringleader, didn't they? They insisted they were just along for the ride. It was all Theo Moseley's doing. Isn't that what they told you?"

"They testified he'd stolen the car," she said. Seeing where this was headed, Lydia added, "but they were willing participants."

"And my client, young Theo here, continues to maintain his innocence, doesn't he?"

"He does."

"These two young men—" he began. *Ah, yes,* she thought. *The other two are grown men.* "—the ones who fingered Theo, they're white, aren't they?"

She struggled to avoid frowning in reaction to the intended slur on her reputation. "Objection," the prosecutor roared. "This is immaterial and irrelevant."

"Sustained," the judge said. "Mr. Goddard, you've established no basis for this line of questioning."

"I apologize, your honor."

"The jury will disregard this question." *Sure they will,* Barnwell thought. *You've given half of them reason to doubt the clear evidence. You think at least one won't be swayed by that?*

"I have no more questions of this rookie detective," Goddard said.

The assistant DA rose to her feet. "I have questions on redirect," she said. Barnwell watched as the prosecutor shuffled her papers, trying to decide which parts of the damage to undo. She knew she wouldn't touch the racial issue. The judge had ruled it out of order, and to question Lydia about anything touching on the subject would not only emphasize it, but allow Goddard to reopen the wound on redirect.

She had Barnwell review what they'd already established, that the prints of all three men were found in the stolen vehicle, and that those of Theo Mosely were on the steering wheel. Then she asked what Barnwell had done before joining the ACPD.

"I spent three years with the Boyleston Police Department," Lydia said.

"What was your rank when you joined the force?"

"Patrol officer."

"And when you left?"

"I was a detective."

"So you were promoted during your time there. How did that come about?"

Lydia explained she'd studied for the detective exam and passed it with the highest marks of anyone taking the test that round. "But passing the exam doesn't make you a detective, does it? What led to your promotion?"

"I uncovered evidence that solved a murder."

"In so doing, what else happened?"

"Oh, you mean—" Lydia began. "It was a twenty-year-old case. Someone had already been charged and convicted of it. He'd been sentenced to death."

The prosecutor faced the jury as she spoke. "So your

investigation into an old murder case freed an innocent man?"

"Yes."

"How many other homicide cases have you been involved in?"

"Three others," Lydia said, "two since I joined the county. I led the team investigating the death of a man who'd bilked five women out of thousands of dollars. As we developed evidence, one suspect died. It was meant to look like suicide, but we proved it a homicide."

"Were these committed by the same individual?"

"No. There were two separate killers."

"And you identified both killers?" she asked.

"We did."

"And when was this?"

"Three months ago."

"Would you call yourself an experienced investigator?"

Lydia looked toward the jury. "I'd like to think so," she said. "I received a commendation for my work on these cases."

"Thank you, detective."

Lydia stood down, proud of her performance, but seething that the defense attorney had dragged race into the case. She glared at him, her intense blue eyes which had disarmed so many reluctant witnesses drilling into him as she left the courtroom.

"HE KNEW WHAT HE WAS DOING." Lydia threw a knotted towel into the sink as she yelled loud enough for neighbors to hear. "He's tainted the jury pool." Calvin Mayfield, Lydia's boyfriend, sat at the kitchen counter, listening to her diatribe. "Aren't you going to say anything?" she asked. She tossed her head with such vehemence that her tight, blond curls pranced across it, threatening to gallop off.

"I was waiting for you to finish." Mayfield was chief of police of Boyleston Borough, the small force Lydia had served until her transfer to ACPD earlier in the year. He looked up at her, taking her in with his brown eyes, and said, "He was doing his job. He uses that trick whenever he faces a white officer. You knew that going in."

"He accused me of racism." Howie, her West Highland terrier, stared up at her, then turned his attention to her partner.

Mayfield sighed and shook his head, allowing his beer's carbonation to bubble off. "I understand why you're angry. You have a right to be. But he uses it because there's a long history of white cops grabbing the nearest Black man to close their case. Even here in Pittsburgh." He draped the last few words in sarcasm.

She looked out the window toward the garden. The evening sun painted her hydrangeas a flaming orange. Her neighbor, Anna Molnar, had helped her conceal the green beans, lettuce, and zucchini behind a wall of rosemary and marigolds to discourage the deer, who roamed the neighborhood as though they owned it. Which they once had, now that she thought about it. "You know what really pisses me off? The jury will release Theo Mosely."

"You can't be certain of that," he said.

"I am. I saw the looks on their faces as I left the stand. Goddard's little stunt worked. Mosely will be back on the street tomorrow afternoon and will probably heist another car before the day's out."

Mayfield made a low moaning sound, accepting her

analysis. "I hope you're mistaken, but there's nothing you can do about it."

Lydia turned toward the range, removed a pot of steaming water, and strained the contents through a colander in the sink. She scraped clams out of a plastic container into a sauté pan in which she'd heated minced garlic, stirred the mixture long enough to warm them, and returned the linguine to the sauce. Only when she'd split the dish between two bowls and topped it with freshly squeezed lemon just and parsley from her garden did she say, "I know."

She poured herself a glass of wine and offered one to Mayfield. "I'll stick with the beer," he said.

She piled into the still steaming dish, closed her eyes as she enjoyed the fragrance, and polished it off with a sip of Sauvignon blanc.

"What will you do now?" Calvin asked.

"I've meant to clean out the attic ever since I bought this place. In another week, it'll get too hot to work up there."

"I wish I could help," he said, explaining he had a meeting in the morning. Boyleston was merging its police departments to create a regional force. He'd been chosen to lead it. "I'm tied up until noon, but after that, I'm your man."

LYDIA HAD BOUGHT the house as soon as she joined Allegheny County. This was the first time she'd owned anything more than a used car. After years of moving from military base housing to one rental after another, having her own place gave her a sense of permanence. She hadn't bought the narrow, two-story house just for herself, however. After her former lover, David Kimrey, had died during a domestic dispute, his father had willed her David's dog, a West Highland terrier named Howie. The animal had been in depression after his owner's death, and something about his estranged girlfriend brought him back to life. After first resisting the offer, she'd relented, adopting Howie. The house had followed, then Calvin. She not only had a home, but the beginnings of a family.

After Calvin left the following morning, she went to work. A door in the spare bedroom opened onto a stairway to the attic. She dressed in jeans, a heavy long-sleeve cotton shirt, a baseball cap, and a pair of leather gloves. Although she'd detected no nighttime scampering, she worried about what she might find up there. She also toted an LED lantern, but was surprised to find a light switch at the base of the stairs. When she flipped it on, a bulb lit up the staircase, another illuminated the rafters overhead, and a roaring sound assaulted her. It took her a moment to identify the noise as an attic fan, which pulled air from the second floor, ruffling her curls.

Howie followed her to the base of the stairs, but she ordered him to remain behind to avoid tripping over him. The first object she found was a drop leaf dining table covered by a quilted cover of the type used by moving companies. A lamp and a box of decorative glass globes lay atop it. She carried them down to the bedroom, placed them on the floor, and returned. She'd wait for Calvin to help move the table.

A rattan bassinet stood in a corner, its white paint chipping off the reeds. She could carry it downstairs herself, but as she picked it up, she was enveloped in a cloud of dust that gave her a sneezing fit. *This may not be my best idea.*

But she'd begun the task. She wasn't about to quit now.

Taking the rickety stairs one at a time, she moved an array of items into the spare bedroom until she could find no more room. Piles of newspapers and magazines stood against one corner of the roof; it took her four trips to carry it all to the back porch, where she'd recycle them. *A fire waiting to happen. Why did they leave all this?*

She stopped for lunch, and Calvin joined her. They began lugging items from the bedroom down to the dining room. "What are we going to do with all this stuff?" he asked.

She replied with an involuntary shrug. "I have no idea." She'd only planned to empty the attic, not what to do with what she found there.

"Let's call Vietnam Veterans," he said. "They pick things up and sell anything of value."

Lydia agreed. "There's one item I want to keep, though. Help me move this table."

Mayfield followed her up the stairs, Howie trailing along behind them, but halted as his owners ascended into the attic. "Place it in that bare corner of the living room. We can put plants and books and stuff on it."

Calvin cleared his throat, ready to argue the point, but gave up, knowing he wouldn't win this one. He picked up one end and she the other, but as they began moving it to the top of the stairs, he stumbled over something and dropped the table to the floor. "What the...?"

He grabbed a canvas duffle bag that had been shoved beneath the table and cast it aside. Backing down the stairs one at a time, calling out each step to Lydia, he maneuvered the table through a path they'd cleared in the bedroom. After taking a slight break, they carried it to the ground floor, placing it in the space she had selected.

Dusting off her hands, she said, "I'll cover it with a tablecloth and put a lamp on this end."

"It's in remarkable condition," Mayfield said, expressing grudging approval to what she envisioned.

She spent another hour cleaning and dusting the attic while he filled plastic bags with dirt and debris. As he hauled the vacuum down the flight of stairs one last time, Lydia carried the canvas bag over which he'd stumbled, placing it on her kitchen counter while he took out the trash. He settled before the TV to catch the last two innings of the Pirates game. She opened the duffle bag, ignoring its musty smell. Inside, she found a drawstring sack whose contents rattled as she lifted it out. It held a cloth cosmetics pouch, whose daisy applique had faded like fall leaves, and a purse.

She set the latter aside for a moment and opened the drawstring sack, withdrawing a handful of costume jewelry, silver earrings that fastened to the earlobe with a set screw, a necklace with a strand of cultured pearls, and a host of small pins that featured everything from inlaid designs to Eastern Star rhinestones. Someone might like these, she thought, but to her they were just junk. The cosmetics bag contained tubes of dried lipstick and a powder compact. Lydia didn't understand why any woman would have kept them, much less stored them in the attic.

She reached for the purse, a bright yellow frame bag whose bottom was wider than the top, giving it a trapezoidal shape. Its jaws were secured with a kiss lock. She first took the exterior to be faux leather, but on examination realized it was the real thing. She found nothing inside but a tag reading Morris White. The label meant nothing to her, but the purse, she told herself, was both old and new, in that it did not appear to have ever been used. Its leather was dry, but otherwise in good condition. Had the attic fan circulated enough air to help preserve it? Perhaps she could restore its luster with leather balm.

Strange, she thought, that the woman had taken an attractive handbag, probably costing a good amount at the time of purchase, and stored it in an attic. Deciding it might be worth something, she put it aside and went upstairs to take a shower.

OFFICER KAY INGRAM jostled the front door of the tavern, making certain it was locked. As she walked through the narrow parking lot toward the rear of the building, her flashlight caught a reflection. The officer leaned over and examined a hypodermic needle. She fetched a pair of puncture proof gloves from her cruiser, brought a disposal kit back to the lot, and placed the needle into the plastic container.

You could at least clean up after yourself, she thought as she returned to her vehicle. Etna, a small borough along the north bank of the Allegheny River, was no stranger to drug use. Named for the Sicilian volcano to honor the blast furnaces that had once dominated the town, Etna was reinventing itself as a family-friendly community. Unlike much of Allegheny County, the average age of the borough's four thousand residents was declining as young families took advantage of the low cost of housing and the proximity to the urban core. It was a decent place to live, and Officer Ingram was distressed to see evidence of open narcotics use. Her immediate concern was not finding the user, but keeping youngsters from finding the needle.

Retracing her steps through the parking lot, she tried the tavern's back door and, as expected, found it locked. She continued up Mount Royal Boulevard, Etna's main drag, and checked both front and rear doors to the local hardware store. It was a quiet weekday evening, one of the last few days of spring, and a breeze off the river helped cool the warm air trapped beneath the layer of clouds. A few cars whizzed by, ignoring the twenty-five mile-per-hour speed limit. She passed a group of teenagers wandering up the street with nowhere to go and nothing on their minds except enjoying the freedom of being out of school.

"Hi, officer," one girl said as they moved past.

"Evening, Morgan," she replied.

They giggled after they'd passed by, as though they'd gotten away with something. And perhaps they had. Did their parents know they were out on the street at this hour?

Her next stop was Tomas Sedlak and Sons, the local funeral home. Tomas was long gone, as were his sons, replaced by grandsons and granddaughters, but the name of the venerable institution was unchanged. Officer Ingram turned the door handle. To her surprise, it gave way. She considered what to do. Perhaps the owners had forgotten to lock up.

She could step inside, engage the lock, and return the next day to advise them to be more careful, but her training kicked in. The entrance was supposed to be secured. Ingram couldn't ignore it.

She was alone. The Etna police department comprised the chief, six full-time officers, and two part-timers. Not enough personnel for two-person overnight shifts. Whenever Etna needed back-up, it called on Millvale, the adjoining borough, an arrangement that worked both ways. Kay now spoke into her shoulder-mounted speaker-microphone to summon help. Five minutes later, Officer Ken Pollard, a veteran cop with twenty years of experience and a gut to match, arrived. He ran his hands through his non-existent hair and listened as she explained the situation.

"Probably nothing," she said.

"But we should check," he finished for her. "Let's go in and turn on the lights to make sure nothing's been disturbed, lock the door, and leave. We'll have checked the place, right?"

While she felt something more than a cursory inspection was called for, the older officer had taken charge. Swallowing her reservations, she agreed. Pollard opened the door and fumbled for the light switch. "Where is the damn thing?" he muttered.

Ingram swept her flashlight along the walls until she found a switch, revealing a reception area painted in a light rose color. Bulbs concealed in silver-colored sconces provided illumination. A long hallway stretched before them. "That's where the chapel and viewing rooms are," Pollard whispered. To the right, a small room lay behind a pair of doors. Its glass panes revealed three comfortable chairs nestled around a table, a box of facial tissue at its center. A heavy wooden door across the foyer concealed another room. She assumed this was the office.

"Everything seems copacetic," he said. "Satisfied?"

"We should check the chapel," Ingram said.

Pollard shrugged. "Your call." He followed her down the hallway, standing behind her as she opened the chapel door. Her fingers found the light switch, and as she eased the sliders up, the small room was bathed in soft light from outlets concealed by the crown moulding. Three pews faced an altar and an open space where the casket containing the remains of the departed was displayed during services. She peered under the back pew while the older officer chuckled to himself. "Satisfied?" he repeated.

"I suppose so." She backed out and extinguished the lights. As they retreated up the hallway, they heard a thump from somewhere beneath them. The officers looked at each other and, without a word, turned toward a pair of double doors at the end. Their flashlights revealed a flight of stairs that doubled back at a landing. They crept down, Ingram wincing at the other officer's heavy tread.

They faced a pair of swinging metal doors with small glass windows similar to those leading from a restaurant into its kitchen. Standing to one side with Pollard opposite her, Ingram eased the right door open. She spotted movement. Certain it was not an illusion created by light streaming in from the stairwell, she pointed at a coffin in the middle of the room, one of six on display from which the bereaved might choose.

Using hand motions, Kay Ingram outlined what she proposed, and the other officer nodded agreement. They advanced on the coffin, both holding flashlights, Pollard's in his left hand and his revolver in his right. She moved behind the casket while he stood before it. She reached over the top with both hands and pulled at the lid.

The coffin flew open. A figure sprang out like a jack-in-the-box, barreling into Pollard, who dropped both his torch and his weapon.

Ingram released her grip on the lid. Pollard called out in pain, but she paid no attention, chasing the retreating figure as he tore up the stairs and through a back door. It didn't register that the alarm had failed to go off as she pursued the intruder. "Stop!" she yelled. "Police!"

The man didn't pause, running across the loading dock and jumping into the alley. She chased through the darkened neighborhood for five blocks, weaving between side streets and another alley. Kay considered himself a decent runner, but he left her behind. Wheezing, leaning forward with her hands on her knees, she spoke aloud. "Now, what was *that* about?"

Allegheny County has 118 municipalities— cities, boroughs, and townships—101 of which maintain police departments. The rest are patrolled by neighboring communities, three regional law enforcement agencies, or the Pennsylvania State Police. The Allegheny County Police Department rises above this hodgepodge, providing investigative services to the smaller towns and handling all serious crimes, such as homicide, outside the City of Pittsburgh. Although the break-in at the Sedlak Funeral Home wasn't a major crime, Officer Ingram requested ACPD assistance. Lydia Barnwell took the call from the dispatcher at 1:05 a.m., was out the door at 1:22, and arrived in her cruiser at 1:45. Ingram greeted her and apologized for the early morning call.

"That's all right," Barnwell replied. "I'm a light sleeper." On most nights, she had nothing to drink, and when she did, she limited herself to one beer or glass of wine. Even after three hours of rest, she awoke grouchy but clear-headed. Ingram led her through what had transpired. "Hiding in a casket?" she said.

"Yeah. As we entered the room downstairs, I thought I saw the lid close, so we tried to surprise whoever was hiding inside. He got the better of us, jumping out as I pulled the top open and knocking Officer Pollard over." She nodded toward an overweight uniformed officer sprawled in a chair like a discarded rag doll.

"I must have interrupted him when I first tried the front

door. He may have crept down the stairs while I awaited back-up, hoping I'd make just a cursory check."

"Can you describe him?"

"I only caught a glimpse from behind, but he's a white male, youngish—mid-twenties. He's taller than me, 5-10 to six feet at most, and slender. I'd put him at 160 to 170 pounds, but don't hold me to it. He wore jeans, a long-sleeve Steelers t-shirt, but no cap, and a pair of trainers."

Barnwell was impressed by the thoroughness of her description, given the circumstances. "I think he had light brown hair," she added, "but the light wasn't too good. I'm an okay runner, but he outdid me."

"How did he get in?"

"We don't know. There's no sign of forced entry. I haven't looked too closely, though. I'll leave that to the crime lab."

Barnwell noticed she'd donned plastic gloves. This officer knew her business. "Any idea what he was after?"

"None. I can't imagine they keep drugs in a funeral home, at least not the sort you'd want to take." She allowed herself a smile. "I peeked inside the office. Nothing seems out of place, but I've alerted the director. His wife says he's on his way."

They heard a vehicle enter the parking lot. Both women stepped outside as a man emerged from a black Escalade. He walked toward them with his head pushed forward, as though battling a headwind.

"Dan Sedlak," he said as the officers introduced themselves. He was in his late forties with thick, salt-and-pepper hair combed back from his forehead. Lydia found him handsome in a rugged way, heavy features in a lean face, giving him a look of authority. He was dressed in a gray suit with a white shirt and pale blue tie. She wondered if he'd taken time to shave, since she'd driven from Carnegie, yet arrived before he had. His brows were knitted in concern as he looked from one of them to the other. "What's happened? You said there's been a break-in."

As the Etna officer described what she'd found, Sedlak pushed past them, heading toward the office to the left of the reception hall. "Don't touch anything," Barnwell warned. "The crime lab is sending an evidence team. We want nothing disturbed."

"My prints will be all over the office," he said as he approached a row of file cabinets fronted with polished walnut.

"You might cover the intruder's prints with your own. Please wait," she said, her voice commanding despite the politeness of her words.

"All right." He stepped back, staring at the wooden surfaces of the cabinets as though they'd tell him something. As he rubbed his cheeks in frustration, his hands trembled.

"Mr. Sedlak," Barnwell said, "why would anyone break in to a funeral home? What would they hope to find?"

"I don't know," he said as he scratched in chin with a baffled expression on his face.

"Do you keep narcotics on hand?" He shook his head. "Weapons?"

"Certainly not."

"Why then?" He shrugged, sending a long strand of hair over his ear. As he pushed it back, he glanced toward the file cabinets again. "What sort of things do you keep on file?" she said.

"Business records, of course. Invoices, payments, balance sheets, tax returns. But also information on the clients we've served. These are confidential; that's why I'm concerned." The funeral home kept track of every action they'd taken with a decedent, he said, from the time the body arrived at the mortuary until the moment they delivered it to the cemetery or placed its ashes in the hands of a loved one.

"But why would that matter to anyone?" she asked.

"I don't know. We don't determine the cause of death or sign death certificates. That's the county's job. We serve families in making final arrangements and play no other role."

"Do you have a burglar alarm?"

"We do, but we couldn't set it last night. It's an older unit. We've had the problem before. I called the security company to service it, but they can't come until Monday."

"Who was the last one here?"

"I don't know. I had an afternoon meeting at church, so I left my sister in charge."

He led them through the rest of the mortuary, opening doors to chapels, visitation rooms, and the preparation labs where the body was readied for burial. "And there are no chemicals here anyone might find useful?" Barnwell asked.

"Nothing," Sedlak said. "Besides, as you can see, everything is secured. Nothing's been disturbed."

Finally, he showed them the cold room, where two bagged bodies awaited the ministrations of the staff. "Could he have been after jewelry?" she asked.

"Valuables are usually removed before we receive the body. If we find anything of value, we secure it until we can return it to family members." He led them upstairs again, approaching the office safe to show it was empty. Again, she had to warn him away.

The crime lab arrived, and the two officers briefed them on what had occurred. As the technicians went about their work, Lydia discharged the Millville officer and sat in the kitchenette, Ingram drinking coffee while Barnwell contented herself with herbal tea.

"What's Sedlak doing?" the Etna officer asked.

"Lurking," Lydia said. "I told him to stay out of their way, but he's standing back from them, watching everything they're doing."

"Creepy," she said.

Lydia was noncommittal. Burglary victims reacted unpredictably. She'd await the verdicts of the crime lab.

Two hours later, the technicians announced they'd finished, having taken prints off door handles, desks, the file cabinets in Sedlak's office, and everywhere else they found them. "How did he gain entry?" Barnwell asked.

The team leader turned at the entrance. "Through here. Your officer discovered the door unlocked. He walked right in."

"My sister," Sedlak said behind her. "Delores can be forgetful."

Barnwell turned to the crime team. "Did you check the alarm box? They couldn't activate it last night."

"We took prints off the cover, but..." Realizing he'd neglected to scrutinize it, he retreated toward the back stairs.

She followed Sedlak as he returned to the office, watching while he opened each of the file cabinets and one built into his desk drawer. He leafed through records, taking his time about it. "Nothing appears to be missing," he said after nearly a quarter hour. "No harm done. I'll speak to Delores about the front door. She needs to be more careful."

He opened the safe. "See," he said, "it's empty."

The crime lab investigator loomed in the door. Barnwell followed him into the hallway, our of earshot. "Nice catch," he said. "Someone cut the wires to the unit."

This was no random event. Someone had planned the break-in.

Sedlak had insisted there was no jewelry on the premises, and Officer Ingram hadn't noticed the intruder carrying anything as she chased him through the deserted street. Someone had broken into this funeral home. But why?

———

LYDIA ARRIVED home to find Calvin sitting at the dining room table across from Tommy Molnar, Anna's fatherless son whom Mayfield had taken under his wing. Howie and Tommy's dog Ginger rested at their feet. Numbered cellophane bags lay to one side while the pair worked on a pile of plastic pieces. "What are you building?" she said.

The ten-year-old looked up, a shock of tousled brown hair obscuring his eyes, and smiled. "Chief got me this LEGO kit," he said, "McLaren's Formula One car."

Lydia wondered how much it had cost, but it wasn't her business. She and Calvin, whom Tommy had begun to call by his title, kept their finances separate. If they ever married, they could revisit the matter. Neither had popped the question to the other, and she wasn't certain how she'd react if he did so. He'd not even hinted at it. For the first time, she asked herself if she'd made him too comfortable with their present arrangement.

Calvin, reading from the instruction booklet that lay crosswise between them, shoved a piece across the table, and Tommy fit it into place. Soon after she'd bought the house during the winter and Mayfield paid his first visit, Tommy's mother had taken him for an intruder and called Carnegie police. Alerted by the flashing lights of the squad car, Lydia charged from the front door, berating the officers while Calvin, bent over the hood of the cruiser as the officers searched him, tried to calm her.

While the misidentification soon resolved itself, Lydia arrived home the following day to find a noose dangling from the second floor bannister. Tommy later confessed to the act, having been goaded by a schoolmate. Calvin took a special interest in the boy, and now that the school year had ended, spent what free time he had with him.

Lydia watched the pair for a moment, then ventured into the kitchen, Howie trailing after her in the hope she might top off his breakfast with a treat. She poured a measure of coffee into her Moka and placed it onto the smallest of the burners. Moments later, Calvin joined her. "I found enough pieces to keep him busy for a few minutes. What happened this morning?"

She took him through her summons to the funeral home. When she described the burglar springing from the casket, Mayfield doubled over in laughter. "But nothing seems to have been disturbed," she said. "We can't imagine what he was doing there."

"Perhaps looking for a place to sleep," he said.

"Permanently," she added. The last wisp of steam escaped from the Moka, and she grabbed a pot holder to lift it from the burner. She let it sit while she frothed milk, then poured both liquids into a cup, closed her eyes, and took a sip. "That's better," she said. Howie looked up at her in anticipation, but all he got for the effort was her hand running from his forehead down his back.

She fixed herself a bowl of cereal and sat at the counter as Calvin returned to the dining room and the project. Lydia had two more cases she was working, but as she ate her late breakfast, she couldn't get the break-in out of her mind. What was the young man after? Her instincts often served her well. She was convinced there was more to this.

The doorbell rang, and before she could leave the counter to answer it, she heard Tommy exclaim, "Hi, Mom!"

Anna Molnar entered, and Tommy showed her the progress they'd made on the racing car. "I feel I should pay you something for this," she told Calvin.

"And I feel you should not," he replied. "I'm having as much fun as he is."

Lydia invited her into the kitchen, offering to make her a coffee, but Anna demurred. "One more and I'll have a buzz on," she said.

The two women sat together, discussing the flowers and vegetables in Lydia's garden and plans for a block party the neighborhood was holding the following weekend. Anna, who had diabetes, was baking sugar-free cookies, while Lydia, whose erratic schedule made anything more involved problematic, was supplying flats of bottled water.

Anna's attention was diverted by an object at the end of the counter. "What's this?"

Lydia reached for the yellow handbag and placed it between them. "It's a Morris White purse I found while cleaning out the attic. It's genuine leather."

"It looks brand new," Anna said.

"Whoever owned this house placed it in a canvas bag, along with several other items. I'm not sure it's ever been used."

"I've never heard of Morris White."

Lydia told her what she'd learned from the man's obituary. "He was known as the Henry Ford of handbags. He'd started selling them from a pushcart and built it into a thriving business until the depression hit. From the quality,

I'd say this wasn't part of his regular line. This is more a Lincoln than a Ford."

Anna reached for the purse, turned it from one side to the other, opened the kiss clasp, and peered inside. "What will you do with it?" she said.

"I haven't decided. Vietnam Veterans are picking up the furniture we found upstairs, but I doubt they'd be interested in a handbag. Do you want it?"

Anna paused, looking first at the bag, then at Lydia. "How much do want for it?"

Lydia didn't know what it was worth, but she also knew this a single mother was living hand-to-mouth. "If you'd like it, it's yours," she said. She explained how a bit of leather cream might restore the surface.

"I can't take it from you. I have to pay you something."

"After all the meals you've cooked for me? Don't be absurd."

Lydia didn't imagine it. The woman's eyes filled with tears.

CHAPTER TWO

MILLVALE OFFICER KEN POLLARD was awakened by the 911 operator at 12:32 a.m. "Reports of shots fired at 340 Ballard Street." Pollard acknowledged the call, shoved his cruiser into gear, and drove the three blocks.

The borough he served had a colorful history. Lying along the Allegheny River, it was the southernmost point of the Venango Path, used by Native American tribes going to and from Lake Erie. It had been home to the Senecas and was the site of a major conflict during the French and Indian wars. The community took its name from a rolling steel mill established by Henry Phipps, who would later join Andrew Carnegie to form a sprawling company that became U.S. Steel.

All that was in the past. The steel industry collapsed following the Second World War, taking Millvale's population along with it. It had become a sleepy residential community across the river from Pittsburgh, its tranquility interrupted on this June night by gunfire.

Pollard stopped before a white, two-story building with a curb front entrance, flanked by a similar house and a more modern brick structure. A few neighbors stood on the street outside the residence, since the sidewalk was too narrow to hold them. No one had entered the dwelling. They stood in the warm night air gawking, as though waiting for something to happen.

"All right, move back," Pollard ordered as he removed his bulk from behind the wheel. Since he'd parked in the middle of the street with engine and emergency lights still engaged, he was drawing even more of a crowd. "What's going on? Who called this in?"

A burly man, his arms covered in tattoos, stepped forward. He was bareheaded and wore a pair of Levis and a gray t-shirt bearing the name of what had once been a local brewery. "I heard three shots ten, twelve minutes ago. They weren't that loud, but I could tell they were gunshots. Took me a minute to pull on some clothes. Ran outside, but didn't see anything. Knocked at Marty's door, but there's no answer."

"Marty...?"

"Sullivan," the man said. "He owns the place. Or did. His mother's gone now. He lives alone. That's why I—"

"Got it," Pollard said. The officer might have slowed down in recent years, but he took pride in knowing most of the 3,200 people in town. He stepped to the door and knocked on it.

"I already tried that," the witness said.

"You're sure you heard gunfire?" Pollard asked.

"I served in Afghanistan."

Pollard accepted the explanation. He was tempted to call Etna for back-up, as they had summoned him twenty-four hours before. Instead, he turned the handle on the screen door and twisted the knob. The door opened with ease. Donning a pair of plastic gloves, Pollard took the flashlight from his belt and stepped inside, closing the entrance partway to shield whatever he might find from prying eyes. The beam of his flashlight showed nothing amiss. The officer trained it on the wall until he found the light switch.

He checked the small dining room and kitchen, then climbed the stairs, wheezing with the effort as he reached the landing. Pollard mounted the last few stairs and paused in the hallway. He had been in identical homes dozens of times. They were cookie cutters, built long before the war to house workers in the industries that once crowded the waterfront. To his left was a main bedroom, to his right a smaller one for children or guests. The only bathroom lay between them.

He first checked the larger room. A single bed jutted from the far wall, flanked by twin nightstands. Above the headboard was the only window. A low chest of drawers stood against the long wall, and a vanity faced the bed, a wicker chair before it covered with a stained pink cushion. The flashlight caught flecks of dust in the air. Pollard coughed and cleared his throat.

The officer backed out without turning on the light and proceeded up the hall toward the second bedroom at the front of the house. The officer swung the door open and stopped, assailed by the acrid odor of gunpowder and blood.

Pollard froze in position for a moment, then found the light switch. He turned and stared at the scene. A body lay against the bed, its knees planted on the floor, the torso flat against the comforter, both arms extended forward. And at least one hole through the skull.

Detective Sergeant Lyle Jeffrey arrived at 1:42, followed by the crime lab from the county medical examiner's office. The crowd had swollen. Jeffrey rose above most of them with his six-foot height, and his hawklike features intimidated the rest. "Move back," he commanded. He motioned the lab's white van to the sidewalk, inching it forward so its rear end just cleared the door. Brandy Timmons, who headed the team, emerged from the vehicle and joined him. "What have we got here?" Jeffrey asked the officer.

Pollard explained what he'd found, insisting to the detective, whose distrust of the competence of local officers was well known, that he'd worn gloves during his search and hadn't disturbed any evidence. Jeffrey sent Timmons ahead to begin her examination and asked Pollard what he knew about the victim. "Name's Marty Sullivan," he said. "Martin. He lives alone here. Mother died of cancer a few months ago."

"February," a neighbor's voice rang out.

"A few months, just like I said," Pollard replied. "He works for a roofing company just off Route 28, but does odd jobs on the side." Jeffrey asked for a description, although he knew the coroner would provide details. "Late twenties, maybe twenty-seven," he said.

Again, a voice called. "He's twenty-five. We went to high school together."

Jeffrey inspected the slender woman with stringy blond hair. She wore a Pirates jersey with Andrew McCutchen's name and his number, 22, emblazoned on the back. "Stick around," he said. "I'll talk to you in a minute." He eased Pollard away from her and, in a quiet voice, asked if the victim had a record.

"Don't think so, and I know most of the people here.

Something of a loner. Dad left the family when he was just a kid. A construction worker. He left for work out of town one day and never came back. Mother raised him. They were real close. Even when she got cancer, he'd take her to Mass every Saturday evening. I heard he cooked for her, cleaned her up. You know how it is."

Jeffrey got the picture. He posed a few more questions, but Pollard had divulged everything he knew. Or everything he could remember.

He turned to find the young woman who had volunteered information on the victim, but she had disappeared. When he asked her name, others in the crowd pretended not to know who he was talking about. He asked Pollard. "Dora," he said. "Macklin," he added when Jeffrey stared at him open-mouthed. She lives at the end of Cecil Street, a block over.

"Why do you suppose she left?" the detective asked.

"It's late. She works mornings. Somewhere across the river."

Jeffrey would have to run her down. She was one more person making work for him. He donned white paper protective gear, entered the house, and ascended to the upper floor, passing the photographer on his way down. Brandy was bent over the body. "Anything?" he asked.

She glanced over her shoulder without straightening up, not making eye contact with him. "I just got in," she said, her voice betraying her exasperation. "Photog took longer than usual. He's half asleep."

Absorbing the rebuke, Jeffrey backed away, but she called out, "I know one thing: he's dead." Which he could tell from what little he'd seen. He looked about the room, containing nothing more than a bed, tall dresser, and a poster of a runner on the wall. The victim appeared to have had simple tastes. "Was the window open when you got here?"

"I haven't touched a thing." Her voice was tinged with resentment, as though he ought to know better. He returned to the street, where a kind neighbor thrust a paper cup filled with coffee into his hands.

"Did anyone see anything?" he asked the crowd that had since dwindled to about a dozen. They shook their heads in unison, responding to some unheard rhythm. "Someone running from the house after you heard the shots?" he prompted.

"We didn't hear nothing," a man replied. "First we knew about this was the flashing lights and sirens." Two others shrugged.

"How's Marty? He hurt bad?"

The detective saw no point in shielding the truth behind the standard "we're continuing to investigate," since at any moment the crime lab would carry the bagged body down the stairs, out the door, and into the waiting jaw of the van. "I'm afraid he's dead."

The group emitted a collective sigh, like a breeze playing through the leaves, had there been any trees on the street to serve as an instrument. "He was shot?" the man said. "Who'd want to hurt Marty?"

"That's what I'm asking. Did anyone know him well?"

"We all knew him, but ... well? No. He kept to himself. Always did, but more so since Grace passed away. That's his mom." The makeshift jury seemed to agree with the assessment. "He was a nice enough guy. I can't think of anyone who'd want to do this."

The detective got no more answers to his questions. It was as though the man had come into the world and left without leaving so much as a footprint.

Jeffrey crossed the street, studying the layout of the block. The victim's house abutted a similar one on the right, leaving no room for passage between them. The rear of the brick building on the left faced Francone Street and left a small path between the two structures. Jeffrey walked to the corner, turned behind the brick building, which he now saw housed a dental office. His flashlight led the way through the backyards of the homes on Ballard and those that ran parallel on Cecil. No fences separated the two rows. Sullivan's killer would have had no trouble exiting the back door and slipping behind the dentist's office to Francone Street or heading south toward an L-shaped court that gave onto Cecil Street.

This didn't mean the assailant had come this way. For all the neighbors had seen, he—or she—might have walked through the front door, exited the same way, and disappeared into the night while whistling a merry tune. He hoped fingerprints would provide some clues.

He returned to the lab's van and waited. It took fifteen minutes for the attendant to carry the body, bagged and buckled to a stretcher, down the stairs and into the rear of the vehicle. Brandy Timmons approached him, peeling off her gloves. "Three shots in all. One went wild, but two entered the base of his skull, traveling upward."

"Gangland style," Jeffrey said.

"Yeah, but mobsters rarely miss, do they? Once the pathologist recovers the bullets, he may be able to tell if they roughed him up before executing him."

"They?" Jeffrey said.

"Could be. We dusted for prints, but I can't yet tell how many individual ones we found."

Jeffrey knew they had also taken those of the victim in order to identify those that didn't belong. He wished the lab supervisor a good night and entered the house, securing the back door, placing a lock on the front, and dressing both entrances in crime scene tape.

STILL FEELING the effects of her loss of sleep the night before, Lydia arose late. Not that eight o'clock was most people's idea of sleeping in. Calvin had already left, having an early morning planning meeting on the consolidation of the three police forces. Since she wasn't due at headquarters until noon, she draped a robe over her pjs and set the Moka over the low flame for her single cup of coffee.

She heard a light tap at the front door. Clutching her housecoat around her, she took the few steps through the hallway and peered through the glass. Anna Molnar stood outside, shivering in the morning air. Lydia opened the door and invited her in. "Follow me to the kitchen," she said. "My espresso's on the stove."

"I'll just be a minute," Anna said as she trailed her. "There's something I want you to see."

After checking to make sure steam was still escaping from the small pot, Lydia turned to face her, noticing for the first time that she'd brought the yellow handbag with her. "Did you take a close look at this?" Anna asked.

"No. Why?"

Anna undid the clasp and opened the bag wide, turning it toward her. "I felt something crinkly along the side and wondered what it is. There's a side pocket, hidden just below the clasp." She slid her hand beneath the metal closure, revealing a long zippered seam. "I had the dickens of a time opening it. The zipper was stuck, so I had to rub WD-40 on it. But once I got inside, look what I found." She extracted a white window envelope, its color faded to a light tan, folded in the middle. "There's a letter inside."

Although the coffeepot was still steaming, Lydia turned off the burner and let it sit while she reached for the envelope. The printed return address was of a real estate office in McCandless, a township north of Pittsburgh, where North Park was located. The cancellation over the four-cent stamp was too faint to tell when it had been mailed.

"The letter's what's important," Anna said.

Forgetting her coffee, Lydia unfolded the envelope, raised the flap, which appeared to have been opened without slitting or tearing it, and removed a single sheet of paper. The recipient and address, positioned to show through the envelope's window, read "Mr. Frank Alberti, 605 Boquet Street, Carnegie, Penn." The letter was undated.

"Dear Frank," she read,

I haven't heard from you, and I'm getting concerned. You've told me how busy your travels keep you, but when you left three weeks ago, you promised to call. I hope you have been truthful with me. You know how devoted I am to you. Timmy and I would be quite hurt if you don't mean what you've said to me all these times.

I love you and look forward so much to our times together. I always show my devotion in every way you ask me to. If you can't call, please just write and let me know you still care for me. I can't imagine you were just playing with me, but if that is the case, please tell me so I can try as best I can to get over you.

I have always enjoyed our nights together. Timmy likes you so much and asks about you. He asked me to thank you again for the set of Matchbook cars.

If your wife won't give you a divorce, tell me straight out

so I can try to get over you. Whatever happens, know that I will never forget the kindness you have shown me and my son. We both love and miss you.

A single handwritten signature at the bottom of the page in blue ink read, "Jane," no surname. Beneath that was a P.S.

I typed this at work and used a billing envelope so your wife won't realize this is a personal letter. I hope this doesn't cause a problem.

Lydia gave her head a violent shake, as though warding off a pesky fly. Her blue eyes flashed.

"Isn't that pathetic?" Anna said. "I felt so sorry for the woman."

"Yeah, this Frank guy must have been a real shitheel."

"Do you think she saved the letter and never mailed it?"

Lydia frowned, trying to determine what she meant, then realized she'd focused only on the message. "She mailed it to this address," she said, smoothing out the letter so Anna could see it. "Frank must have lived in this house, either as an owner or a tenant. I'll look it up when I have time."

She closed her eyes, imagining what must have happened. "Frank's wife takes in the mail. She opens the envelope—steams it open, I think, intending to reseal it. But when she reads the contents, she reseals it. I see her concealing it in this bag, then—what does she do? Carry it around with her? No, the purse looks like it's had little use. She carries it to the attic and tucks it away in a canvas bag."

"Why?"

"Insurance, maybe. She confronted her husband, told him she had the goods on him and that if he ever got out of line again, she'd take him to court. Back then, getting a divorce was no simple matter. This letter was dynamite.

She could have taken him to the cleaners. Instead, she hid the evidence and held it over him."

"What should I do with it?" Anna asked.

"From the stamp, I'd guess this was sixty years ago. Maybe more. It's history."

"Should I toss it out, then?"

Lydia thought for a moment, looking out the kitchen window toward her garden. "No, let me hold on to it." She couldn't have explained why she was unwilling to destroy the incriminating letter. To share a cynical laugh with girl-friends over the foibles of men and the gullibility of women? She didn't know. Something impelled her to keep it, at least for a few days.

IT TOOK SOME INVESTIGATIVE SKILL, but Jeffrey found Dora Macklin serving at an Italian breakfast cafe in Lawrenceville. She spotted him as he entered and scowled. "Can't talk now," she said before he'd asked. "I'm alone here."

"I'll have the bonjour crepe and coffee while I wait," he said.

She sighed and walked away, returning with the carafe and a scowl. He took a seat near the window at a booth meant for two. While he ate in silence, he scrolled through the morning news headlines on his phone, interrupting himself from time-to-time to listen to traffic on his radio. When he'd finished breakfast, he ordered more coffee, went to the bathroom, and returned to his seat, signaling he wasn't about to leave until she spoke to him.

At nine o'clock, the crowd thinned out, and she took the

opposite seat in the narrow booth. "How long will this take?"

"That's up to you," he said.

"All right, let's get it over with."

"Why did you run away from me this morning?" he asked.

"I didn't run. I work here every morning except Monday, when we're closed. I needed my sleep."

"How did you know Marty Sullivan?"

"He and me used to be a thing."

"You went together?" he asked.

"Slept together," she said. At forty-two, Jeffrey still considered himself a young man, but he could remember a time when one didn't kiss and tell. This generation was an open book. No sense of privacy. No shame.

"But no longer," he prompted.

"No." She waited for his next question, and when he didn't pose one, filled in the vacuum. "He got weird when his mother started failing, and after she died, he just crawled into himself. He was always quiet, but then he just clammed up."

"What do you mean by quiet?" A customer came in, and she rose from the booth without answering. The man ordered a latte. She drew it, took the rest of his order, then returned. "He never had much to say. He'd listen to conversations of other people, but didn't offer anything. Politics, sports, whatever. He'd just sit there, tracking their back-and-forth." She allowed herself a small laugh. "He didn't even turn his head. Only his eyes. I just remembered that."

"But after his mother died..." the detective said.

"He totally shut down. It was eerie." A bell rang. "I gotta get this." She brought the customer his frittata, poured coffee into his now empty cup, and resumed her seat.

"It was like he was observing the world without being in it. I couldn't take it anymore. I told him I was outta here. He said, 'Okay,' like it was no big deal." She shook her head. "Bastard!"

"And when was this?"

"His mother died in early February, so it must have been late in the month or early March. Around then."

"And you haven't seen him since?"

"It was over between us. Why would I go back to him?"

"He and his mother were close," Jeffrey said.

"Yeah. He looked after her during her last year. His father walked out when he was young. I don't know if Marty ever saw him again or even remembers him. He didn't talk about it. Didn't talk about much of anything." She gave an involuntary shudder.

"Who would want to kill him?"

She shrugged. "No one I can think of. He didn't bother anyone. Never got into trouble. He worked at the roofing company, did odd jobs on the side, ate, drank, slept. That was about it."

"Any close friends?"

"He was part of our high school crowd, but I don't know he was that close to anyone. A lot of them left town after graduation, some going into the military, others looking for work." He opened his notebook in hopes she'd give him some names. Instead, she asked, "What did they do to him?"

"Did you hear the gunfire?"

"No, but I heard about it. Where'd they get him?"

For the second time that morning, Jeffrey decided not to avoid the question. "Through the back of his head. Three shots, one of which missed."

"So he didn't suffer much," she said. "That's good."

"You've no idea who might've done this? A dissatisfied customer? Someone he owed money to?"

"No." She looked up at a point beyond him, folding her arms across her chest as though hugging herself. "I'm sorry to say this. You're not supposed to speak ill of the dead, you know? But he was a nothing. Who'd bother?"

She rose to give the diner his check, ran his credit card, and scooped up the few dollars he left on the table. When she turned back to the detective, he was gone.

***

Before returning to headquarters, Jeffrey assigned two patrol officers to canvas Sullivan's neighbors for any security footage that might show who had entered his house. In this neighborhood, close to crime-ridden communities, he hoped someone had electronic eyes on the street.

He sat at his desk, ready to rope Barnwell into the case as soon as she arrived so he could grab some sleep. His morning was not over, however, for he found a message to call Tyrell Brown, the county pathologist. "Good morning, Mr. Brown," Jeffrey said, giving the greeting a grandiloquent twist.

"Good for you, maybe."

"Since I've had no sleep, it's not. Whatcha got?"

The pathologist reeled off a series of facts about the decedent: height, age, weight. "He was in great physical condition. Clear lungs, but there's evidence of vaping. No heart problems or sign of any other disease. He had three tattoos on his right arm. Stars, with one point blocked in. I haven't seen the pattern in any gang-related killings. It may just be decoration."

Although Brown would include it in his written report, Jeffrey wrote it down.

"He took two bullets through the base of the skull while he was kneeling on the bed. We recovered both slugs, plus another that went into the wall plaster after grazing his skull above his left ear. Point 22 LR's."

"Small caliber," Jeffrey said.

"You see it in Ruger LCRs. Smith & Wesson 43 C's, and some older Berettas. Ir doesn't make much of a hole, but any head wound causes exsanguination."

"The first shot was the one that grazed him?"

"It had to be in that order. The rug was bunched up toward the bed as though the victim caught his feet on it as he backed up, suggesting a bit of a struggle. He was still facing forward when his assailant fired the first shot. It did only minor damage, but may have stunned or even incapacitated him. He either turned on his own and lay prone on the bed, or the killer turned him over before firing two rounds into the base of his skull. Either could have killed him, but two made sure of it."

"All right, Tyrell, thanks for the quick work."

"Hold on a minute. There is one curious thing."

Jeffrey listened and made notes. The young victim may have been a quiet soul, but he harbored a secret.

LYDIA ARRIVED at headquarters thirty minutes before she was due. Eight detectives sat at their desks in the bullpen, most staring at monitors as they examined evidence. At some, files were neatly stacked to one side. Others looked like a child had gone through the piles, spreading pages everywhere. This was Jeffrey's modus operandi. He glanced up as she entered. He was unshaven and his hair pointed in all directions as though searching for a comb. "I was called to a shooting death in Millvale this morning."

"Etna and Millvale are getting pretty busy for small burghs," she replied.

"That's why I waited for you." She didn't ask what he meant, knowing her partner would get to the point in his own time. He briefed her on Marty Sullivan's murder, then turned to the report from the medical examiner. "They took his prints to confirm the ID and found something interesting. You were called to a funeral home early yesterday morning."

She told him about Officer Ingram discovering the break-in and calling for backup. "They discovered him hiding in a coffin downstairs. When they tried to surprise him, he got the better of them. Jumped out so suddenly he bowled the older officer over. Ingram chased him up a dark street, but he outran her."

"Not for long, as it turns out," he said.

She was way ahead of him. "The shooting victim?"

"One and the same."

She leaned back in her chair. "Whew!"

He waited for her to process the information. "The owner of the mortuary, Daniel Sedlak, claims nothing was taken, and that he can't imagine why anyone would have broken in. But his hands shook as he spoke to me. We need to question him more closely."

CHAPTER THREE

AFTER BRIEFING LYDIA, Lyle returned home for a few hours' sleep, allowing her to continue the investigation. His willingness to leave her on her own was a vote of confidence. When she'd first joined the department months ago, she'd encountered, if not hostility, widespread doubts about her competence from her male colleagues. Superintendent Morris had even put her under Jeffrey's supervision when he felt she'd commandeered too many resources investigating a body found in a culvert in North Fayette.

But Jeffrey didn't share their doubts. He had worked with her on previous cases while she was on the Boyleston force. After he'd recruited her, took her on as a partner and gave her considerable independence in the investigation into the unidentified corpse. With his guidance, she'd eventually solved not one, but two murders stemming from the discovery. That seemed to have allayed most of the questions about her competence. Now, faced with an execution-style slaying, Jeffrey reposed enough trust in her to let her question a suspect on her own.

For Daniel Sedlak was a suspect. Martin Sullivan had

broken into his funeral home. Within hours, someone had shot and killed him. While there was no evidence linking the two, she couldn't ignore the confluence of the events.

She pulled to a stop before Sedlak's and entered the reception area. A subdued piano solo played a song she recognized as "You'll Never Walk Alone" on hidden speakers. A woman dressed in a black dress with a high neckline, puffed sleeves, and mid-calf hem rose from a desk and approached her. "May I help you?" she asked in a well practiced solicitous tone.

"Detective Barnwell," she said, flashing her identification. "Here to see Daniel Sedlak."

"That's my brother. I'm Delores," she said, extending her hand. "Daniel is with a guest now."

"I'll wait," the detective said.

The woman cast a furtive glance around the foyer as though uncertain what to do. Lydia couldn't be the first visitor to have to wait. Perhaps the first cop, however. "Let me put you in one of our reception galleries."

She stepped forward with long strides and threw open a door with glass windows to a room containing three stuffed chairs and a side table with a ubiquitous box of tissues as a centerpiece. "Would you care for a cup of coffee?" Delores said.

"I'm all set," Lydia replied, raising her water bottle in explanation. "How long will he be?"

"I can't say."

"Please let him know I'm waiting."

"Uh — all right." She backed out of the room, leaving Lydia alone. The piano music changed to "How Great Thou Art." She hoped for something a bit more uplifting, like "Always Look on the Bright Side of Life."

She toyed with her phone for a moment, but her

thoughts drifted to the letter Anna Molnar had found in the purse. Why had someone kept it, let alone concealed it in an expensive handbag? She suspected Frank Alberti's wife had intercepted it. Had she confronted him? Who was Jane, the writer? Had she eventually discovered happiness? Lydia had her own mystery to solve. If she found time, she'd look into it.

The piano began playing "Nearer My God to Thee," and Barnwell glanced at her watch. So much of detective work was drudgery and just waiting around. She imagined Sedlak trying to talk a bereaved spouse or child into a larger, grander coffin. Perhaps one with a bar and TV set. The words to an almost forgotten ditty came back to her, something about drum majorettes playing castanets at a funeral.

"Sorry to keep you waiting." Lydia looked up to find Sedlak looking down at her. Had she almost nodded off? She told him she understood and followed him across the reception area to his office.

"What more can I do for you?" he asked, his tone suggesting he'd done quite enough.

"I'm following up on the break-in night before last."

He made a quick dismissive gesture with his hands. "I'm sure it was nothing. Perhaps someone looking for a place to sleep. Homelessness, you know."

"Have you had a chance to go over the facility to make certain nothing was taken?"

"I'm sure of it."

"How about your office? We know he was in here. The crime lab found his prints on your desk and file cabinets."

"I told you yesterday morning," he said. "Nothing was taken. We're not pressing charges."

She tried to intimidate him by giving him the blue-eye treatment, but he looked away. "We also found his prints on the alarm console. He'd disconnected the power supply. That's why you couldn't arm it." She paused again.

"You're saying he planned this?" He waited for a response and got none. "Who would do that?"

"Someone with the skills of a handyman," she said. "Someone who knows how to unlock doors."

"Who might that be?" He brought his hands together and allowed his fingers to dance with each other. Like all detectives, she wore a body camera. She could detach it from her blouse by pulling it away from its magnetic backing, then used it to tape interviews. She wished she'd thought to record this, for she suspected he was hiding something.

"Where were you just past midnight this morning?"

He jerked back as though slapped. "What kind of question is that?"

"One I ask anyone involved in a homicide, no matter how tangentially. So where were you at the time he broke in?"

He reached up and adjusted his blue tie, which was not out of place. "At home asleep. Why do you ask?"

"Can anyone vouch for that?"

"My wife." He raised his voice and leaned toward her. "What is this about?"

"Do you know a young man named Martin Sullivan?"

Sedlak shook his head. "I don't think so. Why?"

"You're certain? You've never heard of him?"

"Is that who broke in?"

"We identified him through his fingerprints. He goes by Marty."

He frowned and shook his head. "I don't recall anyone by that name, but I meet so many people here. I suppose it's possible."

"What could he have wanted? What might he have been looking for?"

"I have no idea. The safe was empty. You saw that. I thought he was just trying to get in off the street, that he was homeless, but if he planned this…"

"He has his own home," she said. "Had."

Sedlak blinked, catching the meaning of the change in tense. "Has something happened to him?"

"Someone broke into his house early this morning and shot him. He's dead."

Taking a deep breath, he sat up straight in his chair. "That's why you're asking where I was? You think I had anything to do with this? I don't know the guy. I don't have a clue what he thought he'd find here."

"Doesn't it seem odd he'd break in to a funeral home one night and find himself *in* it the next?" Sedlak said nothing, crossing his arms and staring her down.

"Could he have been doing a job for someone else? There must be something here worth taking." When he didn't respond, she said, "You told me you don't keep narcotics here and have no weapons."

"Apart from a handgun, which I keep locked in the desk drawer."

"You said yesterday you don't have any firearms on the premises."

Sedlak shrugged. "I thought you meant rifles, semi-automatics. This is just a pistol."

"May I see it?"

He looked beyond her for a moment, then said, "No. I'm not sure where I stand here, but I don't care for the way this conversation is going. I think you need a court order to search my desk. I keep the handgun solely for my protection. I don't carry it, so I don't need a permit. I won't produce it until you have a court order. Even then, I'll want to speak to our attorney. "

"I'll seek a warrant," she said, getting to her feet. "Meanwhile, give this some thought. Why would a young man have forced his way into your funeral home? He'd gone to some trouble, disarming the alarm system and prowling around in your office. This was not a random event. He had a reason."

As she left, the piano music had returned to "You'll Never Walk Alone." It was a loop, playing over and over again, just like this interview.

WHEN LYDIA LEFT the mortuary at half past one, she was hungry. She could have crossed the Allegheny River to one of the Italian eateries in Lawrenceville. Instead, she drove west on Route 28 to Aspinall, parked on Commercial Street, and walked around the corner to the Cornerstone Restaurant. She and David had often had lunch there, but she hadn't returned since the young officer's murder.

She found a table near the window and ordered the lamb burger. As she waited for her food, sipping at an herbal tea, she asked herself why she'd taken such a dislike to Sedlak. His surprise at learning of the murder of the man who'd broken into his business seemed legitimate. His insistence that he didn't know Marty Sullivan seemed persuasive. Still, Lydia was convinced he was hiding something. Her instincts sometimes led her in the wrong direction, but this one was overpowering. Even if he'd had no involvement in Sullivan's murder, Sedlak knew something he didn't want her to discover.

She added a few notes to those she'd taken during the

interview, again ruing the fact she hadn't recorded it. The server returned with her order. "We haven't seen you in a while."

Lydia smiled, hoping the subject of David Kimrey wouldn't come up. "I live in Carnegie. I rarely get out here."

"And I'm sure it's difficult, after ..." She let the thought float in the air.

"Yes," Lydia said. "It is."

There it was. She couldn't escape the events of the year before. She wondered if she ever would. In the days following David's death, she and Calvin had tumbled into bed in what she assumed would be a one-night-stand. It was a bad idea. They worked together, and it had taken no time for other officers to figure out what was going on. Particularly Mark Ewer, their fellow detective, who probed into everyone's business like a woodpecker tapping at siding to excavate insects.

Chief Karol Novak had used a light touch to put Ewer in his place whenever he issued one of his inappropriate comments. An icy stare often worked. Ignoring him as though he hadn't spoken. Sometimes just the words, "To continue ..."

A lot had changed over the past six months. Novak had retired, Lydia had transferred to the ACPD, and Calvin had been promoted from deputy chief to the top job. She wondered how Ewer was taking this. She'd have to ask. Calvin was working long hours running the department while creating the new regional agency. He had no time for foolishness.

She finished her lunch, thinking about how far Calvin had come: a Black man who'd had to force his way onto the discredited police agency of a small community under Pittsburgh's shadow, promoted to detective, then deputy chief, and finally the top job. He was now poised to lead a department that would bring a more professional approach to three South Hills jurisdictions.

Lydia paid her bill and returned to her vehicle, reflecting that both she and Calvin had chosen well, though she wished he'd be more assertive in their relationship. She'd been the one to suggest they move in together. It was time he demonstrated some of his leadership skills at home.

Coppola Roofing and Siding operated out of a white building resembling a Quonset hut off Route 28, just inside the Etna town limit. Three tall garage doors faced the street, with a single metal entryway in the right corner. Stacks of building material rested against a concrete wall on the left side of the parking lot.

Lydia entered and found herself at one end of a long, unattended counter. Five large photos of roofing projects adorned the wall behind it, framing a single windowless door that presumably led to the garage area. An open door at the far end of the counter led to a corridor, but she heard no activity inside. She stood alongside it and studied three frames containing a business license, building permit, and a registration certificate in the name of Walter Coppola.

"Hello?" she called. No one answered. She called out again. Only the roar of a roof-mounted air conditioner interrupted the silence. She entered the narrow hallway and found small offices off to the left side.

"What are you doing here?" A dark-haired woman who appeared to be in her early fifties emerged from a cubicle. She was about five-six, stocky, but not overweight, clad in a pair of worn denims and a sleeveless t-shirt bearing the numbers 4 1 2, Pittsburgh's area code. "No one's allowed back here."

Lydia flashed her ID and introduced herself. "I'm looking for Walter Coppola," she said.

"What do you want with him?"

"Who are you?" the detective asked.

"Maria Karras. I'm the bookkeeper. Is this about Marty Sullivan?"

"You've heard what's happened to him?" Barnwell asked.

"Of course," the bookkeeper said. "Etna's a small town. Flashing lights and sirens. The coroner pulling a body bag out of a house in the middle of the night. What do you think?"

Unlike Calvin, the woman was too aggressive. *Just answer my questions, and I'll be on my way.* "Is Mr. Coppola here?"

"No, he's on a job. We've got good weather. Every crew is out. Walter's floating between the projects to make sure everything's being done right. Some of these workers ... You gotta watch them. They show up hung over or sneak off during working hours to smoke grass. They get up on a ladder and first thing you know, they slip and slide. Then OSHA comes down on us." She planted her hands on her hips and snorted. "No one wants to work any more, in case you haven't noticed."

"Did that include Mr. Sullivan?"

"No, I can't say that. He was an okay worker. Did his job. Collected his pay."

"How long had he worked here?" Barnwell asked.

She scratched her head. "Seven years, maybe? Ever since he got out of high school. I could look it up."

"Please do." Maria Karras retreated to her office, shuffled through the bottom of a two-drawer file cabinet behind her, and emerged a minute later. "Yeah, that's right. Started working here in June seven years ago."

"How well did you know him?"

The woman shrugged. "Kept to himself, particularly after his mother died. I knew her. Everyone here did. She'd been a schoolteacher. It was a slow decline. Cancer, you know. Marty took good care of her. I'll say that much for him."

And nothing more? What does that mean? "Is anyone else here now?" she asked. "Someone who knew the victim?"

"No, it's just me. Everyone's out, like I told you."

As Lydia returned to her vehicle, she thought about how much of her time was spent chasing after things just out of reach. A witness, a source, a clue. Not at all like on TV.

JEFFREY HADN'T SIGNED BACK in. Barnwell barked a request into her APX-4000 for another detective to join her at the victim's home and drove to Millvale to await his arrival. Crime scene tape was draped around the front entrance, which was protected from curiosity seekers by a security lock. She drummed her fingers on the steering wheel while she debated what to do, then got out of the car and approached the house next door.

Getting no answer, she tried the next one. An older woman came to the door, her white hair undone. As she peered out at the detective, her lips trembled, and her eyes blinked as though unaccustomed to the light. Lydia smiled and flashed her ID. The woman's shoulders sagged, her fear dissipating. "You're here about Gracie Sullivan's boy," she said. "Awful thing. We're all terrified something might happen to us."

She pivoted, using her cane for support, peering into her house. "You'd better come in. It's hot out today."

"I'm waiting for a colleague," Lydia said. "I'll just take a minute of your time."

She accepted the woman's offer of iced tea, having left her water bottle in the cruiser. As she hobbled to her kitchen, Lydia regretted putting her to the trouble. The detective glanced around the living room, which was filled with so much furniture she didn't know how the woman could navigate it. Though the room could not have been more than sixteen by twelve, it contained two sofas, three chairs, a coffee table, and two end tables, the bottom shelves of which were stuffed with old newspapers and magazines.

One chair was turned away from the room, angled so it afforded a view of the street. Lydia imagined the woman spending her days observing the comings and goings of her neighbors, always on the lookout for intruders and subjects for gossip.

The walls were covered with photos of people Lydia assumed were her parents, a late husband, children, grand-children, and two infants who might well be her great-grandchildren.

"My name is Margaret," she said as she returned to the room. "O'Dowd," she added as though it were an afterthought. "Everyone calls me Maggie." Seeing the detective examining her photos, she said, "I've lived here all my life. My father helped build these places. The mill provided them for their workers. It's long gone, of course, but I stay."

Lydia took a sip of her tea and hid her distaste when she

discovered it was so sweet it was almost syrupy. "You knew Martin Sullivan?"

"Not really. He kept to himself, but I knew Grace, his mother. I called her Gracie. I knew her from the time she was a little girl."

"What was she like?"

"Well…" Barnwell half-expected her to proclaim she didn't like to speak ill of the dead. Instead, she said, "She had a rough life."

"How so?"

"First, she loses her baby girl. She'd had Marty first, but when he was one, she got pregnant again and gave birth to little Florence. Named after the grandmother, she was. Gracie's mom?" She stated it as a question, as though Barnwell might have remembered her. "She died in her sleep, from—what do they call it now?"

"SIDS?" Barnwell guessed.

"That's it. They didn't have a name for it back then. Others thought she was at fault. She blamed herself and got depressed. She was a basket case, poor thing. Then her no-good husband left her. Ryan was his name. I don't know what became of him. I don't much care." She sniffed to show her contempt.

"So she raised Marty as a single parent?" Barnwell asked.

"Yes. Did it all on her own. I don't know what gets into men to think they came just walk away from their families. Can you imagine what that does to a child—a young boy in this case—to realize his own father doesn't care about him?"

Unfortunately, Lydia could. In her brief career in law enforcement, she'd seen it many times. And her father had been distant after her mother's death, never accepting the role of parent.

"Then she took up with this Polish fellow. Petrosky, maybe? I can't remember. She just called him Sid. I only met him once or twice. Big man. Totally bald. He's a vet."

"Army," Lydia asked. "Marines?"

"Animals," the woman said.

Lydia, the military brat, smiled. "A veterinarian."

"That's what I said. I don't know what she saw in him, but he was always giving her presents. Once he gave her a necklace with a huge diamond in it. Gracie showed it to me like it was the best gift she'd ever received. Maybe it was. Another time, it was a fur coat. He always showered her with gifts, lots of little things, too. Maybe that's what attracted her." She sniffed again.

"Did he live with her?"

"No," she said, shaking her head as though to perish the thought. "No, he just came and went. He drove this expensive SUV, but never parked in front of their house. Always down the street. That's a risky thing to do in this neighborhood."

Meaning, Barnwell thought, that he was hiding something. "When he spent the night?" she asked.

Maggie O'Dowd nodded her head, then lowered it, looking up at the detective to convey the shame of it. "But he always left before dawn. If he'd still been there, I'd have noticed."

Lydia was certain of it. "Did he and Marty get along?"

"No." Her answer was clipped, dismissive. "Gracie told me he didn't like it when Sid was around, and that Sid didn't care much for him. It was tough on her, but she told me once, 'He's grown now,' meaning her son. 'I've earned a right to some life of my own.'"

Lydia felt she was getting somewhere. "What's become of this Mr. — what did you say his name is?"

"It's something Polish. Starts with a P." Her face brightened. "Petarsky. I have to remember she worked with pets and put the Polish ending on it."

Lydia made another note and reframed the questioned she'd been asking when she interrupted himself. "Does he still come around?"

"Not since Gracie got cancer."

"Since she died, you mean?"

"No, like I said. When she got that breast cancer and it spread all over her body, he stopped coming. Just like her husband, he was. She knew how to pick them. Marty, on the other hand, he took good care of her. He was devoted to her. A good son. So something worked out for her."

Lydia's radio crackled, telling her the other detective had arrived. She rose and thanked the woman.

"Just once," she said.

"I'm sorry?"

"The boyfriend came by one afternoon after she died. This time, he parked right in front. I saw the car pull up through the window and stepped outside to see what was up. He charged into the house like he owned the place. He was in there about two, three minutes, then came storming out, carrying some bulky package wrapped in plastic. Jumped behind the wheel of his car and made that squealing sound with his tires like kids do when they're showing off."

"And what did Marty do?"

"He wasn't home. Working, I think."

"So Petarsky had a key to the house?"

"I guess so. How else would he get in?"

"You took long enough." Detective Scott Ullrich stood outside the Sullivan house, sheltering from the late afternoon sun.

Lydia didn't feel the need to apologize, but explained she was questioning a neighbor. "We may have a suspect." She returned to her cruiser, removing evidence bags and gloves, which they donned. She stripped the crime scene tape from the front door, broke the seal the crime lab had left in place, and opened the lock.

They began their search downstairs, leaving the room where the murder had occurred to the end. "What are we looking for?" he asked.

"CSI found Sullivan's computer, but not his phone. I doubt we'll have better luck, but we can try. I'm also looking for financial records and a will." With both Grace Sullivan and her only child dead, Lydia wondered who would inherit the house. Would the errant husband, Ryan Sullivan, reappear to claim what was left?

Ullrich worked the kitchen and dining room, pulling out drawers and searching the pantry, while Barnwell went through the living room. She found no papers stashed away and riffled through the outdoor magazines left on the coffee table without result. Fifteen minutes later, they took the stairs to the top floor and entered Grace Sullivan's bedroom.

Lydia ran her hand over the pink bedspread, stirring up a cloud of dust. Both she and Ullrich buried their mouths in the crooks of their arms as they sneezed in unison. "This place hasn't been cleaned in a while," he said between coughs.

"Five months," Barnwell said. She pictured Marty Sullivan making the bed after his mother died, then closing the door, never to reopen it. While Ullrich checked the nightstand, she went through the chest of drawers. She found nothing more than what she expected: tops and bottoms, sweaters, panties, but no bras. Maggie O'Dowd had told her Grace had breast cancer.

In the vanity, she unearthed a variety of cheap cosmetics and a two-tiered box in faux leather filled with costume jewelry. None of it, she judged, was worth more than a few dollars. She turned to the small closet, combing through dresses, jackets, and pairs of women's shoes, most of which were made for comfort. "Did you check the downstairs closet?" she asked.

"I thought you did."

Her curiosity aroused, she returned to the ground floor and opened the narrow cubby inside the front door. She found jackets, a long wool women's coat, several pairs of shoes and a pair of work boots on the floor, a vacuum cleaner tucked against the back wall, and an assortment of baseball caps and women's hats on the top shelf. *Strange,* she thought.

She returned upstairs and went through the bathroom drawers, finding nothing of interest. Finally, both detectives entered the smaller bedroom at the front of the house.

Dried blood stained the light green comforter, and blood splatter had painted a Jackson Pollock design on the wall behind it. The rug in front of the bed was stained by different substances, as Marty's bowels and bladder had released their contents. The county didn't clean up after a gruesome murder. That was left to a private company "specializing in homicides, suicides, and accidental deaths," as the wording on their trucks proclaimed. But who would summon them, and who would pay them?

Lydia would have expected to see posters of Steelers or Pirates players. Perhaps a rock band. The only thing interrupting the blank walls of the room was a photo of a runner wearing a yellow shirt bearing the word "Oregon."

"Steve Prefontaine," Ullrich said.

The victim's wallet and keys rested atop a tallboy dresser that rocked as she reached for it. She pushed on the edge, and it returned into place. "Sturdy," Ullrich sneered.

"She was a single mom, and when she fell ill, he supported her," Lydia said. "They weren't rolling in money." Still, she thought, Marty was a handyman. He could have braced it. *The cobbler's children have no shoes.*

She opened the leather wallet from which the gloss had worn off in two places, extracted a twenty-dollar bill and three ones, and replaced them. In the two side pockets she found a driver's license, credit and debit cards issued by a local bank, a library card, and the advantage card from the grocery chain. She placed the wallet in a plastic evidence bag, sealed, and signed it.

While Ullrich searched the closet, she turned to the chest of drawers. Socks in the top drawer, underwear in the second, tee and polo shirts below that, then shorts. As she opened each of them, she supported the tallboy with her free hand, which made searching difficult. Asking the detective to brace the highboy, she knelt to sort through the bottom drawer. It contained a bit of everything: torn tee shirts, a cut-off sweatshirt, heavy woolen socks for winter. She removed every drawer and found nothing more.

With the drawers removed, the tallboy regained its precarious balance. Barnwell reached beneath it and found a shim. She slid it into place and steadied the chest. Who had removed it, and why? She knelt and tapped the underside, being careful not to slide her hand for fear of picking up splinters. As she probed at the wood, she touched something smooth.

"Scott, come brace this for me again?" Ullrich braced the dresser again as she lay on her back, studying the foreign object with her flashlight. A plastic sleeve was taped to the bottom, its open end pointing out. Probing with her fingers, she withdrew a dog-eared blue file folder. She set it aside so she could get to her feet, retrieved the folder, and sent Ullrich back to the closet.

The label contained a handwritten address, but had been crossed out. Had the young man salvaged this from his work? She laid the folder on the end of the bed and opened it. Inside she found a deed to the house, a copy of the previous year's federal and state tax returns, paid invoices for various items of lumber and hardware, a contract for cremation services, and several sheets of glossy paper containing specifications for roofing materials. Why had the victim gone to so much trouble to hide seemingly innocuous items? She emptied the contents into another evidence bag.

"Find anything?" she asked Ullrich.

"Just what you'd expect, jeans and cotton slacks, a suit and two dress shirts, and several pairs of shoes."

She crouched again and searched beneath the bed, scanning her flashlight from one corner to the other. She found two yellowed books on accounting. Their labels showed they'd come from a second-hand bookstore in Ross Township, north of Millvale.

"Not much," Ullrich said.

"He had to have a cell phone," she said. This was one of the first things investigators took from a scene. If a phone was still running, they rushed it to headquarters and plugged it in, keeping it active until they'd thrown passwords at it to crack it through what they called "brute force." Someone—either the killer or someone else—had taken it.

"I'm just as interested in what we didn't find." Ullrich raised an inquiring eyebrow.

"Grace Sullivan's boyfriend is supposed to have given her a diamond necklace and a fur coat. Where are they?"

"Her son must have sold them," Ullrich said.

"Maybe," she said, "but he hadn't touched anything else." She was dissatisfied with the explanation.

———

BARNWELL RETURNED TO HEADQUARTERS, knowing she'd had to write formal reports of her three interviews before she could leave. As her fingers danced over her keyboard, another detective interrupted her, informing her a man was at the front door looking for whomever was in charge of Marty Sullivan's murder investigation.

She picked up the phone to the call box in the small entrance area. It offered visitors three options: general investigations, narcotics, or homicide. She identified herself, and a man's voice said, "I saw Marty Tuesday night at a funeral home. I don't know if it's important."

The department had released no information about Sullivan's breaking into Sedlak and Sons the night before his murder, so this sighting might be significant. "I'll buzz you in," she said. "Have a seat in one of the green chairs and I'll be right down."

She took the stairs to the ground floor and entered the reception area, where a young man with a mop of chestnut hair pulled back into a bun awaited her. His skin was toasted a deep brown, and he wore a sweat-stained, sleeveless shirt emblazoned with the name and logo of a big box hardware chain. "Jerry Mullins," he said, extending a beefy paw.

Barnwell introduced herself, asked for his ID, and invited him to follow her. "I would have come in sooner, but I had to work," he said as they entered the conference room. Inverting his hands, he pointed to his outfit as confirmation. Seven tables covered in a birch wood laminate were anchored together to form a large conference table, lined with black armchairs with mesh backs.

"Have a seat," she said.

"I'm, uh…" He ran his fingers alongside his clothing, showing how dirty and sweaty he was.

"Don't worry about it. I thought you'd be more comfortable here than in one of the interview rooms upstairs. They're pretty spartan." According to his driver's license, he lived in Etna. He'd gone to some trouble to come here in the late afternoon traffic. She aimed to make this as painless as possible.

She detached her body worn camera and set it before him, explaining how it worked. As she fumbled with it, Mullins stared ahead at the side wall, dominated by a large TV monitor, then at the two monitors on the back, and finally at the lectern in front, flanked by the ACPD logo and the US and Pennsylvania flags.

She offered water, which he refused, and initiated the recording. "I don't know if this means anything," he said, "but seeing as how someone killed Marty, I thought I'd better say something. He was acting kind of strange."

Mullins told her he'd gone to a visitation at Sedlak Funeral Homes three nights before for a woman who'd been his teacher in middle school. He'd run into Sullivan, who'd been in his same class and later on the high school track team. "I knew his mom had died a few months ago, so I asked him how he was doing. He said fine, but it was clear he didn't walk to talk about it. We stood there looking at each other. I couldn't think of anything to say, and he looked like he wanted to get away. It was awkward, if you know what I mean."

"I do. I've been in that situation myself. Was that what you meant by his acting strange?"

He looked off to toward the lectern as though hunting for the right words. "It was what happened next. He walked away, and I followed him with my eyes. He has this girl-friend, Dora, who I haven't seen in a while. I thought he was looking for her and I could say hello?"

He made it a question, making certain she was following his story, while a curious expression came over his face. "But he wasn't," she prompted.

"No." He let out a slight whistle as though he were relieved she'd helped him explain. "Instead, he wanders up the hallway, looking in one room and another. He turned around at one point like he wanted to see if anyone was following him. When I saw him turn. I made like I was heading for the front door."

"So he didn't notice you?"

"I don't think so. Anyway, I turned at the entrance and saw the rear door close. I assumed he'd gone through it, 'cause there was no one else there." He leaned toward her and lowered his voice as though imparting a confidence. "I've been in that funeral home a few times. They took care of both my mom's folks when they died, and we lost a friend in an auto accident a few years back, so I know it's not a public area. I'm not sure where it leads, but it's not to a chapel or anything."

She waited, but he'd said what he'd come to tell her. "What do you think he was doing?"

Mullins rubbed his hands together as he considered the question. "It seemed like he was looking for something, if you know what I mean. But that's crazy. What would you find at a funeral home? Do you think this has anything to do with his murder?"

"We're investigating everything he did in the days leading up to his death. Every bit helps."

She asked him what he knew about Sullivan, but learned nothing others hadn't already told her. He'd always kept to himself, hanging out with those his age, but not really a part of them. He was devoted to his mother and helped support the family. Mullins hadn't seen Sullivan since his mother's death, but when he was out in public, he was often with Dora. "She's his one friend," he said, "or was."

The better term, Lydia thought, was "had been," but she kept that to herself.

LYDIA PLANNED to meet Calvin for dinner, so after she showed Mullins out, she returned to writing her reports. Before she had completed the second, however, her cell phone made its distinctive ring, telling her he was calling.

"I know we'd planned to meet at Sarafino's..." he began.

"But something's come up," she finished.

"Yeah, Alton Borough's public safety committee wants to meet with me about the consolidation plan."

"I hope they're not getting cold feet," she said.

"I do, too. Doug Lentz," he said, referring to Boyleston's council chairperson, "keeps acting like we're taking them over rather than forming a combined command. I think they want some reassurance. At any rate, I'm sorry."

"Don't be. I'm tied up here, too."

With her evening cleared, she opened the evidence bag

and studied the documents she'd found concealed beneath Sullivan's unstable dresser. The tax return was unremarkable. The victim had reported $39,760 in income against $3,000 in withholding. He'd taken the standard deduction, giving him a refund of $909. She noted he hadn't claimed his mother as a dependent, which, at that point, she must have been. *You should have gone to an accountant.*

She studied the invoices for his home repair side hustle. Something didn't add up. She reopened the tax return. *No wonder you didn't have someone prepare this. You were being paid under the table.* Here was another sign that Sullivan was something other than a model citizen. First the break-in and now evidence he was dodging taxes.

She turned the pages of the roofing specs and was about to cast them aside when she noticed someone had circled two different grades of shingles, penned in their per-bundle cost, and entered a series of calculations along the margin that totaled $4,298. Were these a comparison for a client? Wasn't that the job of Maria Karras, Coppola's bookkeeper?

She turned to the cremation contract. Dated eighteen months before, the agreement was between Grace Sullivan and Sedlak Funeral home for $1,375. Her signature was at the bottom of the second page, along with that of Delores Sedlak. *How thoughtful. Marty's mother made her own arrangements, knowing she would soon die.*

Lydia studied the fine print. Although she'd never read such a document before, she found it remarkable. She was about to close the file when something caught her eye. She stared at the signatures, held them up to the light, and turned them sideways.

She would check with Ross Sutton, who headed digital forensics. While this wasn't his area of expertise, she hoped he'd confirm this document was an original, rather than a copy. What was it doing in this folder? Shouldn't Grace have had a photostat?

Lydia thought nothing more about it, returned the documents to the plastic bag and resealed it, then returned to her reports, which, given her conversation with Jerry Mullins, had now increased by one. Before leaving for the night, she emailed Jeffrey, calling his attention to Grace's erstwhile boyfriend, Sid Petarsky, his hurried visit following her death, and the missing gifts. She also referenced Jerry Mullins' statement placing Marty at the funeral home hours before he broke in. She'd left plenty for her partner to chew on.

CHAPTER FOUR

"YOU HAD A BUSY DAY." Lyle Jeffrey removed the reading glasses he'd just begun wearing and massaged the bridge of his nose. Although he wore dark glasses on the cloudiest of days, he hadn't become accustomed to the cheaters.

"Everyone I spoke with is on the same side of the river, just a few miles from each other," Barnwell said. "I didn't have to waste half my day traveling." The two rivers bisecting Pittsburgh make the distance a crow might fly irrelevant. Almost anywhere you travel means crossing a bridge or two, often backtracking to something within sight of where you began.

"You did well. Have a seat," he said, dragging her chair alongside his desk in the detectives' bullpen. The wall ahead of them held the "Baltimore Board," two white boards side-by-side that listed every homicide the twenty detectives had worked that year, color coded to indicate whether a case was still open or had been solved. The name came from a TV series, *The Wire*. One of their colleagues had seen it on the show and replicated it. So far, most of the entries were green. Only the Sullivan case and five others broadcast their status in bright red.

"We've retrieved security camera video from two homes near Sullivan's house." Jeffrey angled his computer screen to share it and punched a few buttons on his keyboard. The first was from a doorbell camera at one of the few residences on Francone near its intersection with Ballard Street. "This house backs up to Sullivan's, so if anyone came from that direction…"

The detective scrolled to a point fifteen minutes before the neighbor had reported shots fired. It showed an empty street with no activity. He advanced through the clip until they saw a vehicle cruise by heading west. He backed it up. Because the view was from the opposite side of the street, the image wasn't clear. In the dim light from a streetlamp half a block away, the four-door sedan, either gray or light blue, appeared to have a man at the wheel. His face was shrouded in darkness.

"I think it's one of those Korean jobs, maybe a Kia, and not a late model. Sutton will enhance this for us." But since the camera showed only the side of the car, the plate wasn't visible until it was almost beyond the frame, and then too blurry to be made out. "Pennsylvania tag, but that's all," he said.

Unlike Photoshop, the AMPed5 software used by the forensics team couldn't create details that weren't there. While it could lighten dark areas, increase contrast, and sharpen the detail, it couldn't add pixels or change the underlying image. These restrictions allowed its images to be admitted as evidence, and most defense attorneys had ceased challenging it in court.

Jeffrey resumed the video. Three teenagers walked by.

Their features were indistinct. Eight-seven seconds after it had passed headed west, the same vehicle returned the way it had come. Nothing else transpired until seven minutes later when a police car raced by, its emergency lights flashing like an Independence Day celebration.

He brought up the second video, taken from a house four doors southwest of Sullivan's house on Ballard Street. "This came from an older system," he explained. "The image is low resolution and black and white." As he had done before, he raced through the sequence until he caught movement.

An image of a person wearing a ball cap passed on the side opposite the house. The outfit, jeans or slacks and a shapeless shirt of some sort, gave no clue whether its wearer was male or female. Barnwell put her nose to the screen, but the person's features were concealed beneath the cap.

"Who'd be out for a walk at this hour?" Lydia said.

"It had been a hot day. Perhaps someone waited until it cooled off before going for a stroll."

"Maybe," she said, her tone conveying skepticism. Seconds later, a vehicle drove by. "Isn't that the same car we saw in the other sequence?"

"It looks like it," he said, but the image was even less clear, so they couldn't be sure. The driver didn't appear to stop, although Sullivan's house was four doors away, out of the frame.

Lydia recorded the time stamp and had Jeffrey replay the sequence from the first house. She pulled up a map of the area on her own monitor. "Whoever was behind the wheel didn't have time to stop. They may have driven a block beyond Ballard, turned here on Easton, then circled the block."

"Why take such a circuitous route?"

"Perhaps the driver was lost and made a wrong turn," she said.

Jeffrey resumed the first video and watched as the sedan returned the way it had come. They compared the time-stamps from the two videos. Eighty-eight seconds had elapsed. "Whatever he was looking for, he didn't have time to enter Sullivan's house, so it doesn't help us."

He returned to the second video on Ballard Street, stopping when the three teenagers they'd caught walking west on Francone passed. Once more, the time stamps suggested the youngsters hadn't had time to enter the house.

As they continued watching the screen, a man came running from a house across the street, holding a cell phone to his ear. The figures in the upper right showed the time was 12:31 a.m., four minutes after the teenagers had passed by. "There's the fellow who called it in."

Three minutes later, the Millvale officer arrived on the scene, and all hell broke loose. "What do you think?" he asked.

"Not much to go on."

"We'll see what Sutton and his crew can make of this, but otherwise, it's a nothingburger."

Investigations on TV shows were much more exciting.

"WHAT'S OUR NEXT STEP?" she asked.

"You're the detective. You tell me."

She beamed, her bright blue eyes flashing in recognition of the faith he'd placed in her. "Sullivan's boss, Walter Coppola, is on a siding job this morning, but he's agreed to meet with us at two. In the meantime, I'd get Ross Sutton looking into Sullivan's bank records and cracking his email account."

"Done." So her partner had already spoken to the forensics detective. She wondered what else he'd been up to while working from home the day before.

"Next, we should interview Sid Petarsky, Grace's former boyfriend. He's supposed to have showered her with expensive gifts. We didn't find them, and we know he let himself in and carted something away while her son was at work."

Jeffrey agreed. "How about returning to the funeral home to ask the owner more questions?" he said.

"He knows more than he's telling us," she replied. "Sullivan breaks into a mortuary. He has to have a purpose, but Sedlak claims nothing is taken. Hours later, someone murders him."

With his reading glasses perched on the edge of his nose, Jeffrey held a pencil between his hands as though waiting for more. "Still," she said, "Let's examine Sullivan's bank records before we go back to him."

"Correct," Jeffrey said.

Barnwell realized he'd been testing her. "Let me find this Petarsky fellow."

"He lives in Mars," Jeffrey said, "but runs a veterinary clinic in Cranberry." Once again, he'd anticipated her suggestion.

IT TAKES nine months to make the 140 million mile trip from Earth to Mars, but only thirty-six minutes to travel the twenty-seven miles from ACPD headquarters to the suburb of the same name in neighboring Butler County. The borough acquired the name in the late nineteenth century. No one knows why. It has no apparent significance, but serves the well-to-do avoiding Allegheny County taxes.

Just before ten, the detectives arrived before a glassed-in storefront in an upscale strip mall off the interstate. Four customers occupied Scandinavian designed leather sling chairs in the lobby. One held a cat in her lap, another had hers in a carrier at her feet. On the opposite side of the entrance, a tired-looking cocker spaniel rested at the feet of a young man who appeared to be in his early twenties, while an older man alongside him held the leash of a reddish dog of indeterminate breed whose eyes followed every movement in the room.

Jeffrey flashed his credentials to the woman behind the sliding glass window and asked to speak to Dr. Petarsky. Behind her, a chorus of dogs howled in unison. "He's with a patient right now," she said, "and these people are waiting."

"We need to speak to him," Jeffrey insisted.

"May I say what this is about?"

"Police business."

She gazed at him, demanding more information. When he didn't budge, she snorted, slammed the window shut, and heaved herself out of her chair. A minute passed, then another. Finally, she opened the door from the waiting room, leading them down a hallway lined with examination rooms. The smell of wet fur, urine, feces, and disinfectants enveloped them as she led the two detectives to an office at the end of the hall. A desk faced the back wall, a high-backed swivel chair in white leather before it, and a single guest chair nestled alongside it.

Jeffrey motioned Lydia into the chair. Instead, she turned and examined framed documents and photographs beside the door. His diploma, dated in 1988, and his 1990 doctorate were from Ohio State—*The* Ohio State University, as it now insisted on being called. Beside the two certificates was a color photo of a young man in a white coat. He had a long, thin face and big ears with a thatch of dark hair sweeping across his forehead. Not a handsome fellow, she decided.

Above and below them were photos of children with dogs, cats, two horses, and a rabbit. Happy testaments to the veterinarian's work.

She turned back toward the desk where Jeffrey was studying more pictures: a young woman beaming as she was flanked by two small boys, an older woman holding a grandchild, and a shot of the couple in late middle age on the deck of a boat of some sort with the massive, baroque Buda Castle behind them. Scenes from a life.

The door opened and the man in the photograph entered the room, still wearing a white lab coat, which was now stained in yellow and brown, with the same long face, drooping ear lobes, but whose salt and pepper hair had eroded since the images were taken. He frowned as he stood at the entry, glaring at them without closing the door. "What is it?" His tone was sharp, demanding.

Jeffrey introduced them and turned on his body cam. "We're here about the death of an acquaintance of yours, Martin Sullivan."

He stared at Jeffrey for a moment and closed the door. "I heard it on the news this morning. Tragic thing. But I hardly knew the young man. What do you want with me?"

"How did you know him?"

Petarsky hesitated, clasped the fingers of his right hand in his left and massaged them. "I knew his mother. They came to me about a pet."

"A pet?"

"A cat, as I recall. I see a lot of animals." He seemed to consider his answer for a moment. "This tabby had feline leukemia virus, which affected her kidneys. They'd let it go too long, so she was quite weak when they visited. I don't think they were well off. They probably delayed coming to me until it was too late. I had to put her down."

"And they came all the way from Etna." Jeffrey's tone was innocuous, an observation rather than a question.

"I seem to recall a friend had recommended me." He displayed a small smile and nodded, satisfied with the explanation.

"Mrs. Sullivan came alone, or was her son with her?" Lydia kept a straight face, but couldn't believe how agile Jeffrey was in reeling out his line.

"He drove her."

"And from that, you began seeing her." Jeffrey's tone was unchanged, but Petarsky blinked as if he had discharged his service weapon.

"I, uh—Yes, I was helping the family. As I mentioned, they were quite poor." Jeffrey cocked his head to one side as though questioning the response. Petarsky frowned, perhaps realizing his answer made little sense.

Barnwell stepped into the crevice her partner had created. "We have it from a neighbor that you spent many nights there. You even had a key to the house."

"Who says so?" Neither detective responded, and after looking from one to the other, the veterinarian collapsed into his chair. "All right. Yes, we—Grace and I had a brief affair. She was quite lonely. My wife and I were going through a rough patch at the time."

Since neither detective had taken the remaining chair,

both towered over him. "But you dropped her after she became ill," Barnwell said.

He held up both hands, halting oncoming traffic. "It wasn't like that."

"How was it?"

"I'd been trying to end it for weeks. Months. Elena and I had reconciled. I didn't want to give up on my marriage."

"And Grace was diagnosed with cancer."

"There was no connection." He crossed his chest with his right arm and placed his hand over his heart, the picture of wounded innocence. "The timing was less than ideal, but it was something I'd been considering."

Less than ideal? "How did she take it?" Barnwell asked. "She couldn't have been pleased. She gets this diagnosis, and her lover takes this moment to walk out on her."

His face was the color of a ripe orange. A scowl split his forehead. "I don't see what any of this has to do with—"

"After her death," Jeffrey said, "you broke into Marty Sullivan's house one afternoon and carried away the presents you'd given her."

"How did—?" He stopped, momentarily flummoxed, but soon recovered. "They were mine. She was gone, so I wanted them back."

"Technically, they were part of the estate. If Sullivan had wanted to press charges, he could have. I don't know what a diamond necklace is worth, but if you include the mink coat, we're talking grand larceny."

"All right. He was angry. Threatened me. Said he'd turn me into the cops." The doctor snorted. "He never did."

The detectives avoided making eye contact. "Why not?" Lydia said.

"What was he going to do with them? Besides, I told you, they were mine."

The pair fell silent again. Petarsky seemed to take the lull as an accusation. He hugged himself, rocking back and forth in his chair. "She found out," he said in a low voice.

"Your wife?"

"Some time before, Elena had noticed credit card payments to a jeweler and a furrier and confronted me. I told her I'd intended them as gifts for her, but took them back because she always insisted I was too extravagant. She kept looking in our accounts for the refunds. When they didn't turn up, she badgered me about for an explanation. I was forced to tell her the truth and promised I'd end it."

"And she wanted the jewels and the coat," Lydia said.

He looked away for a moment. "Yes, but I couldn't do that when Grace was alive. Once she was gone, I asked Sullivan to return them, but he wouldn't."

"Did you threaten him?"

He averted his gaze again, looking past them toward the door. His right heel tapped a rhythm on the floor. "Of course not. I just asked him to return them. He refused. I knew he worked days. We close the clinic Wednesday afternoons. I play golf if the weather's good, but I skipped this day, drove down to Etna, and took back what was mine."

"And he let that pass? He threatened to bring charges against you, but never did. That's your story."

He looked up at them and spread his arms as though saying search me. "It's the truth," he said.

"When was the last time you saw him?" he asked.

"Not since I broke up with Grace. We talked by phone, but never met in person."

"Where were you two nights ago, shortly before midnight?" Barnwell asked.

"At home. We had guests over for dinner. They stayed late. We couldn't get rid of them."

"Your wife will corroborate this?"

"I'd rather you spoke to our friends. They'll confirm it. Let me give you Barry's number." He turned and began writing on a prescription pad.

"You don't want us speaking to your wife," she said.

"I'd prefer you didn't," he told her. "Elena's still upset with me. It's an open wound. Raising it again would threaten our marriage."

Jeffrey asked if he owned weapons. Just hunting rifles, he said, insisting he hadn't touched them in two years. "I have no free time since we opened this clinic. And now," he said, struggling to his feet, "if you have nothing more, I have a room full of sick animals and an overworked assistant."

"We're checking your story," Jeffrey said. "If we find one word of what you've told us isn't true, we'll be back. And this time, we'll bring a warrant."

Petarsky nodded, and the detectives left. Neither spoke until they were a mile down the interstate. "What a load of garbage," he said.

"His story or the man himself?" she asked.

"Both," he repeated.

THE DETECTIVES GRABBED A QUICK BITE, sharing their reservations about the veterinarian's story and considering what they'd learned about Sullivan. A pattern was forming of a lonely young man who'd withdrawn even further after the death of his mother, for whom he'd cared during a long illness. He'd cut corners on his taxes, broken into a place of business, and quarreled with his mother's lover over gifts he'd bought her. This raised more questions than they could answer. What had he been after at the funeral home? Why hadn't he turned Petarsky in to police? The more they learned, the more they needed to know.

A few minutes before one, they arrived at Coppola Roofing and Siding and found the same empty counter Barnwell had confronted the day before. She eased open the door to the garage. Finding no one in the work area, she led Jeffrey into the hallway that flanked the row of small offices.

Maria Karras sat at her desk, working her way through a sub sandwich. She put it down as they stood in her doorway, wiping either mayonnaise or mustard from her mouth. A stain on her t-shirt, either the same as or identical to the one she'd worn the day before, suggested it was the latter. "Back again?" she said.

"We have an appointment with your boss. Where is he?"

She rubbed her chin with her hand as though to remove remnants of the sandwich. "He's out on a job. I don't know when he'll be back."

"You know how to reach him?" Barnwell said.

"I call him," she said.

"Then do so. He's agreed to meet us."

"You can't just come in and order us around. Walter's having enough trouble hiring workers to do his jobs. With Marty gone and all—"

She interrupted her protest as the sound of one of the three garage doors sliding back on its rails drowned her out. "There he is now."

They withdrew from her cubicle and stood in the hallway as a beefy man with brown stubble and a shaggy mustache slouched into the hallway. "You the cops?" he said.

Jeffrey introduced the two of them. "Come on in," he

said, pushing both hands before him to herd them down the narrow corridor. They were almost at the rear door when he paused and turned a key into another cubicle, this one about half again the size of the bookkeeper's. He seated himself behind a desk whose surface was obscured by file folders and stacks of papers. A computer rested on a wing. Its screen came to life as he settled into his chair, displaying the logo of an earlier version of the Windows operating system.

He waved his hand toward the two chairs in the room, red plastic seats on thin aluminum frames, and removed his cap, emblazoned with the trademark of a brand of shingles. "I'm sure you've come about Marty. Damned shame."

"How long had he worked for you?" Jeffrey asked.

"Ever since he got out of high school. That would make it, I don't know. Six, seven years?"

"What sort of worker was he?"

"Reliable. Always arrived on time. Showed up sober." He issued a wry snort. "That counts for a lot around here. Did his job. Never screwed up. Never a do-over."

"What sort of person was he?" Barnwell asked.

"Marty?" *Who else?* she wondered. "Quiet kid. Had little to say. Came into work, went out on a project, did as he was told, and went home. Didn't talk much. Some of these guys love to talk about the old days. High school stuff. You know the Springsteen song?"

"Glory Days," Jeffrey offered.

"Yeah, that one. Marty wasn't like that. He had a job to do, did it, and that was the end of it."

"Did he have had friends here? Someone he hung out with during his off hours?"

"If so, I never saw it. You know his mother was sick? She had cancer. He spent the last couple of years taking care of her. Didn't have time for much else."

"But before that?" Jeffrey asked.

Coppola scratched at a scab on his nearly bald head. Barnwell guessed more than one pre-cancerous cell basked in the sun of late spring. "He once had a girlfriend, but I haven't seen her around in a while. Mackey? Something like that."

Jeffrey supplied Dora Macklin's name, and Coppola confirmed the identification. "What about guys?" he asked. "We all have friends."

"I can't think of anyone."

Jeffrey shook his head in frustration. "How did he get along with the others? Were there any disagreements?"

"Nah. Marty didn't engage in anything like that. If someone had tried to pick a fight with him, he would have walked away."

"Did he have any enemies?"

"You mean someone who would have killed him?"

"Anyone at all. Someone who felt he was doing too good a job, speeding things up when they were trying to drag the job out."

Coppola snorted and flashed a sardonic grin. "No one here pulls that stuff. Anyone who tries doesn't stay around."

"Can you think of any reason someone would have wanted to harm him?" Jeffrey persisted.

"Marty? Nah." The man seemed to think about it for a moment. "After his mother died, he changed. Didn't say two words. Just came in, worked his shift, and left. He'd always been like that, but after his mom died, he built a wall around himself. Death changes people, you know? He had no father, so they were real close. When she got sick, he devoted his life to her. When she passed away, it was like he had no purpose. Just came and went."

Jeffrey flipped his notebook shut, but Barnwell wasn't

finished. "When I went through his things, I found what looked like a spec sheet for roofing materials. He'd circled two and done some calculations that seemed to show the cost differential for different grades. Do you have any idea what that's about?"

"No. He didn't deal with that kind of stuff. That was my job. Mine and Maria's."

"Then why write those figures down?" she said.

"Wait a minute. He was doing some projects on the side. Maybe he did an estimate for one of his customers."

"He was working here, but doing roofing jobs on his own?" she said. "He was competing with his employer, and you were okay with it?"

"He didn't do roofing projects. Just little jobs too small for us. I threw him a few things. I'm sure that's what he was doing with that spec sheet." He nodded his head and smiled at her. "If you want, return it to me and I'll take a look."

She thanked him, but was noncommittal as they left the office.

"Something doesn't add up," Lydia said as they returned to the cruiser. "Coppola says he was only handling minor jobs, not roofing projects, but suggests that's why he was comparing the cost of shingles."

"Oh, Barnwell, you have a suspicious mind," Jeffrey said with a chuckle. Their levity was interrupted by a call on Jeffrey's Motorola. He listened for a moment and asked a few questions. "Head to a brew pub called Julio's," he told her. "On Canal Street in Sharpsburg."

The bar was only a mile from the roofing company. Four minutes later, she pulled to a stop before a gleaming aluminum and glass building along the main drag of the borough where Henry J. Heinz built a glassworks with which to bottle his pickles and, later, catsup, the first two of what would become 57 varieties.

Jeffrey opened the door and held it for Barnwell. Only a few customers were there at this hour: two men sitting at one end of the long bar, a woman scrolling on her phone at the other end, and three women huddled at a table by the window. A young man with a handlebar mustache and shoulder-length hair parted in the middle glanced up and nodded without identifying himself. "I'm taking a break," he said to the woman at the end of the bar.

He led the detectives toward the glassed-in brewery, opened the door, and hollered, "I'm using your office for a few minutes, okay?" Without waiting for an answer, he ushered them into a small room. Through its floor to ceiling panes, they could see tanks and pipes gleaming in the sunlight that streamed through the transparent panels in the ceiling.

The room had no desk, but a round table with four chairs. A credenza, its shelves crammed with notebooks, held a notebook computer. The one wall not glassed in was festooned with posters and stickers from craft breweries from Maine to Alaska.

"I'm Seth," the young man said. "Goodman," he added. "It's tough getting hold of you folks. First, I called the Etna Police Department, and they referred me to the county. I had to talk to three people before someone understood me."

"You say you knew Martin Sullivan," Jeffrey said, ignoring his complaint.

"Marty," he corrected. "We went to high school together, but that's not why I called. For the past few months, he'd come in after work for a slice of pizza and a beer. Never more than that. He'd have one and if he stayed beyond that, switch to water. He was always alone and had little to say. If there was a baseball game on, he'd watch it, but mostly he just sat there."

Barnwell wondered where this was leading.

"A lot of folks get talkative after they've had a few. Not obnoxious or anything. Just loosening their tongues and getting friendly with anyone who'd listen. And since Marty sat alone at the bar, people sometimes chatted with him."

"And he engaged with them?"

Goodman chuckled, curling his mustache while he considered the question. "No, they engaged with him. They'd start talking, and he'd just sit and listen. He'd nod a bit, say little things to keep them going, but mostly he just let them say whatever was on their minds. Folks like to talk about themselves after they've had a few drinks."

In Lydia's experience, few people need alcohol to find themselves an object of endless fascination.

"A few nights ago, this man comes in. Older guy, needed a shave, ruddy face like he'd been drinking most of his life. You know the type?"

"We do," Jeffrey said.

"So he asks for the name of the young fellow he'd been talking to the week before. And then I remembered the same guy had been bending Marty's ear a few nights earlier. So I said, 'You mean Marty Sullivan, the roofer?' He asked me to describe him. When I did, he said that was the one he meant. He asked if I knew where he lived. Etna, I said, and he wanted an address. He didn't say please. 'Where in Etna?' he said. I got a bad feeling, like I'd said too much already. If he'd talked to Marty that long, why didn't he know his name?"

As the bartender unspooled his story, Lydia felt her

breath quickening, but she kept her bland face. "Did you get his name?" she asked.

"No. I didn't think to ask."

"Had you ever seen him before?"

"Not that I recall, but I've only worked here a year."

"Who else might remember him?"

Goodman walked to the door and called out for someone named Donna. The woman who'd been playing with her smartphone called out, "What is it?"

He left to question her, and Lydia followed. The woman didn't recall the incident and said it might have been her night off. Since Goodman couldn't remember the date of the conversation, he didn't argue the point, but his slight shrug suggested she might have been too busy on her phone to notice anything. Barnwell asked if she knew anyone matching the bartender's sketchy description of the man. "That fits half a dozen guys," she said. "Especially the red face."

"Do you keep security tapes?" she asked, her eyes picking out the cameras mounted above the bar. When he confirmed it, she said, "I want you to go through the videos and see if you can find this man."

He agreed. They tried to dredge more information out of him, but he was a dry well. Jeffrey turned to questions about Sullivan's background—what he'd been like in school, what his interests were—but Goodman said he hadn't known him well. "He was an outsider. Didn't talk to many of us. Didn't belong to a club. I don't think he even went to the prom. He hung around with one girl, Dora Macklin. I don't know if they're still together."

"Anyone else?" Jeffrey asked.

"You've talked to Al Kuczienski, haven't you?" Jeffrey shook his head. "They worked together at the roofing company. Marty got him the job there. I think they were on the track team together. Back then, they were thick as thieves."

Lydia took down the man's information, and they left. "You know what I'm thinking?" Jeffrey said as Barnwell turned onto Route 28 and the inevitable late afternoon funnel onto the Fort Pitt Bridge.

"The same thing I am," she said. "If he's so tight with this Kuczienski fellow, why wouldn't Coppola have mentioned him? We asked him who Sullivan was close to, and he implied he had no friends on the crew."

Ross Sutton, the digital forensics detective, was waiting for them when they returned to headquarters. He was a big man, looking more like he could break down a door than into a computer, but, as she'd learned months before, his appearance was deceiving.

"We're still trying to ping his phone to find it," he said. "Chances are, whoever took it turned it off, maybe even removed the SIM card, if they know what they're doing. If we can't recover it, we'll get a court order for his digital records from his cell carrier."

Such records could show where Sullivan had been and who he'd talked with, but not what was said. Even given this limitation, they might learn something helpful.

"We haven't gotten into his computer yet, but we will," Sutton said. "We now have his bank records. He had two checking accounts, one for personal use, the other for business. At irregular intervals, he'd get income from one of his side jobs. He purchased materials and equipment from Home Depot and charged it to a credit card.

He paid the card off each month through this business account."

"Nothing out of the ordinary, then?" Jeffrey said.

Sutton's face broke into a conspiratorial smile. "On most of these side jobs, he was paid by check. The transactions will show you the names of his customers. They range anywhere from just under $300 to $800. But he also made several deposits in cash, and they tended to be higher. For one job last year, he deposited over $5,000."

"He didn't report that on his tax returns," Barnwell said. She'd already told Jeffrey Sullivan was being paid under the table.

"What's more interesting," Sutton said, "is his personal account."

Both detectives leaned forward, knowing from the way Sutton teased out his stories that something big was coming. The detective rubbed his hands together, savoring the moment. "His current balance is just over $6,400, which is a lot to keep in a checking account. The more interesting thing is how it's fluctuated over the past four months."

He handed them each a printout of Sullivan's banking transactions since the start of the year. Lydia ran her eyes down the sheet. He'd hadn't earned much during the frigid weather in January and February. Beginning in mid-March, he'd received paychecks every two weeks from Coppola. While the precise amount varied, the usual deposit, after withholding for federal and state income taxes and FICA, was just over $3,000.

What stood out to her, however, were seven cash deposits ranging from $3,000 to $8,000. "I'll save you the math," Sutton said. "Over a four-month period, he took in $37,000."

"Exactly that amount?" she said. "All these entries are in round numbers."

"You noticed that?" *Of course I did*, she thought. *I'm a cop*. But she didn't rise to the challenge, waiting for his conclusion.

"But as fast as it came in, it went out. Only $6,000 left in the account. Where's the remaining $31,000?" Sutton waited while she studied the sheets. "Oh, I see. He was paying hospital bills."

"Yes, his mother had put her assets into a living trust," the detective said. "It transferred to him as soon as the death certificate was filed, avoiding probate. Unfortunately, apart from the house, which she owned outright, her medical costs had consumed her savings. Sullivan inherited not assets, but debts. He's been paying them off as more bills come in."

"Where did he get all this cash?" Jeffrey said.

"I'm unable to tell. We're working on it."

"Cash payments in round numbers," Lydia said. "Not just where did it come from, but did he intend to declare it on his taxes?"

"If he didn't," Sutton said, "he was foolish to put it in the bank. He may not have been the brightest star in the firmament."

She continued studying the sheet. "Look how evenly some of these are spaced. Three thousand one week, four the next. A month later, he deposits $8,000. Two weeks later, another $8,000."

"What are you thinking?" Jeffrey asked.

"He may received a large lump sum but split it into two deposits to avoid triggering a CTR." US banks and credit unions are required to file a Currency Transaction Report with the federal government on any single transaction of

$10,000 or more, a requirement meant to identify drug dealing and money laundering.

"Good girl," Sutton said. *When will he stop patronizing me? He stops just short of saying something actionable. Not that I'd report him. He's too damned good at his job.*

"And you're certain it didn't come from his mother's estate," Jeffrey said.

"No," he replied. "Grace Sullivan knew her days were numbered and planned for it. She'd put the house into the trust and sold her automobile when she got too sick to drive,. What little cash remained went to pay her medical bills and funeral expenses. But after her death, hospital bills kept piling up."

"What funeral expenses?" Lydia said. "She had a cremation contract. I filed it in an evidence bag. She'd paid $1,350 more than a year before she died."

Sutton fumbled through her copy of the report for a moment and drew a two-sided pen from his pocket, using one tip to highlight a $1,500 payment to Sedlak Funeral Home.

"How do we explain this?" she said.

"Additional expenses?" Jeffrey asked. "She'd paid for the cremation, but Sedlak charged her for a memorial service?"

"That was held at St. Stephen's," she said. "I found the clipping in Sullivan's file."

Affecting the accent Desi Arnaz had used on an antediluvian comedy show, Jeffrey said, "Sedlak has some 'splainin' to do."

So did Walter Coppola, who'd denied Marty had any friends on the crew, when he'd hired Al Kuczienski on Marty's recommendation.

Now, thanks to the information Seth Goodman had

provided, they had a stranger who'd tried to identify Sullivan days before his murder. Why did everyone they interviewed have something to hide?

———

Lydia bought two walleye fillets and a half-pound of asparagus at the market. She measured rice into the cooker and turned it on, trimmed the spears and painted the fish in olive oil, then fired up the grill on the back deck while she waited for Calvin.

When he arrived at six, he changed from his uniform as she prepared dinner. He opened a bottle of Chenin blanc, and they sat at the small table on the deck, brushing away insects as they discussed their days. The sun was still high in the sky and wouldn't set for another three hours. She stretched out her long legs, luxuriating in the warmth. It had been a harsh winter, and both felt they'd earned this evening.

"Four suspects," he prompted.

"I can't call them that yet. We have four people acting suspiciously." She said laughed at her artificial distinction. "The owners of the funeral home and roofing company are withholding information. Whether they've lied, we don't yet know. The veterinarian is a scumbag and a thief who tried hiding his relationship with Grace Sullivan. He doesn't want us speaking to his wife, despite saying he's confessed all." And did it make sense, she asked herself, that she would await Grace Sullivan's death before reclaiming the diamond necklace and mink coat Coppola had given her? No, she would have demanded he act now.

She emptied her wineglass and held it out for a refill, something she seldom did. "Now we have this man who jawed with the victim and returned days later eager to find him. Why? What was he after?"

Lydia told him about the cash deposits Sullivan had made. "We can't find where they came from."

"Lots of questions," Mayfield said, "but no answers."

"But we will get them." She held her glass up to the sun and watched as it splintered the light into patterns on the table's surface. "I'll get them."

As Calvin cleaned up, Lydia sat at the table in the dining room and made notes of all she'd learned since the break-in at the funeral home three days before. What she had were shady characters providing untrustworthy information, but no motive. Why had anyone wanted to kill Marty Sullivan? He was a cipher, a gentle wave surrounding sand castles but never inundating them.

Follow the money. Chief Novak had always counseled that. Whether she dealt with a drug deal or a love triangle, money was always involved. Large quantities of cash, expensive gifts, stealing a loved one's assets—avarice always played a role. She thought about the cash Sullivan had deposited in his personal account. Was this drug money? They'd seen no evidence he was using, let alone dealing. Gambling winnings? They'd seen nothing to indicate he played the horses or entered the casino. Where had all this cash come from?

After an hour's work, she had no answers, but she had framed the questions she needed to ask. As she set her notes aside, her fingers touched a file folder in which, the day before, she'd deposited the letter Anna Molnar had found in the yellow handbag. A woman named Jane had written a letter to Frank Alberti, pleading with him to contact her. Lydia was certain Alberti had used and then discarded her.

But who had placed the letter in the handbag and

hidden it? And why? Anna had suggested Jane hadn't sent the letter after writing it, but she clearly had. It had been sent to this address and, sixty years later, turned up concealed in a handbag in the attic of this home. Lydia's money was on Alberti's wife. She'd opened the letter and hidden it away for reasons of her own.

She couldn't resist a mystery, even if it didn't involve a crime. She knew she'd have to solve this one, if only she could find the time.

CHAPTER FIVE

JEFFREY TOOK his family to early Mass each Sunday, after which he'd meet Lydia at headquarters. On this morning, Calvin arose at dawn to take their neighbor boy, Tommy Molnar, fishing. As Lydia cleaned up the breakfast dishes, she smiled to herself, picturing a Black cop and a white youngster spending a morning together, fishing poles dangling in the water while they enjoyed each other's company. *It's the way things should be.*

This left her with an hour of free time. She opened her notebook computer and logged on to her account at headquarters to research the dead man's father. From the moment she'd learned that Ryan Sullivan had abandoned the family when Marty was only a child, Lydia wondered what had become of him. He'd moved to south Florida, and she began searching there.

She found him almost immediately. Rather, she found lots of them. It was a popular name. She logged on to the Allegheny County Real Estate portal and searched the ownership records. Ryan John Sullivan and Grace Evans Sullivan had purchased the home in 1996. The deed had been transferred to Grace in 2002 as part of the divorce degree. Marty would then have been four years old. She wondered if he'd even remembered his father.

Armed with this information, she narrowed her search to Ryan John and Ryan J. Sullivan and came up with five matches, two of which had no number listed. She dialed one of the remaining three. When her call went to voice mail, she left a message. A woman answered at the second number, said her husband was at work, and no, he'd never lived in Pennsylvania. At the third, she spoke to Ryan J. Sullivan himself, but three minutes chatting with an elderly gentleman with hearing difficulty told her she had the wrong man.

Lydia would find another way of locating him. He might want to know his son was dead. Perhaps they'd been in contact, and he could shed light on where Marty had come up with the cash payments found in his account. Who would inherit the house now that both Grace and Martin were gone? She checked Pennsylvania law and learned that if a child died intestate, a divorced parent would not inherit unless he'd provided child support for at least a year. From what others had told her, this was not the case.

She returned to the real estate portal. She'd promised herself to investigate the letter Anna had found in the yellow purse. What better place to begin than delving into the history of her own house? Entering her lot and block number, she studied the history of ownership. It had changed hands four times since 1996, when Emilia Alberti had sold it for $83,000. Going further back, she learned the title had transferred from both Albertis to Emilia alone three years earlier.

The site listed property transfers only since 1986. For older records, it directed her to another page containing photocopies of earlier deeds. She filled out the required form and found Frank and Emilia's names on a deed dated November 1969. They'd paid the original owner—or rather his estate—$31,350 for the structure he'd built in 1932, the height of the Depression. She could imagine someone with a bit of money taking advantage of the distressed economy to build more house than he might otherwise have afforded.

She closed her computer and thought about what she'd found. Frank Alberti and his wife had bought the property in 1959. Twenty-seven years later, Emilia had sold it. Jane, Frank's jilted lover, had mailed her letter between 1958 and 1963—a range shown by the cancelled four-cent stamp.

What had become of Frank? Once Emilia opened Jane's message—which Lydia was certain had happened—had she divorced the man? Had he left her? Had he passed away?

ALLEGHENY COUNTY's crime lab never sleeps. An examiner had worked on Saturday and provided a report both detectives found when they arrived at ten. Sitting alongside each other at Jeffrey's desk, they read the results in silence.

The team had discovered three sets of fingerprints in Grace Sullivan's bedroom—hers, her son's, and a third unidentified sample. "Doctor Petarsky, I'll bet." Jeffrey looked up and nodded in agreement. They'd also found three sets of DNA on the headboard, nightstand, and closet door. Two belonged to Grace and Marty. They assumed the unknown sample was that of the veterinarian. This proved nothing, since the man had spent many nights there and had returned after her death to reclaim his gifts.

In Marty's room, they found his own prints and an

unidentified pair, which did not belong to Grace. *Had she never entered?* Had Marty cleaned his room, washed his clothing and sheets, and vacuumed? Grace Sullivan had been ill for the last two years of her life. Did that explain the absence of her prints? Barnwell had no answers.

The DNA results complicated the picture she was forming. The lab had identified traces from both mother and son, as well as a third, unidentified sample differing from the third set taken from Grace Sullivan's room. They'd found strands from both unknown individuals on the front door frame and the bannister leading to the upper floor.

As they contemplated what the trace evidence told them, Jeffrey's computer called out a siren song. Opening the inbox, he said, "Ballistics report. They're busy down on the Strip." The medical examiner's office sat along Pittsburgh's Strip District, which was also home to some of its best ethnic food stores, two fish markets, restaurants, and a forest of new high-rise apartments housing young tech workers.

Jeffrey opened the pdf and read its contents aloud. The ballistics lab had examined the three slugs. The two fired into Marty Sullivan's skull were too damaged to be of use, but the errant shot found in the plaster behind his bed contained rifling consistent with a Beretta 71. Jeffrey knew his weapons and didn't need to research the history of the handgun. "It's a version of the Model 70 whose weight was reduced by using an aluminum alloy frame instead of steel. It was manufactured from the late fifties until some time in the eighties and marketed here under the name Jaguar."

"An old weapon, then?"

"Yes, but plenty are still around. They're prized by collectors. But one could just as easily have sat in a drawer or a safe somewhere for sixty years and remain serviceable."

"Reliable enough to kill a man," she said.

AL KUCZIENSKI, whose given first name was Aleksy, had agreed to meet them after Mass. He sat in a folding chair on his front porch, a beer in his hand, as they pulled to the curb. "Okay to sit out here?" he said. "The baby's sleeping."

Barnwell was happy to comply. She'd seen enough of windowless offices, barking dogs, crematoria, and garages full of roofing materials to last the month of June. Kuczienski unfolded two more chairs and arranged them in a triangle. "I've known Marty since high school, although we weren't were never what you'd call close," he said without waiting for the question. "I guess I should say 'knew.'"

"What sort of person was he?" she asked.

"Quiet, introspective. He was a ghost, the kind who could walk into a room unnoticed and leave just as quietly. Have you discovered who murdered him?"

Jeffrey spilled the air from his lungs like an untied balloon. "That's what we're trying to learn. Do you have any ideas?"

He shook his head without answering.

"You say you didn't know him that well before you started working together," she said.

"We sometimes hung out together with a couple of other guys, driving around on summer nights looking for girls. But I didn't really *know* him. I'm not sure how to explain it."

"I think I understand."

"We were on the track team together before he had to drop out. He was a middle distance runner—the 800, 1,500, and 3,000. He had the speed and talent to have made state, if he'd stuck with it." He leaned back, folded his arms, a vacant look taking over his features as he recaptured a memory. "Coach tried to get him on the relay team, but he wasn't having it. I guess that tells you a lot about him. He always ran alone."

"You said he had to quit," Jeffrey said. "For what reason?"

"No one understood why he dropped out, and he never explained it. Then I saw these flyers around the neighborhood offering home repair services. I spotted him at his locker a few days later and said something about going into business for himself. He looked at me kind of funny and said, 'I have to. We need the money.'"

Kuczienski stroked his narrow wisp of a beard. Lydia detected tears in his eyes. "That's when I found out about his family, his dad leaving them and all."

"He told you this?" Lydia said.

"Not then. Someone else mentioned it. A girl he's going with."

"He has a girlfriend?"

"Yeah. Dora, Dora Macklin."

"She says they broke up some months ago."

"Did they? She's friends with Shari, my wife, but hasn't been around lately. Anyway, it was after we started working together that he mentioned it. We were having a beer one evening. My dad was over at the time and brought a twelve-pack, since we weren't old enough to buy it ourselves. The three of us were sitting around talking about the Steelers, what their prospects were for the coming season, that kind of stuff. Dad went inside to help my wife wash the dishes, and Marty said something to the effect that he acted like he's one of us. I didn't get what he was saying. How else was he supposed to act? That's when he told me he'd never had a father, so he assumed mine was more like an authority figure. I asked a few questions and, since we'd both had a couple of beers, it all came out."

"He was resentful?" Jeffrey asked.

"You know it. He hated the guy. Called him selfish. Said he was living the high life down in South Florida while his mother worked to support the two of them. That's when he told me he'd dropped out of track to help her."

"He had a chip on his shoulder," Jeffrey said.

"Yeah. He never mentioned it again. Maybe he sobered up the next morning and regretted he'd said anything. Not that we were drunk. Dad wouldn't have let us have that much." The man closed his eyes and shook his head.

"When his mom got sick, I could tell it got to him. Now, he was working to support both of them. And when she died, he'd get angry over nothing. I thought if he didn't get help, he was going to do something, either to himself or to someone else."

Jeffrey asked how the two of them had found their way into Coppola's company. Kuczienski said Sullivan had worked taken a summer job there between his junior and senior years and planned to go full time as soon as he gradu-ated. "A couple weeks before school was over, he asked me if I'd lined anything up. I hadn't. He said this roofer was looking for help and was I interested. I signed on for what I thought was a few months. I'm still there."

He crushed the empty beer can with one hand and scratched the back of his neck with the other. "I gotta find something else to do, though. This guy's a sleaze. I need to find a union job."

"A sleaze?" Jeffrey said.

"Cuts corners on everything, and drives us workers like

shit. Doesn't pay overtime. Says he knows how much time a job should take, and if we don't finish by then, it's because we're screwing around. Which I wasn't doing, anyway."

Something in his tone caught Lydia's attention. "But Marty?"

Kuczienski paused, his eyes darting around as though he'd been trapped. He took a deep breath. "All right. He'd gotten sloppy the last few months. It was like he didn't care any more. He was always on his phone, setting up one of his private jobs."

"Why did Coppola allow that?"

Kuczienski seemed to consider again, his eyes shifting back and forth. While he'd been voluble when he started speaking to them, they were now pulling words out of him. She sensed they'd entered a minefield. "You'll have to ask him. Something was going on there. I couldn't figure out what. Anyone else, Coppola would have fired weeks ago, but he let Marty get away with it. I don't know why, but I do know one thing."

Lydia raised her brows, her blue eyes drilling into him as she posed the silent question.

"It wasn't out of the goodness of his heart," Kuczienski said. "That SOB doesn't have one."

Ross Sutton had accessed Grace Sullivan's bank records, and what he'd found sent the detectives rushing to Daniel Sedlak's home. They arrived in Fox Chapel just as his Escalade pulled into the garage. A curved driveway arced before a sprawling house whose two levels fit the contour of a tree-lined hill. They followed him into the driveway as he was preparing to close the door, a woman and two teenagers scampering up the indoor stairs. "What is it this time?" he demanded.

She introduced Jeffrey. "We have another question for you."

He stood with his hands on his hips, flaunting his annoyance. "So, ask it."

"I'd prefer we sat down somewhere," Jeffrey told him.

"We just returned from lunch. We always go after church." When Jeffrey didn't move, he said, "All right. Come in. But make this quick. We're changing and heading out to North Park."

He led them up the paved walk to the front door and unlocked it. "Police," he told his wife, who stood in the living room wearing a question mark on her face. "It's about that burglary."

She turned and walked away without a word. Barnwell thought she detected a strained dynamic between the pair, but wasn't prepared to pursue it. Sedlak motioned them to a long sofa facing the window and took a chair before it. "So, what's your question?"

"In going through Marty Sullivan's records, we found he'd paid $1,500 for his mother's cremation."

"That's our standard basic charge," he said. "No frills. No urn. We place the cremains in a heavy plastic bag and enclose it in a cardboard box."

"Then how do you explain this?" Jeffrey handed over a document sealed in a clear folder.

Sedlak appeared to study it. With the sunlight streaming in behind him, Lydia couldn't make out his expression. He returned it and leaned back in the chair, crossing one ankle over the other. A man at peace, she thought.

"It's a contract for cremation services, executed over a

year ago and signed by you and Grace Sullivan." When Sedlak remained stoic, Lydia said, "When she learned she was dying, she began planning for her last days to spare her son the trouble. She came to you and arranged for her own cremation." *Had she told her son what she was doing at the time, or had she informed him after the fact? She might never know.*

Cocking his head to one side, the mortician frowned. "I don't believe she ever paid us."

"She did." Jeffrey presented him with another transparent folder containing a bank record, the entry highlighted in yellow.

While they couldn't read his expression, Sedlak's hands twitched as he returned the folder. "I'll have to check our records. This was some time ago."

"Is this why Marty broke in four nights ago? Was he trying to prove he'd paid for something his mother had already arranged?"

He responded with silence.

"She paid you $1,375 sixteen months ago, but when she died, her son had to ante up $1,500. Either they paid twice, or inflation is more rampant that I thought."

He looked off the one side for a moment, then, in a low voice reflecting all the spite he could muster, he said, "I've told you all I know. If you have further questions, go through my attorney."

"We need to speak to your wife," Jeffrey said.

"What for?"

"To corroborate your story about where you were on the night Sullivan was murdered."

"I won't permit that. Speak to our lawyer. You're treating us like suspects when we're the victims. This man Sullivan broke into our establishment, for what purpose I don't know. He took nothing. That's the end of the story. This interrogation is over."

He escorted them to the front door and slammed it behind them.

"What do you think?" Barnwell said as they walked down the path to the driveway.

"Guilty as hell," he said. "Of something, at least."

Jeffrey backed out and paused before putting the cruiser into drive. He looked out at the spacious home looming over the top edge of the windshield. "What do you suppose this is worth?"

"A million?"

"Maybe more. We're in the wrong business, Barnwell."

BECAUSE DR. PETARSKY hadn't wanted the detectives to interview his wife, he'd given them the name of a friend, Barry Goldstein, to confirm his alibi for the night of Sullivan's slaying. Back at headquarters Sunday afternoon, Barnwell made the call, with Jeffrey listening on speaker phone.

"Sid said you'd be calling," Goldstein told her.

"Did he say why?"

"Just that you wanted to confirm that Rachel and I had dinner at their place Thursday night."

"And did you?"

Goldstein laughed. "You might say that. Elena's not much of a cook, but they're nice people. We enjoy their company, so we put up with the chewy chicken." He chuckled again, amused at his cleverness.

"And when did you leave?"

"It was late. After ten. We tried to make our exit after

dessert, but Sid kept telling stories about animals he'd treated and their owners, some of whom needed treatment."

Barnwell resisted the temptation to remark that this was great dinner conversation, asking if he could be more specific about when he and his wife had left. Goldstein responded by calling, "Rachel, what time did we leave Petarsky's Thursday night?" He waited a beat and said, "She says it was around ten thirty, because it took us fifteen minutes to drive home, and she noticed it was almost time for the late news."

Lydia glanced at Jeffrey. That left plenty of time for the veterinarian to have made it to Etna. Jeffrey tapped the fingers of his right hand against the thumb. She frowned until she recognized he was imitating a mouth speaking.

"And Dr. Petarsky kept telling stories, you said?"

"As though he didn't want us to leave."

Lydia's breath caught in her throat. "Does he always do that?"

"Sid loves to talk, but this was a bit more than usual." He lowered his voice to almost a whisper. "I don't think the two of them have much to say to each other, so when they have company over ..."

"I understand," she said. She raised her eyebrows at Jeffrey, who shook his head. She thanked the man and ended the call.

"So the good doctor's alibi isn't one," she said.

"And they didn't overstay their welcome, as he claimed. He held them there."

"As though he was creating a cover story," she said. She took a long swig from her water bottle. "We need to speak to his wife, whether he likes it or not."

Lydia's cell phone chirped as they returned to headquarters. It was a number she didn't recognize. As soon as she answered it, a voice said, "I found it."

"I'm sorry, but who is this?"

"Seth Goodman. From Julio's? You asked me to check the security videos to see if I could find the man who was looking for Marty. We were too busy last night, so I came in a couple of hours ago and found it."

Lydia told Jeffrey to turn around. They were about to enter the merger with I-279 heading toward the Fort Pitt Bridge, but Jeffrey crossed a lane of traffic and exited toward the David McCullough Bridge, executed a U-turn on Canal Street, and headed back the way they'd come.

Goodman was waiting for them, standing with both hands placed flat on the bar as though locked in place. He led them toward the office overlooking the brewery, where they'd spoken the day before. "It only took a few minutes to find the scene where he came looking for Marty, since that was just Monday evening. It took me longer to locate their original conversation. I thought it was just the week before, but turns out it was June 2nd, a Friday night."

He first brought up the video of the man who'd returned to the brewpub to locate Marty. The image was clear, but the camera's location, above the bar and taking in most of its length, made it difficult to detect his features. He had a slender frame, but as he mounted the stool, Barnwell noticed a bulging waistline that spilled over his belt. He wore a gimme cap with a logo of some sort—a company, she thought, not a sports team—and bowed his head. Was this his natural bearing, or was he trying to avoid the camera? Either way, the video didn't tell them much. Still, they'd subpoena the hard drive on which it was stored to see what Ross Sutton could make of it.

Goodman hit the escape key and rolled the thumbnail images back to June 2nd, picking a sequence beginning at 9:13 p.m. From the four-way split on the screen, he selected the image of the camera over the bar. Every seat was occupied, and several people stood behind, drinks in hand, as they chatted with each other. At one end, almost out of the frame, a lone figure stared straight forward as another, the man in the earlier video, engaged him in conversation. He appeared to shout, since his listener, Marty Sullivan, recoiled at certain points.

This his demeanor changed. Instead of ignoring him, Sullivan turned toward the man, whose hands painted images in the air as he spoke. His movements became exaggerated, and he seemed to wobble on his stool. "He's drunk," Jeffrey said.

"Keep watching," Goodman replied. "Something happens I didn't notice that night. I was busy as hell and wasn't paying much attention to them."

The man held up a finger and pointed to his empty glass. They watched as Goodman refilled it. "I think he'd been drinking before he came in," he explained. "I should have cut him off."

The two men resumed talking, and Sullivan appeared to interrupt the monologue with either questions or comments. The man waved his hands in the air and laughed. Sullivan leaned forward, wagged a finger in his face, and turned to look behind him. "He's trying to hush him up," Lydia said.

Sullivan said something to the bartender, then reached into his pocket and peeled off several bills from a roll. "Until I saw this," Goodman said, "I'd forgotten Marty paid the bill. He told me to keep the change. I went on to the next order and didn't see what followed."

The younger man looked behind him, stood up, and motioned for his companion to follow, grabbing his drink as he did so. The drunk rose unsteadily and followed Sullivan as they left the frame.

Goodman returned to the four-way split and switched to a camera overlooking a set of tables. As the pair wandered into view, the older man stumbled against the edge of a chair. Sullivan grabbed him with one arm while setting the drink down with the other. The two sat together for twelve minutes, and though Sullivan's back was to the camera, he appeared to be pumping his companion for information of some sort. He reached for something below the table.

"He's making notes on his phone," Barnwell said. Jeffrey grunted in agreement.

The older man said something, pulled his chair back, and made his lopsided way out of the frame. Another camera caught him disappearing into the men's room. Sullivan reached across the table and pulled something toward him. He concealed beneath the table, stared down, appeared to fumble through it, then returned the object.

"His wallet," she said. "Marty went through his wallet." They watched as Sullivan tapped something into his phone.

Another two minutes passed, and the man returned. Sullivan signaled for a server, but she ignored him. "We cut him off," Goodman said. "If we know he's drunk, and he kills someone while driving home, we're responsible."

After three more minutes of conversation, Sullivan rose from the table and said something, clapped the man on his shoulder, and left. A few minutes later, his companion did as well, weaving his way out of the picture. Goodman selected an exterior shot, which showed the man lurching toward his car.

"An older Kia," Jeffrey said. It took over a minute before

the vehicle left its parking spot. "Freeze the frame," he ordered. "Can you enlarge it?"

"No," Goodman said, "this system doesn't allow us to do that."

"We can." Jeffrey asked the bartender how long the videos were kept before the system overwrote them. Satisfied that the thirty days were enough, he said, "We're going to subpoena these images. Meanwhile, let nothing happen to them."

The detectives thanked Goodman for his diligence and left the pub. "What do we have here?" Jeffrey said as he returned to headquarters.

"A man who's had too much to drink tells Marty something. Sullivan finds it sufficiently interesting to pay for his drinks, take surreptitious notes, and rifle through his wallet. Two weeks pass, and the man returns to the bar to find him. Forty-eight hours later, someone breaks into Sullivan's house and murders him."

"Agreed," he said. "Who he was and what he told Sullivan we have no idea, but we need to find out."

"CHECK YOUR INBOX," Ross Sutton commanded over the radio.

"Don't hold us in suspense," Jeffrey replied. Lydia suppressed a chuckle, for that's exactly what the digital forensics detective enjoyed doing. He would dangle a revelation out of reach, like a person teasing a cat with a ball of feathers at the end of a wand.

"We unlocked Sullivan's computer and found some interesting emails. I've uploaded them to his file."

"That was quick." Sutton's team was talented, but it

could take them anywhere from a few days to weeks to crack a password-protected computer.

"Getting in was no problem," he said. "You want to guess his password?"

"'Password'?" Jeffrey suggested.

"Close, but no cigar. Barnwell, you want to take a shot?"

She thought about what she'd learned about Sullivan. "His mother's name."

"Bingo! Followed by the numbers 0354, the month and year of her birth. You're pretty good. You want to move across the hall and work with us?"

Lydia didn't respond, knowing the offer was meant in jest. She was thinking about what this told her about the murder victim. It was not unusual for an unmarried man in his mid-twenties to be attached to his family, but everything she'd heard or observed told her he was more than a mommy's boy. His devotion to Grace bordered on obsession. What role could this have played in his murder?

"We still don't have a motive." Jeffrey seemed to read her thoughts.

"Maybe those emails will tell us. Ross called them interesting. Is that an understatement?"

"He doesn't work on Sundays without a reason." Jeffrey pulled into the police lot and double-timed it to the entrance, Lydia in tow. He sat at his desk, pulling her chair alongside his, and opened the computer file on the Sullivan case. Sutton had attached a long thread of emails sent and received by the victim, but in a second file, he had isolated three of them.

The first was from a Gmail address they didn't recognize, just a jumble of letters before for the at sign.

I won't pay you another dime, you damn fool. I've told my wife everything. You have no more leverage over me. If you contact me again, I'll report your blackmailing ass to the police and relish every day you spend in prison.

The second was from Sullivan's account to the same address:

I don't believe you. You wouldn't dare admit this to your wife. She'd sue you for divorce and take everything you're worth. Don't tell me you'll go to the police, either. You stole my mother's mink coat, diamond necklace, and the string of pearls. You're the one headed for a cell.

I never blackmailed you. I asked for your help to pay her medical bills. You gave her plenty of money in the past, so I knew you could afford it. I asked you to show me a kindness. Instead, you treat me like a criminal.

And finally, this response.

My wife is a fine woman, very understanding. We were going through a trial separation when I met your mother. I wandered, and so did she. You have nothing on me. As for the gifts, I only took what was mine.

Don't try claiming me you weren't extorting money from me. Yes, the first time you called, you said you were just asking me for a favor. When I refused, you thought it over and called back, saying you were calling my office rather than the house. "I know you wouldn't want your wife finding out." Those were your words. That's extortion.

Never contact me again. Do not call my wife. If you make any further attempt to blackmail me, you will suffer the consequences.

Jeffrey leaned back in his chair and hissed, "Jesus!"

Lydia nodded as though she'd suspected something of the sort. "Now we know where he got that cash. Did it all come from Petarsky?"

Jeffrey stroke his cheek and opened another file from Sutton. "Does it seem reasonable that he'd pay out $37,000 over a series of weeks and only then end it? Hold on a sec." He wrote a date on a notepad and returned to the emails. "Petarsky's last message—if we confirm this is his account—was on May 17th. Sullivan was still depositing cash payments in June, the last one two weeks ago."

Lydia let out a long sigh. "Right. We'll need to subpoena Petarsky's bank records."

"One thing's for sure," Jeffrey said.

"Our innocent little introvert was an extortionist," she finished for him. "Could this explain why he was talking to our mystery man in the bar, and why he came after him? Did the old man tell him something he later regretted?"

"He wasn't blackmailing just Petarsky," Jeffrey said.

"This may be why he broke into the funeral home. He wasn't just after reimbursement. He wanted something he could hold over Daniel Sedlak's head."

This email exchange had added an important element to the case. At last, they had a motive ... and an abundance of suspects.

———

LYDIA ARRIVED at the Italian restaurant in Bridgeville before Calvin, found a table near the window, and had a glass of iced tea while she waited for him to arrive. A family occupied the next table: a mother and father and two children, a girl of elementary school age and her brother sitting in a booster chair. She smiled at them and studied the menu.

Calvin passed by the window, having parked down the block. She waved as he passed, so he joined her without waiting to be seated. "Ordered yet?" he asked.

"No, but I've settled on the linguine with clam sauce."

He buried his head in the menu. As he did so, she saw the woman at the next table nudge her husband and nod in their direction. He looked, but returned his attention to the dwindling slices of pizza. The woman scoffed and must have darted her eyes at her daughter, for she looked in their direction and giggled. Her mother shook her head. No use making a show of it.

On most occasions when Lydia and Calvin went out, it was at the end of a workday, so he was still in uniform. People ignored them, figuring they were on official business. This being Sunday, he wore civilian clothes. This made them a couple and provided the woman with an opportunity to teach her child how to hate.

Seeing her frown, Calvin said, "What's wrong?"

"I'll tell you later."

He glanced at the table and, under his breath, said, "Oh."

While she understood that he'd lived his life with racism and was thus inured to it, she was not. She longed to turn to the woman and say, "Yes, we're a couple. I'm with him because I love him. And I love him because he's the kindest, most thoughtful man I've ever met. He cares for me and is attentive to my needs. So what's your fucking problem?"

She would have concluded her speech by reaching over and shoving the woman's face into her salad. Instead, she turned and stared at the woman, peering at her until she locked eyes with Lydia's piercing gaze, the intense blue daggers that had vanquished many a recalcitrant witness.

As though reading her thoughts, Calvin whispered, "Don't make me arrest you."

"I'd resist," she said, not bothering to lower her voice. "You'd have to handcuff me."

The woman gathered her family and left, her husband standing at the cash register waiting for his bill. Lydia reached across the table and covered Calvin's hand with her own. Something positive had emerged from this disturbing encounter, for it was the first time she'd admitted to herself that she was in love with him.

CHAPTER SIX

CALVIN HAD BEEN CALLED back to work the night before on a shooting in neighboring Byers Township, one of the three communities that would become part of the regional force, so he was sleeping in. Lydia crept downstairs, put the Moka pot on the stove, and opened her computer. She typed "Frank Alberti" into the search bar. The page filled with links to a swimmer, a private detective, and others with the same name, but not a trace of the former owner of her house.

She leaned back and thought while the espresso pot bubbled. Of course. By 1996, Frank's name was no longer on the deed. Many newspapers had not digitized their archives before that year. Standing over the stove, she recalled someone telling her how to access photocopies of old articles.

Lydia steamed milk and prepared her morning coffee while she tried to remember. An answer came to her. She returned to the computer and typed, "News stories from years ago." Instructions began loading even as she entered her query. She clicked on the listing for the site's archive and entered Alberti's name. The page filled with news pages containing stories about people mentioned in the text. As she scanned the headlines, she realized she should narrow the criteria. She added the word "Carnegie" to the search terms.

The site presented ten articles, three of which were irrelevant. But the remaining seven were not. Her breath quickened as she made her way through the first story. Since these were photocopies of news pages, they were difficult to read. Type was faded in some images, and where the original document had been folded, portions of the text were out of focus. But what it told her was clear. Her skin grew cold, as did her coffee, while she perused each article, printing them out as she went. Lydia reached for the copies and found they'd only printed thumbnails. "Damn," she said.

"What's wrong?"

She'd been so preoccupied, she hadn't heard Calvin's heavy tread as he made his way down the staircase and into the kitchen. "Sit down and read this." She opened the third article, which was the most complete, and watched as he studied it.

"Murdered," he said.

"Yeah. He was found in a motel in Ross Township. Someone broke into his room and shot him dead."

"Who?"

"As far as I can tell, the case was unsolved. Local police questioned a former girlfriend, Jane Quinlan."

"The Jane who wrote the letter?"

"Possibly, but if they charged her, it's not mentioned in any of these articles." She buried her face in her hands. "I don't have time for this. Now that we have a motive for Sullivan's slaying, we need to re-interview all our suspects."

Today, they would check Petarsky's alibi, question others at the funeral home, and ask Marty's employer why he'd failed to mention his best friend. Jeffrey would seek to subpoena the veterinarian's bank records and the bar's videos. She would ask the public's help in identifying the stranger in the bar. Something else was tugging at her memory, something that had awakened her before sunrise.

"I guess it will have to wait," he said.

She folded her hands against her mouth as though in prayer. "I know you're busy…"

"No," he said, waving his hands to forestall the onslaught. "We had a shooting last night, I'm still two officers down, and I have so many planning meetings for this transition I don't have time to run the department. What's so urgent about it?"

"I can't let it go, Calvin. A man who owned this house was murdered, and it looks like they never found his killer. We're cops. We hate loose ends. Besides," she said, "even if I had time, if Jeffrey knew I was taking on a side job while we're in the middle of a murder investigation, he'd be furious."

He shook his head in frustration while she turned to the stove and began making breakfast. While she broke eggs into a pan, he slid two slices of bacon into the microwave and bread into the toaster.

Feeling her steely blue eyes on him, he said, "Why don't I ask Tommy to go through these articles and summarize everything in one document?"

She suppressed a derisive snort. "He's too young to take on something like this."

"He asked me to look over an essay he had to write for fifth grade English. I didn't change a thing. He's sharp, well organized, and writes well. He can start with this third article, lay out all the facts, then go through everything else and add whatever he finds on the other pages. Meanwhile, I'll call county and see if they still have a file on it. I'll keep you out of it."

"Thanks," she said. "I knew I could count on you."

"And," he said, "you take advantage of me because I can't resist you."

Lydia's cell phone chimed. She leaned over the screen, saw assistant medical examiner Brandy Timmons was calling, and paused the eggs mid-scramble. "You're handling the Sullivan murder?"

"Detective Jeffrey and I, yes."

"We have a walk-in who wants to view the body. Says he's his father."

Ask and ye shall receive, Lydia thought. "Hold him there. I'll be in as soon as I can."

She summoned Calvin, who sat at the kitchen counter swiping through his phone. "I have to run. Keep stirring these until they firm up. Don't turn up the heat."

"You think I don't know how to make scrambled eggs?"

"Just don't let them get tough," she said. "Keep stirring. If they cook too fast, take them off the burner for a moment."

He chuckled and shook his head while she ran upstairs to pour herself into her clothes. She returned five minutes later, puffing out her curls with her hands, to find a mound of shimmering pale yellow on a plate alongside a slice of toast and a strip of crisp bacon. She shoveled the eggs into her mouth, took a bite of the toast, and raised her fork in salute. He could finish the bacon, as he always did.

LYDIA KNEW BETTER than to join what had become a parking lot on Parkway West at this hour. Instead, she took Noblestown Road into Crafton and picked up Route 60 to the West End Bridge. Twenty minutes later, she pulled to the curb in front of the medical examiner's long building on Penn Avenue. A man sat in the lobby lounging against the arms of the chair with his legs extended before him. He wore khaki-colored shorts and a T-shirt bearing the name of a seafood shack at Ponce Inlet. Lydia had been there. "Ryan Sullivan?" she said.

He looked up at her and nodded. "You the cop?" He rose to his feet. Sullivan was of medium height, with sandy brown hair streaked by the sun. He was tan as a pecan, but his skin glistened, and he smelled of coconut oil.

Barnwell introduced herself. "Can I see the body now?"

"I need some identification."

He pulled a wallet from his hip pocket that held a few credit cards on the left and his cell phone on the right and fished out his Florida driver's license. She looked it over and returned it to him. "We've already identified your son through his fingerprints and DNA. We don't need you to formalize it."

"I'd still like to see it."

It, she thought. *Not him.* "The medical examiner performed an autopsy," she told him. "I'm afraid his body's not in condition to be viewed now."

The man scowled and puffed out his chest. "Who gave them permission to do that?"

"It's required under Pennsylvania law. Whenever there's a homicide, the coroner performs a postmortem examination."

Sullivan frowned again, but didn't pursue it. "What about his things? What's happened to the house?"

"I'm not an attorney, but you and your wife divorced twenty years ago. When she died, she left everything to your son. We haven't found a will, so he may have died intestate. In this case—"

"I was his father." He clenched his fists as she spoke to him. Veins stuck out on his neck. If the sun hadn't grilled his skin like a slice of melba toast, his face would have been red.

"In this case," she continued, as though he hadn't interrupted her, "the estate will go into probate. The court will search for all claimants and determine who inherits. It's not for me to say."

"I bought that house. It's mine."

Barnwell knew he'd made the down payment, but Grace had paid off the mortgage months before her cancer diagnosis. She took a chair and motioned for him to sit alongside her. In a different tone of voice, she asked, "How well did you know your son?"

"My ex-wife wouldn't let me see him." Barnwell had read the divorce decree. He had visitation rights. Had he not exercised them, or had Grace ignored the order?

"When's the last time you spoke to him?"

"Aw," he said, waving a hand in the air as though the matter were of no importance. "A while back."

"He told a friend you left when he was just a child and he hadn't seen you since."

"Grace kept us apart." He leaned into his fist, hiding his mouth with his knuckles that displayed a ring she took to be gold. "Besides, I had a new family to support. I couldn't be racing back and forth between here and Florida."

"So you haven't been in touch with him since the divorce?"

"No," he admitted. "But I was still his father. And I bought that house. I only want what's coming to me."

Barnwell wanted the same thing, but the result would have been different. She asked where he was staying. He gave her the address of a cheap motel out on Route 60, near where she lived. "But I can't stick around," he said. "I need to get this cleared up so I can go home."

"Will you make funeral arrangements before you leave? I don't know when the medical examiner will release—"

"Won't you folks handle it? He was murdered. Don't you take care of victims?" She gazed at him until he looked away. "I guess not, huh? Well, I don't have the money to do that. If we'd been close..."

Hiding her aversion to this little man, she asked how he'd traveled to Pittsburgh; he said he'd driven. "When did you arrive?"

"Last night. I drove straight through."

"Where were you last week?"

"At home in Daytona." He drew himself up and curled his hands into fists. "You trying to tie me into this? You can ask my girlfriend."

She noted the probability he'd been through another divorce. Perhaps more than one. "You work in construction?" she said.

"No," he said, shaking his head vigorously. "I had an accident a few years back. I'm on disability."

He looked fit to her, but she'd learned not to judge. He might have some underlying illness or injury. More likely, she thought, he's a con artist, livin' la vida loca, spending his days on the beach, drinking beers at midday while Jimmy Buffett plays in the background.

As Barnwell turned west on 16th Street toward the David McCullough Bridge, a car in front of her bounce as though tossed by a mighty hand, then crawled to a stop, blocking traffic. A woman got out, wrapping a rain jacket around her as the morning drizzle enveloped her. She looked at the right front and threw up her hands. Lydia turned on her emergency lights and joined her.

"I don't know what happened." Her shrill voice quaked as she battled tears.

"A pothole," Lydia said. "We grow them. We've had a bumper crop this spring. Turn the corner into Mulberry and pull to the curb? You're blocking traffic." Despite her flashing signals, drivers leaned on their horns as they inched past, as if the sound waves would push her vehicle out of the way.

"I'm trying to cross the bridge," she said. "I'm running late."

"You're not going anywhere on a rim. Please move it, and I'll take a look."

The woman got behind the wheel and made the turn into what amounted to an alley. At least it was out of the way. Lydia drove past and parked in front of her. She had the driver open the trunk, saw she had no spare, and summoned both Pittsburgh police and a tow truck. She waited until a uniformed officer arrived, then continued through the alley, returning on Smallman to cross the bridge.

Something about the encounter clicked, bringing back the memory she'd lost during the night. The woman's car was a Kia.

At headquarters, she checked Jeffrey's schedule and saw he was at the DA's office. She walked to the rear of the bullpen and into Ross Sutton's lair. His bulky shoulders were hunched over an electronic device of some sort, his desk, as always, littered with the detritus of past intrusions into recalcitrant cell phones. "You interruptible?" she asked.

"Seeing as how you just did so."

"You once told me that, given the make of a car, its location, and the time, you can trace where it goes."

He put down whatever he was holding and turned to face her. "Not its final destination, but the last camera-equipped intersection it passed."

"Even without a license number?" she asked.

"If you know when it left its last location, all we need is the make, model, and color," he said. "What you got?"

She had his interest now. "I'd like you to trace two paths. One is the blue or gray Kia that passed in front of the murder house on Ballard Street Thursday morning."

"It was gray," he said. "We've enhanced it."

She tucked that away for future reference. "The other is a similar car that left a brew pub on the night of June 2nd. We have it on security footage. Jeffrey's seeking the warrant now."

Sutton grinned, displaying his glee for have something more to do than cracking electronic devices. "I'm on it."

"And one more thing," she said. "Is it possible to discover what materials Marty bought from Home Depot?"

"Of course it is," he said. "I suppose you want me to do that, too."

She smiled and left his office without responding.

———

Jeffrey was still at the DA's office and radioed Lydia to check Sid Petarsky's alibi with his wife. As she drove north on the interstate, she considered how to approach the veterinarian's affair. Best to ask questions, she decided, allow Elena to answer, and see where it led her.

Their home was a large, white structure in a new development atop a hill that overlooked a remaining patch of woodland. A gust of wind tore at the hood of her jacket as she left her cruiser, and the downpour drowned her curls. As nasty as this was two days before the start of summer, but she'd be less happy to live here in mid-January.

The woman who answered the door appeared to be in her late forties. She had wiry, salt and pepper hair, a pallid complexion, and downturned lips. "Elena Petarsky?" Lydia said. She nodded without answering.

Lydia introduced herself. "Okay," she said, but she stood in the doorway with no sign of laying out the welcome mat.

"May I come in? I have a few questions to ask."

Elena peered behind her. "The house is a mess."

"I don't mind," Lydia said. "I live in a pigsty." This wasn't true, but she'd dealt with witnesses long enough to know that standing on the threshold was no way to conduct an interview. It put the subject in charge.

A gust of wind blew rain through the front door, settling the issue. Elena tossed her head toward the interior. Lydia entered and passed a spacious living room to the left. Nothing appeared out of place, and the furniture was many steps above Ikea. She glimpsed cream-colored walls adorned with seascapes as she followed the veterinarian's wife past a long dining room and into a smaller eating area alongside the kitchen.

"I suppose I should offer you coffee," she said without enthusiasm.

"No, thank you," Lydia gestured with her water bottle. "If you have a cloth, though..." The woman pulled a wad of paper towels off its roll and extended it to her, unwilling to soil one of her expensive cloth towels. As Lydia wiped her hair and neck, Elena poured herself a cup, looking out toward what remained of another patch of forest behind the house.

"Sid told me the police might ask me some questions. I was expecting a phone call." Her face wore a rebuke, but Lydia ignored it.

"Did he explain what this is about?"

"Yes. One of his patients was murdered, and you seem to think he's involved. He wasn't. He was home that night."

"Thursday night?"

"Yes. We had company. They stayed late, so we turned in as soon as they left. I didn't even tackle the dishes until the next morning."

There it was again. Petarsky and his wife blamed the hour on the Goldsteins, who claimed the doctor had kept them there. "You and your husband share the same bedroom?"

Elena Petarsky seemed to melt, hugging herself and rocking back and forth. "Why do you ask? What difference does it make?"

Without meaning to, the woman had answered her question. "So he could have slipped out without your knowing."

"He didn't. I'm a light sleeper. He snores. That's why he has his own room."

"Your children...?"

"Are at camp this week, but they left only this morning." She looked toward the window again. "They can't be having much fun in this weather."

She waited for the next question, but Lydia didn't give her one, using the weapon of silence. "Why are you so insistent? It's too bad about the woman, but she was just a patient." She raised her voice at the end of the sentence, as though stifling the urge to pose it as a question.

"That's what your husband told you, that she was just a patient?"

She lowered her head, looking up at Barnwell from beneath her brow. "What do you mean by that?"

Lydia pretended to study her notes, flipping over a few pages. She nodded as if satisfied and looked up at the woman. "He told us he was seeing her while the two of you were separated."

"Were—" Her mouth dropped open, and she gave the slightest of snickers.

"Are you surprised?"

"I'd like you to leave now." Elena Petarsky stared down at her trembling hands, on the verge of tears.

"I'm sorry," Lydia said, "but you now understand why I have to ask these questions."

"He was here that night. He didn't go out. I would have known if he'd left. Now, please leave." With that, the tears overflowed her eyes. Lydia reached for a tissue from the box on the counter, but the woman waved her off, choking on words she couldn't make out.

"All right. If I have other questions, I'll have to return." She made for the front door on her own and sat behind the wheel for a moment. While she loved her job, certain aspects turned her stomach. Chief among them was conveying bad news to someone, whether a death or a betrayal.

I shouldn't have had to do this. But one thing's sure: That son-of-a-bitch lied to us.

As she made her way back to headquarters on the south side, Barnwell replayed their interview with Daniel Sedlak the day before. A thought flashed across her mind. She peeled off I-79 at the junction with I-279, then headed northeast along Route 28 to Etna. Entering the funeral home, she opened the door to the director's office and flashed her ID to his secretary. "Mr. Sedlak is busy," she said.

"That's fine. I just want to confirm some information he's given us." She reached in her notebook and showed her a photo. "Have you ever seen this person?"

"Isn't that the man who was killed last week?"

"Yes, Martin Sullivan. Do you recall his visiting here?"

"Sure. It was around February, I think. After the holidays, anyway."

"He came to see Mr. Sedlak?"

"And his sister. He spoke to both of them."

"How did he seem?"

She turned and looked over her shoulder as though someone might be listening, but there was no one else present. "He was polite to me, real nice. He seemed sort of —" she paused as though looking for the right word.

"Was he angry?" Barnwell asked.

"No. Confused, I'd say. His mother had just died, and they'd brought her body in downstairs. He'd already made arrangements, I think."

"This was his second visit?"

"Yeah. He'd come back for some reason."

"He didn't seem upset, perturbed?"

"No, like I said, he was real polite when he came in. He asked to speak to Mr. Sedlak. They went into the office and spoke for a few minutes, then Delores came in, and they talked some more."

"Did they raise their voices?"

"No, not that I can hear much out here. But it seemed like a normal conversation. They walked him out here. He shook his head like he was confused, but he thanked them and said he'd look again. That's what he said, 'I'll see if I can find it.'"

"Do you recall anything else about his visit?"

She seemed to give the matter some thought. "He even thanked me as he left. A nice young man. I was shocked to hear someone killed him."

Lydia thanked her and turned to leave. "You won't tell them we talked, will you?"

A strange reaction. "Relax. You haven't told me anything except that he was polite." She smiled and nodded.

As she made her way back, Lydia combined what she knew with what she surmised. Sullivan had called the funeral home to collect his mother's body, come in to arrange for her cremation, then was quoted a cost. Convinced his mother had already paid for the service, he'd searched for her contract. As she'd suggested to Sedlak, when he couldn't find a copy, he returned to speak to him and his sister. They denied she'd made any such arrangement and told him if she had, she would have kept a copy of the agreement.

Marty had left, shaking his head, but promising to search the family records more closely. Months later, his confusion turned to anger, and he broke into the funeral home to find evidence they'd defrauded him. While she was speculating, one thing was certain: Sedlak had lied when he said he didn't recall meeting the victim.

"You saved me," Jeffrey said as he mopped his brow and lowered himself into his chair. "Jesus, it's wet out there. Is this how it'll be all summer?"

"Saved you how?" she asked, having no interest in being sidelined by a discussion about the weather.

"Melissa Dawkins is handling the case." Dawkins was an assistant district attorney, a meticulous prosecutor who dotted every i, crossed every t, and then checked her spelling. "She kept me waiting, as she always does, trying to show who's in charge. When you called, she'd okayed the search warrant for the bar's hard drive, but declined to go after Petarsky's bank accounts. She said we didn't have enough."

"Which we could only get if she okayed the warrant," Barnwell said.

"Right, so when you called to tell me he'd lied to us, I did an about-face, barged into her office, and changed her mind."

"You're welcome," she said. "How long will this take?"

"By the end of the day, if we're lucky. If not, tomorrow."

Hating inactivity, she heaved a sigh. "What do we do in the meantime? Petarsky's our lead suspect. He lied to Marty Sullivan to end his blackmail. I understand why he did so. But he also lied to his wife, then to us. We can't believe anything he's told us."

"You're right, but until we have proof Sullivan was blackmailing him, we're in a holding pattern."

"We wait," she said, repeating his mantra.

"Yes, but if Sullivan was blackmailing the vet, he may have done so to others."

They discussed what she'd learned about Sullivan's two visits to the funeral home. "If he'd had a copy of his mother's cremation contract, he wouldn't have had to shell out the $1,500. He was forced to pay for something she'd already purchased and broke in to find proof."

Jeffrey rose from his desk and ran his hands through his hair as he stared across the bullpen. "What was he going to do with it? Come to us to file criminal charges?"

Lydia emptied her water bottle. "Or blackmail him."

"Perhaps he'd already called Sedlak, told him if he didn't want this becoming public, he'd have to pay. So Sedlak breaks into Sullivan's house the next night and shoots him."

"But wouldn't he have searched for the contract and destroyed it?" she said.

"Let's try this," he said, waving his pen in the air like a conductor. "He confronts Sullivan, says he wants the contract back. When Marty refuses, he draws a weapon and threatens him. They struggle, the gun goes off, Sullivan is grazed, but he's conscious. He still won't surrender the contract, perhaps even tells him he'll get him for assault with a deadly weapon. Sedlak orders him to turn over on the bed, puts the gun against his head, and threatens to kill him. Marty thinks he's bluffing, so he still resists. Sedlak fires two shots."

Barnwell nodded as he spoke, picturing how it might have happened. "Once he's done so, he fears the shots have alerted neighbors. He runs from the house without bothering to search for the one piece of evidence that can tie him to the murder," she said. "The question is, what do we do about it?"

And another thing troubled her. If Sedlak had come to Marty's house, why was there no trace of him on the surveillance cameras? Or anyone else, for that matter. Had he come through the alley? Then it hit her. "We're putting too much weight on this security footage. It shows a gray

Kia coming and going, but no other vehicle. Route 28 is the most straightforward path to the neighborhood, so we conclude no one else did so. I've looked, and there are at least three other ways to reach the house. They're not as direct, but they get you there." She angled her screen to show him a map. "If the killer came from the north, he might not have passed the camera on Francone Street. He could have parked north of it, entered the house, and left the way he came."

She showed him two more ways to get there. He traced all three routes with his finger. "Let me refuel." He picked up his coffee mug and headed into the canteen, buying time while he thought about what she said. He returned less than a minute later, waving his mug with so much force she feared he'd slosh coffee over the monitor. "You're right. We can't exclude any suspect based solely on videos that don't even show Sullivan's front door."

"Or the rear," she added.

He gulped his coffee and grimaced. "So it's back to basics. We need to get the funeral home's records. If Sullivan's extorted money from one person, he's done it to more."

"Will Dawkins go for it?"

He lowered himself into his chair and upended his coffee mug. "Not as long as we're awaiting Petarsky's records. 'You're on a fishing expedition,' I hear her saying. No, let's take these one at a time."

"And we need a warrant for his handgun," she said. In neighboring New York, they would have been able to search gun registrations, but as Sedlak had reminded her, Pennsylvania required this only for handguns being carried. And even if the state required handgun registration, it didn't mean a gun owner would comply.

"Don't forget Coppola," she said. "He also lied, telling

us Marty had no friends, while his high school buddy Kuczienski is working alongside him. He told us Marty had gotten careless about his work, but that Coppola let him get away with it. 'There's something there,' Kuczienski said."

"Blackmail?" Jeffrey asked.

"That's what I'm thinking, but we have no proof. Coppola seems the type who would have reached a breaking point and set out to end it."

"Where was he the night of the murder?" he said, scrolling through his file.

"Save yourself the trouble," Lydia said. "We didn't ask."

"We had no reason to suspect him at the time."

"Still..." she said.

"You're right. But it's not too late. Let's circle back. This time, we'll press him on why he let Marty take on these jobs. He made us think they were inconsequential, too small for his outfit, but that may not be the case."

"I've asked Sutton to find out what materials he bought from Home Depot. It may tell us what sort of projects he took on."

"Since he was operating in cash," Jeffrey finished for her, "leaving us no way to check with his clients."

"The butcher, the baker, the candlestick maker."

"What?" he said.

"I'm thinking about our three suspects: the roofer, the doctor, the undertaker. Plus, the stranger Sullivan met at the bar."

"The drinker," Jeffrey said, providing a name for the mystery man. "Our public information officer has sent his photo to both newspapers and the TV stations. They'll be on the noon news."

"And people will start giving us leads," she said, "most of them amounting to nothing and wasting our time."

Coppola's bookkeeper had told them where he could be found. They drove to his worksite in Pittsburgh's Stanton Heights neighborhood, across the river from Etna. The rain had stopped, but the temperature was in the low sixties. He sat in his heated pickup truck with the engine running while his workers toiled on the roof. Jeffrey tapped on his window. He rolled it down a crack and said, "Hop in."

It was awkward, interviewing a man sitting in his vehicle, but it beat standing in the chill. Jeffrey took the passenger seat while Barnwell sat in back, moving a stack of plans and roofing brochures out of the way. "What do you want this time?" Coppola asked. "One more question, just like Columbo."

"More than one, actually," Jeffrey said, setting his body worn camera on the dashboard. "When we spoke Saturday, you told us Sullivan had no friends. But Al Kuczienski works for you. You hired him on Marty's recommendation. They were close."

"Were they?" The roofer snorted. "He brought him on, but I don't know how they knew each other. I pay no attention to my workers' private lives."

"They were high school classmates. Are you telling us you were unaware of that?"

"No idea. What difference does it make? You suspect him now?"

"He's not a suspect," Jeffrey said, emphasizing the pronoun, "but we're curious why you'd tell us Sullivan had no friends when his best buddy worked alongside him every day."

He opened both hands and gave a slight shrug. "I didn't, okay. I'm busy here. You have any more questions?"

Jeffrey often provided Lydia a chance to change the tempo of the interview, but with her in the back seat, it was awkward. She let him continue while she riffled through the papers she'd moved to one side. "We've learned he was extorting money from at least one person."

"Marty?"

"Was that what was going on here? We're told he wasn't as attentive on the job as he'd been in the past and that you let it slide. Was he blackmailing you, Walter?"

"Don't be ridiculous. What could he possibly hold over me? I'm married with three kids, all grown now. Want no part of construction." He snickered. Lydia watched as his right shoulder twitched. "I'm a churchgoer. Ask my priest. I have nothing to hide."

As though the priest would violate the confessional seal, she thought. She leafed through a brochure and a contract as her partner continued his questioning. "Where were you Thursday night between eleven and midnight?"

"Me? At home with my wife. She's quite ill, and our son was visiting with his daughter. His wife's about to have another kid. We have a lot going on."

"We'll check on that," Jeffrey said.

"You do that. Meanwhile, I have work to do."

They emerged from his truck. Jeffrey headed toward their cruiser while Barnwell crossed the street to the house where workers stapled shingles onto the roof. She studied the project for a moment, then walked behind the dwindling stack of asphalt strips, snapping a photo out of sight of Coppola's vehicle. She looked up at the workers and called, "Slippery up there?"

"You said it, lady," one shouted. "Cold, too."

She returned to the cruiser and slid into the passenger seat. "What was that about?" Jeffrey said.

"You remember that spec sheet we found in Sullivan's bedroom, the one where he'd circled two grades of shingles and done some calculations?"

"Okay," he said, catching her drift.

"Our church-going friend is giving his customers a lower grade of material than they're paying for. That's why Marty kept made those calculations on the brochure. He uncovered Coppola's scam, did the math, and held it over him."

"How? If he was extorting money from the man, how could he continue to work for him? It makes no sense."

She didn't respond for a moment as he crossed the 62nd Street Bridge. "Perhaps there was more to be made in using Coppola to build his own business. And less risk if he was caught."

"Makes sense," he said, turning onto Route 28 toward the I-376 interchange.

"What do we do now? I took a shot of the contract, but we should contact that homeowner and get the physical copy."

"Whoa," he said. "We need to focus on Sullivan's murder. One of our detectives, Pat Corrigan, is a former accountant. He handles fraud cases. I'll have him look into it."

"But isn't this a motive?" she asked. "Perhaps Marty was milking him for money, and he got fed up."

"It could be, but now that we have a motive, let's let Corrigan investigate. Meanwhile, we'll keep our eyes on the prize."

She didn't like it. She'd found the evidence and, since she was still trying to prove herself, resented others taking credit.

Sensing her mood, he said, "We can't do it all by ourselves, Barnwell."

He was right. With three suspects and the strange behavior of the mystery man in the brewpub, they had enough to contend with.

———

"It looks like a guy who used to live near us. I don't remember his name or know where he's gone, but you can check."

Lydia listened to the voicemail message and said, "Very helpful. Not."

This was one of seventeen tips phoned in by those who'd seen the televised photos of the man who'd engaged Marty Sullivan in conversation t the brewpub.

"When was this taken?" another asked after leaving his name and phone number. "He looks like my uncle, but he died last year." Which meant he wouldn't have been chatting with Sullivan in a bar unless he'd risen from the dead.

She listened to eight more, two of which seemed worth pursuing. One said the photo looked a bit like his neighbor. "He's always skulking around," the caller said. "We think he poisoned our cat last year." This could be nothing more than an escalation of a neighborhood dispute. It was not unusual for someone to make a police report to settle scores. Still, the caller had left enough information to merit her checking it out. And the neighbor lived north of the river, meaning that it wouldn't be unusual for him to stop at Julio's for a few beers.

The other caller furnished a name, Ezekiel Henry, known as Zeke. "He lived in our apartment complex after he got out of prison," the woman said. "I don't recall what he was in for, but he acted weird all the time, spent a lot of time trying to talk to kids in our building. We kept calling the cops. He finally left. I guess we chased him out."

She logged on to the National Crime Information Center database, entered the name and community, and found the match. The man had a long and storied history, jailed for assault in his twenties and for theft days after he was released. He'd been involved in one shady operation after another, culminating in a fourteen-year sentence for armed robbery—the maximum for a first offense. He'd been released after ten years and put on probation for the duration of his sentence. NCIC had nothing more on him.

Lydia found the number for Zeke Henry's probation officer, but only reached his voicemail. She left a message, then studied his photograph. He did not appear to match the images they'd taken from the bar videos, but these were grainy. Henry was in his late forties, while the man Seth Goodman described was older, a fact even the poor photos seemed to confirm.

It was late in the day, and she'd have to fight rush hour traffic, but Barnwell pursued the one lead she could either confirm or cross off her list. She returned the way she'd come an hour before, taking North Avenue off Route 28 to a nondescript neighborhood on Pittsburgh's north side. On the way, she messaged the Zone 1 police station and asked for an officer to provide backup.

When the officer arrived, they parked across the street from the man who'd phoned in the tip. It was an old, narrow, two-story structure of the type built a century before to house steel workers. The moved lawn was bordered by a row of flowering bushes, a burst of color from roses, hydrangeas, and geraniums. The home to the left was a mirror image, for its lawn, if it could be called that, was overgrown with weeds, and what grass existed had turned brown. As she opened the door, she heard a dog barking from behind a chain-link fence visible behind a corner of the house. She left the officer in his cruiser and knocked. The door opened as though the man on the other side had been watching and waiting. "Sheldon Weinstein," he said, extending his hand. "Call me Shelly. You didn't waste any time."

"Tell me about this neighbor," she said.

Weinstein invited her in. "I don't want Cyril to see me talking to you, though it's probably too late for that." He sighed, and his wife appeared behind him wearing a shapeless dress and holding a gray tabby. A fan roared in the window, and Barnwell realized they had no air conditioning. "Cyril Strange," he said, referring to the neighbor. "The name fits. You probably saw the house next door. It's a blight on the neighborhood. He has a leak in the roof he's never repaired."

Lydia didn't ask the man how he knew this, but listened as he recited a history of problems with the neighbor and his dogs. The city of Pittsburgh had cited the condition of his yard, "but they don't have time to enforce it with all the condemned housing across the river." Animal control had been out more than once as the dogs whenever the dogs had run loose and attacked other animals in the neighborhood, "but that went nowhere."

Lydia heard him out, summoned the Pittsburgh cop, and knocked at the neighbor's front door. For more than a minute, nothing happened. Then it opened a crack. "Mr. Strange?" she asked.

The man acknowledged as much and asked what she wanted. "That Jew sic me on you?"

Barnwell had no interest in stirring up more trouble

between the two. She reached for her phone and opened the photograph of the stranger in the bar. "No, we're looking for this man who we believe lives in the neighborhood. Do you recognize him?"

Strange squinted, fished a beaten up pair of readers from his shirt pocket, and lowered his head until it almost touched the screen. "Never seen him. What do you want him for?"

"We need to question him in a case we're working on," she said. She thanked him for his time and left. The man in the bar had a florid face and, despite his protruding stomach, a slender build in the way of those who take their nourishment from alcohol. Cyril Strange was short, overweight, and had a pallor that suggested he was suffering from some disease.

She thanked the officer and made a show of knocking at the next door, only to remove any suspicion Strange had that Weinstein had reported him. When no one answer, she breathed a sigh of relief and left, wondering how many more blind alleys she'd have to explore.

Ross Sutton now had the video from the brewpub. She hoped he could pinpoint where the gray Kia had traveled when the mystery man left.

CHAPTER SEVEN

LYDIA FOUND a message from Ross Sutton asking the two of them to come to his side of the second floor as soon as they arrived. She left the bullpen and entered. "What'cha got?"

"I'll wait for your partner to show up, so I only have to go through this once."

"I think he's at the DA's office," she said, though she had no clue where he was this morning or when he'd arrive. Whatever Sutton had discovered, she wanted to know now.

"All right." He heaved a deep sigh to display his annoyance. Was it because he'd have to repeat whatever he'd found to Jeffrey or because he still couldn't adjust to working with a woman? She neither knew nor, at the moment, cared.

"We got Petarsky's bank records. Three months ago, he withdrew $8,000 in cash. There's no record of where it went. Last month, he took out the same amount. Again, it disappeared."

From the email thread, they already knew Sullivan had extorted money from the veterinarian. This seemed to confirm it. The forensics detective peered up at her, his eyebrows raised as though waiting for her to say something. And she got it. "That's it? No more?"

"We searched for any activity to account for the remaining $21,000 Sullivan deposited, but found nothing. No big ATM withdrawals or unexplained checks. We looked for every way he might have hidden more payments, laundering the money through credit card payments, gambling, all the usual dodges. Nothing."

"Which means," she said, "Sullivan got—"

"Five additional payments totaling $21,000 from somewhere."

"Or someone," she said. She still wondered if he'd split a larger payment into several to keep below the $10,000 CTR threshold. Even if he had, some bank official should have been suspicious over a 25-year-old male making large cash transactions.

"Is there anything on my Kia search yet?" she asked.

"That's next," he said. "I'll give you what I have by tonight."

She thanked him and was about to return to her desk when Jeffrey entered, sprawling into a vacant chair. "What's this?"

Before she could cover herself by telling her partner she'd thought he was at the courthouse, Sutton dived into his explanation. Either he'd known Lydia was lying or didn't care. She noticed he delivered this rendition with greater enthusiasm than when he'd told her minutes before. He didn't even bother to wait for Jeffrey to reach his own conclusion. "This means your victim got the rest of the $37,000 from somewhere—or someone—else."

"I see that," Jeffrey said. He thanked the detective and,

as they return to their desks, said, "Funny he shared this with you before telling me."

"Wasn't he supposed to?" she said, alert to any suggestion other officers were withholding information from this new female recruit.

"It's just not in his nature. Ross sits over there with his crew, staring at computers all day. He lives for the approval. I guess he respects you."

"I didn't give him much choice," she said.

Jeffrey snickered. "You'll go far here. All right, where does this leave us?"

"I still think Dr. Petarsky's our top suspect. We see how angry he was in the email he sent Sullivan. He lied to him, to his wife, and to us, which suggests he's guilty of something."

"But..." Jeffrey said, and she realized that once again he was testing her, seeing if she could sort through all the implications.

"But $21,000 remains unaccounted for," she said. "This may mean Sullivan had at least one other person on the hook. We need to work that angle as well. Can we get the bank records of Coppola and Sedlak?"

"Not yet," he said. "It was tough enough getting Dawkins to issue the order on Petarsky. Let's focus on the horse doctor for a day or two. Talk to neighbors, associates— These guys have to network with other vets, don't they?— find out everything we can about him."

"Maybe Margaret O'Dowd wasn't the only one who saw him coming and going. Remember, he used to park his car down the street when he visited Grace."

"I should have thought of that," Jeffrey said. "Meanwhile, what's the latest on your mystery man?"

"I haven't had time to check. I spotted Sutton's message the moment I arrived."

"Follow up, then, but don't get immersed in it. Some calls will be from people trying to be helpful. Even more will be from those craving attention."

BARNWELL'S first task was to learn if Petarsky had worked with other veterinarians. As she donned her jacket, however, she received a call from Ezekiel Henry's probation officer. She explained they were investigating a person who'd met with a murder victim days before his death.

"Is this the man whose face you've plastered on the local news?" the officer asked. She confirmed it. "He doesn't look a thing like Zeke Henry. Your man appears to be slender, while Henry bulked up during his time behind bars. He's working in a gym doing fitness training. You can talk to him if you want, but you'll waste your time."

Which was one thing she didn't have. She thanked him and turned to the two dozen tips phoned in overnight. Two callers wanted to know why they were after the man. A youthful voice identified a high school teacher. Another insisted he recognized the man in the two images. His name, he said, was Elvis, and he'd never died.

"Thanks, jerk," she muttered under her breath. There were others like that, but three callers mentioned specific names—Rocky Sasak, a retired carpenter, Tracy Lambkin, a used car dealer, and Paul Welch, whom the caller identified only as retired. A fourth didn't have a name, but said a man matching the description drove for Uber.

She entered these leads into the file. She'd slog through

them when she had time. Now, however, Jeffrey stood at her door. "Let's go see a woman about a dog."

───

Cynthia Bowman had a small clinic along McKnight Road in Ross Township. During their drive, Jeffrey told Barnwell how he'd learned about her and what to expect. The frosty greeting the doctor gave as the receptionist ushered them into her office came as no surprise. As had been the case at Petarsky's clinic, their conversation was interrupted by a canine chorus whose barks and yelps penetrated the walls.

"I only have a few minutes," she said, "so let's get down to business."

"You and Sid Petarsky were in practice together until five years ago," Jeffrey said. "Then you went your separate ways. Why?"

"Did the state board send you?" she said. "It's taken them long enough."

"No, we're here on another matter," he said. "Why did you end your relationship?"

"What other matter?"

"His name has come up in an unrelated investigation," Lydia said. "We're trying to get background on him."

The veterinarian looked at her without smiling. "It's all in the record."

"You said you only have a few minutes. Why not save us all some time and answer the question?"

Barnwell sensed that the slender woman with tight black curls could handle herself in a cage fight, but faced with an equally tenacious opponent, she yielded. "I learned the other practitioner was making sexual advances to some of our owners."

"By owners, you mean your patients?"

"The animals are the patients. The humans are their owners."

"Making advances, you said. Did it go beyond that?"

"In at least one case, yes."

"What was her name?" Lydia asked.

"I prefer not to say."

"Grace Sullivan?"

She frowned and shook her head. "No. It was another woman. Why do you mention Grace?"

Lydia glanced at Jeffrey, who gave permission with a flick of his eyebrows. "She died a few months ago. She and Dr. Petarsky were involved with each other before she fell ill."

"Sh—!" She stopped herself before letting the word escape her mouth. "Another one? I wish I'd known. I might have gotten more traction with the board."

"You filed a complaint against him," she prompted.

"I already told you that. When I learned the other practitioner was having an affair with an owner, I warned him to stop. Then another woman asked if she could transfer care of her toy poodle to me. We didn't normally do that, so I asked her why. She told me the other pract—that he had commented about her appearance, getting more specific each time she brought Inky in. I agreed to assume care for the dog and spoke to … him about it. He claimed she was imagining things."

"Hmm," Lydia said with a sardonic smile. She'd heard that one before.

"That made me suspicious. We'd had two women take their animals elsewhere over the past several months. I called each of them and asked why. One was eager to recount what she'd gone through. I had to pry it out of another who feared her husband's reaction if he found out. The other practitioner had pulled the same stuff on both of them. I told him I was going to file a complaint with the State Board of Veterinary Medicine. He begged me not to, but I did. Then I told him to take his practice elsewhere."

"Rather than you leaving?" she said.

"I own this building and all the equipment. Our names were on the building, but we operated independently."

Lydia decided she liked the woman even more, noting with amusement her refusal to refer to Petarsky by name. "Was his wife aware of his activities? She must have found it odd when you forced him out."

"I can't say. If you've met her, you know she's somewhat aloof. But in case you haven't figured it out, she's the one with money. I suspect she's behind that grand facility in Cranberry."

Jeffrey posed a few more questions, but other than saying he'd never come on to her— "I would have shot him down so far it'd take his head off"—she had nothing more to add.

"What do you think?" Jeffrey said as they sat in the air-conditioned cruiser outside Bowman's clinic.

"That he's a shit," she said, "but she answered a question that's bothered me since we learned about his affair with Grace Sullivan."

"Which is?"

"How they met. It never made sense that a woman living on the edge would bring her cat from Etna all the way to Cranberry. She didn't. She drove the few miles up the road to Ross Township."

"If Petarsky's wife holds the purse strings, it gave him a motive to buy Sullivan's silence."

"He'd shelled out $16,000," Barnwell replied, "but Sullivan kept demanding more. Perhaps he shut him up for good."

Jeffrey drove in silence for a minute. "What do we do now, detective?"

"It's time we confront him. Tell him we know he's lied, that we know Sullivan was blackmailing him, and make him account for his time. If Elena learns how long he's been cheating on her, she may be unwilling to give him an alibi."

"Agreed," he said, "only this time we do it on our turf."

***

WHILE JEFFREY SUMMONED Petarsky to headquarters, Barnwell went over the leads phoned in by those who'd seen the images of "the drinker," the man Sullivan had met at the brewpub. A woman had offered the tip on Rocky Sasak, the retired carpenter, but had not left her name. There was nothing unusual about that. Most people didn't want to get involved.

She found his address and phone number in Whitehall, which was in the South Hills, far from the Sharpsburg brewpub. A woman answered, and Barnwell asked to speak to Sasak. "He can't come to the phone right now. Who is this?"

Barnwell identified herself. "What do you want with *him*?" the woman asked, her tone suggesting no one would ever want to speak to Sasak. In the background, she heard a man's gentle voice giving instructions of some sort. These were punctuated by an occasional groan.

"I'd prefer to speak to him myself," she said.

"Well, he'll have to call you back when he finishes his treatment."

"Treatment?" Lydia said.

The woman explained the man had COPD. "His home healthcare nurse is with him now. He visits three times a week. Rocky's always worn out when he leaves."

"Are you his wife?"

"Daughter," she said. "Madge died years ago. He's all alone now."

Barnwell conveyed her regrets and asked a few more questions about the man's condition. He'd smoked all his life, his daughter said. His wife had died of lung cancer caused by the second-hand fumes. Bitterness crept into her voice as she gave the explanation. "Now, he's confined to the house."

"How often does he leave?"

"Almost never. He has a portable oxygen..." She broke off, her voice taking on an edge. "Why all these questions?"

"I'll explain in a moment. Just hang with me for a bit. He doesn't get out at all?"

"Not unless I take him to appointments. I do the shopping for him. I have two full-time jobs. One doing accounting for clients, the other taking care of dad. Why do you ask?"

Lydia apologized for calling, saying it was clear she had the wrong man. "May I ask what this is about?"

She explained an anonymous caller had identified her father from a photograph posted on newscasts. "Who would have done such a thing?" the daughter said. "Was it a woman?"

"I'm afraid I can't say."

"Mrs. Wasserman. She was a friend of mom's. She's had

it in for dad ever since she died. Pay no attention to anything she says."

Lydia thanked her and disconnected. The next tip came from a caller who had identified himself, saying the man shown on TV resembled someone named Tracy Lambkin, who'd sold him a used car months before. The lot was on Sawmill Run, which was also in the South Hills, but close enough to Sharpsburg to make it worth the call.

This also proved to be a dead end, however. The owner said Lambkin had worked for him for years, but left three months before to move to South Carolina. "He has family down there. I talk to him every so often. We're still buddies. I was sorry to lose him."

"You're certain he hasn't returned for a visit?"

"Naw, he woulda called me if he were in the Burgh."

She was about to reach for the phone again when Jeffrey poked his head in the doorway. "Petarsky's coming in with his attorney at one," he said. "We had quite a tug of war. He said he didn't have to talk to us, that he had nothing more to say. I told him we had some new questions for him and could either come to his house tonight or ask them here. If he didn't like those choices, I promised to issue a subpoena. That broke the dam."

"What do we do until then?" she asked.

"Let's grab a bite and plan how we handle him."

LYDIA RETURNED FROM LUNCH, convinced they were at the end of this case. Petarsky had reason to silence Marty Sullivan. His alibi was shaky, so he may have had the opportunity. As for means, he had a key to Sullivan's house, had been there many times, and seemed to know a bit about the young man's schedule. As for a weapon, they'd issue a search warrant once they concluded the interview.

His guest, Barry Goldstein, said he'd drawn out the after-dinner discussion. This suggested he was trying to establish an alibi. His repeated lies showed he had something to hide. *Yes*, she thought, *I think we have him.*

He'd promised to arrive at one o'clock, but made them wait twenty more minutes. When he arrived, accompanied by a man in his late twenties with a tailored suit and a buzz cut, he introduced Brendan Frazier as his attorney and said their lateness was because he was meeting with another client.

The veterinarian seemed to have lost none of his swagger. "I demand to know why you've brought me here. Why have you questioned my wife, something I told you not to do?"

This was not the opening the detectives had planned over lunch. Petarsky was trying to seize the initiative, but Jeffrey was up to the challenge. "This is a murder investigation, doctor. We decide who we interview and when."

The attorney took over. "I remind you that Dr. Petarsky is here voluntarily. He is under no obligation to answer your questions."

"You can leave whenever you wish," Jeffrey said. "We will then seek a warrant for your arrest. It's that or he answers a few questions."

Petarsky made a dismissive motion with his hand. "Ask away." He smoothed back what little hair remained.

"As you know, we subpoenaed your bank records," Jeffrey began.

"Yes, and I resent that. You have no right to go searching through my private affairs." Barnwell thought he might have chosen a better word, but let it pass.

"We also found messages on Martin Sullivan's computer telling him you'd no longer submit to blackmail."

The veterinarian looked from one of them to the other, but said nothing. She could sense his blood pressure rising.

"That conversation took place on June 16th, just three weeks before Sullivan was murdered. On April 2nd, you withdrew $8,000 in cash from your personal checking account. Three days later, Sullivan deposited the same amount in his account. A cash transaction."

He slid copies of the entries across the table. The veterinarian folded his arms and ignored them, but the attorney drew the photostats toward him and studied them. "This proves nothing," he said.

"A month later, you withdrew another $8,000." Jeffrey tapped a highlighted entry on the document. "Four days later, Sullivan made a deposit in the same amount, again in cash. Another month passed, and you sent this email to Sullivan, stating you'd revealed everything to your wife and you'd no longer pay hush money."

Neither man spoke, so Barnwell joined in the attack. "That was a lie. She claims she knew nothing about your affair. You lied to her, and," she said, leaning forward and speaking slowly, "you lied to us."

"I—" The attorney reached for Petarsky's arm before he could speak.

"You have a key to the victim's house. You've been there many times. Spent the night more than once. So let's go over your movements on the morning of Jun 16th. Where were you?"

"I was at home, like I said."

"We know Grace Sullivan was not your first inappropriate relationship with a client. Your womanizing cost you your partnership."

His face took on a florid hue. "We weren't partners. I rented space from another veterinarian, a most unpleasant individual. We—my wife and I decided I'd be better off on my own."

"Did Elena know about your womanizing?"

Frazier waved a hand in front of his client to prevent him from blurting out a response. "Dr. Petarsky is attempting to cooperate with you. All you've done is hurl accusations at him based on circumstance and innuendo. If you have solid evidence, present it in a court of law. Meanwhile, he has nothing to say to you."

Barnwell didn't take her eyes off the man. In a low voice that contained a hint of menace, she said, "Will she continue to stand by your alibi when she finds out? What will that do to your practice? She owns it, doesn't she?"

She had confronted raw hatred before, but the look Petarsky focused on her equalled the worst she'd ever seen. "You do that, and I'll sue both of you. I'll—"

"Quiet, Sid," Frazier said. "They can't be sued for how they ask questions, and they know it. We'll just leave."

He didn't move, glowering at her. She didn't break her gaze. Her blue eyes could be just as intimidating as his stare. It was Petarsky who broke the deadlock, but only because his attorney grabbed his elbow and nearly lifted him to his feet.

Jeffrey spoke into the microphone. "Interview concluded at 1:58 p.m." They followed the pair into the hallway and trailed them as they stalked toward the entry area.

"That went well," she said.

"He's guilty as hell."

"What now?"

"We get a search warrant for his house. We need to find that gun before he can conceal it."

WHILE HER PARTNER phoned the assistant DA, Lydia recorded the information from the caller who'd identified "the drinker" as Paul Welch. She called the number he'd given, but after six rings, it went to voicemail. She left a message asking him to return the call.

The next informant had been hesitant about the identification. "He looks like an Uber drive who took me to the airport about three weeks ago." She'd left not only her name and number, but her address. The woman answered on the first ring. "Carla Cerrillo," she said, trilling the r and turning the double-l into a y.

"Hola," Lydia said, slipping into the language she'd learned first in Spain and honed during her father's posting to what was now Joint Base San Antonio.

"That's all right," she said. "I speak perfect English. I was born here."

"Sorry," Lydia said after identifying herself. "I don't get enough chance to use my Spanish. You called about the person we're looking for."

"I'm not certain it's the same, but he looks like a man who drove me to the airport a few weeks back. I didn't get a close look at him until he helped me with my bags. The photos you showed were taken from above, and something about them reminded me of the moment he leaned over to get my suitcase out of the trunk."

This was a first for Barnwell, an ID based on the top of a man's head. But then she explained. "It was his cap. It had the same design on it."

"Logo," Lydia said.

"Yes. The letter D in some sort of script. But it didn't look like the Detroit Tigers. I used to live there, so I spotted the difference."

Lydia asked if she recalled the driver's name, but she did not. She thought for a moment. "You're speaking to me on your cell phone? I want you to open the Uber app." She talked her through how to scroll through the activity tab.

"Here it is. UberX ride with Paul." Barnwell took down the date and time of the ride, her pickup and drop-off location, the cost of the trip, and the none too generous tip she'd given. It wasn't much to go on, but perhaps Uber would help identify the driver.

"Hold on a minute," she said. "Go to your message app and see if you find a number you don't recognize."

"I clear most of these things off."

"Still," she said, "This was only three weeks ago. Give it a try."

She waited while the woman searched, listening as she muttered to herself, only some words distinguishable as she discarded one after the other. She stopped. "Here it is. May 28th." She read off the number and the message. "Paul will pick you up at the designated location. Gray 2016 Kia. License number..."

Barnwell thanked her, told her she'd done well, and signed her computer into DMV records. A few seconds later, the registration popped up on the screen, and she gave a low whistle. The car was registered to a Paul Welch, whose address was in the Sharps Hill neighborhood, less than a mile from Julio's Brewpub. "Found you," she said.

Before she could act on the information, however, Jeffrey interrupted her. "Petarsky just called," he said. "He has something to show us."

If Sid Petarsky had known what he was doing, he could have mailed it in. Instead, he urged the two detectives to hurry to his residence in Mars. "I need you to see this before my wife gets home. It will answer all your questions."

Jeffrey had asked him if his attorney would be present, and the veterinarian replied, "That won't be necessary." He gave no further hints about what they would find.

He greeted them at the entry as though he'd been waiting for them, grinning like a boy who'd just been gifted a baseball glove. "C'mon in. You gotta see this."

They followed him to a small bedroom on the second floor that served as an office. A laptop computer was open, showing a nighttime image taken from the front door. "Look at the date and time," he said.

Barnwell did so. This was security camera footage taken on the night Sullivan had been murdered. He tapped the right arrow button on his keypad, and they watched as Barry and Rachel Goldstein left the house. He switched to another camera, which showed the pair walking toward their Mercedes in the driveway. As he held the door open for his wife, he said something, and she seemed to laugh. Barnwell would have given a lot to know what they were sharing.

He brought up a third camera mounted in their garage. Two vehicles, an Audi sedan and a Lexus TX, sat side-by-side. "That's mine." Petarsky pointed to the larger vehicle. "I often have to haul animals or medical equipment in it."

Was he apologizing or bragging for having a luxury automobile? It made no difference. As the minutes ticked by, Petarsky inched the video forward at five- or six-minute intervals, past 11:00, then 11:30, and on to midnight. When the clock reached 12:15 and the date rolled over to June 16, he turned with a look of triumph. "See," he said, "I never left the house. You can watch the whole thing if you have the time. Neither car moved, and the front door cam will show no one left after the Goldsteins. We went to bed, and I didn't leave until seven the next morning."

"I want to forward this video to our forensics team. Will I need a subpoena?" Jeffrey asked.

"No, just show me how to do it."

Jeffrey took his place in the swivel chair and uploaded the video from the drive to an ACPD server that could accept such a massive file. "Satisfied?" Petarsky said, the right side of his mouth cocked in a smirk.

"Thank you," the detective said. "If we have further questions, we'll let you know. We have nothing else right now."

He snorted. "Well, if you do, give them to my attorney. I've done nothing wrong and have nothing more to say to you."

Jeffrey looked him in the eye. "The next time someone tries to blackmail you, save yourself a lot of trouble by reporting it."

Not to mention money, Lydia thought.

BARNWELL RODE HALFWAY BACK to headquarters in silence. As he took the I-279 spur into Pittsburgh, Jeffrey said, "What are you thinking?"

"I don't see any way he could have done it. Unless he hired someone."

"No, I think we have to take him off our list."

She pounded her fists against each other. "I thought we'd solved this one. "

"I did, too. But it's not as though we don't have other suspects."

"Still the baker, drinker, and candlestick maker," she said. Jeffrey turned toward her in confusion, then chuckled as he remembered her characterization.

As they sat in the long line of traffic toward the Fort Bridge and the tunnel, she told him she thought she'd identified the man who'd tried to find Sullivan after meeting with him in the Sharpsburg brewpub. "His name is Paul Welch. He drives for Uber these days, though I haven't had time to learn much more about him."

He told her they'd follow up on it tomorrow. "Let's start the day by going through the entire case. Then we can plot our next steps. Meanwhile, get some rest. We've been at this for a week now. Dropping it for a few hours sometimes brings clarity."

She offered to write the report of their meeting with Petarsky, and he agreed. "My son has a baseball game tonight. I miss too many of them." It took her more than a half hour to complete the task, detailing first the formal interview and the subsequent examination of the security videos. She attached a reference to the files they'd downloaded from his computer.

As she was about to leave, Sutton emerged from his lair. "Still here? Good. I've traced the routes that Kia took. You were right. It's the same vehicle."

He took Jeffrey's seat and scooted it next to hers. "We can't pinpoint exactly where the car ended up both nights. We only have the last intersection through which it passed. But we know he was headed for—"

"Sharps Hill," she said.

"Or near there," he said, expressing no surprise that she was a step ahead of him. "But beyond that, we can't tell."

She told him about the conversation she'd had hours before with Carla Cereillo. "She got his plate number off the Uber app, so I've found his address. I would have mentioned it earlier, but I had to be sure it was the same Kia."

"The reason we couldn't identify it through his plates is because he's obscured it."

Since the Turnpike Authority had installed cameras that captured tags for automatic billing, some drivers had painted out parts of letters and numbers to confuse the system.

Lydia thanked him and sat at her desk for a moment, trying to decide whether to pursue the matter immediately. She elected not to. Calvin had called to say he had something to show her. Paul Welch could wait until tomorrow, she thought, a decision that was to prove a mistake.

Calvin had brought takeout from an Asian restaurant, sweet and sour pork for him, sushi for her. As she picked at her tuna roll, she rewound the tape of the day's events. "Depending on how you look at it, we're not at a dead end but in a traffic circle with too many roads leading out of it. Jeffrey wants to start over tomorrow."

"Good idea," Calvin said. "Sometimes we get so involved in a case we can't see what's right in front of us." He dragged a file folder from across the small table and placed it before her.

The first two pages were Tommy Molnar's summary of the news articles about Frank Alberti's death. It was succinct and well written. On April 13th, 1963, Alberti had checked into a motel on McKnight Road, which had since become a major thoroughfare to the region's largest shopping mall. Shortly after nine o'clock that evening, a guest in a nearby room heard what sounded like gunfire. He was watching television and hadn't bothered to investigate. Seconds later, however, he heard tires scratching off in the parking lot. He threw open the door and saw a late model vehicle—a Ford Fairlane, he thought—pull into southbound traffic, causing a delivery truck to hit its brakes. Returning to his room, he'd found a door two rooms down from his ajar. When he looked in, he found a body sprawled on the floor and called police.

In subsequent news stories Tommy had researched, a Ross Township detective had questioned a woman, Jane Quinlan. The story didn't disclose what her relationship was to the dead man. The youngster had gone far enough to find news articles from months and years later, but no one had ever been charged.

"He writes well," Lydia said.

"He's an amazing kid."

"Did you edit this?"

"Nope. It's all his work, and as you read it, you see it's no cut-and-paste job."

"You're a good influence on him, Calvin." She reached out a hand and covered his.

"I take joy in it. My dad worked two jobs to keep clothes on our backs and shoes on our feet. I didn't see much of him. I'm trying to share what I never had."

He turned the page, revealing the first of what appeared to be police reports. "Now, read this. Better yet, let me explain it to you. When the Ross Township detective investigated, he found no luggage in the room. The clerk said the dead man paid in cash for only one night. She didn't recall if he'd had a suitcase with him, but since guests pulled their cars in front of entrances to their rooms, she wouldn't have been able to see. Take that and the fact his house here is only a dozen miles away--"

"He'd arranged to meet someone," she finished for him.

"A woman, they figured, but they couldn't prove it. They went through his appointment book, talked to his wife, but never discovered who he was meeting or why. One woman came into the picture almost immediately, however."

"Jane Quinlan."

"Yes. She worked in a real estate office in a nearby township. A caller reported she'd had an affair with the victim. They questioned her. She admitted she'd been involved with him, but said she'd spent the weekend with her son's grandparents in Erie. They confirmed the story."

"So that cleared her?"

"They kept her on their radar, but couldn't link her to the slaying. The case remains unsolved."

Lydia ran her hands through her curls and gripped the back of her neck. "We can't let this go," she said. "We need to find out what happened. I wish we both weren't so damned busy."

THE ALBERTI CASE kept Lydia awake until the early morning, but, as she told Mayfield over breakfast, she had no time to spend on it. Even a sixty-year-old mystery deserved to be solved, but her immediate focus was on a death which, if you counted it from the night Marty Sullivan had broken into the funeral home, was just a week old. She fed Howie and took him for a walk around the block, drank two cups of coffee, hoping the caffeine would carry her through the day, and was at headquarters by eight thirty. Jeffrey had not yet arrived, so she sat at her desk and listed the three remaining suspects.

Three because she now had a name for the man who had met Marty Sullivan at Julio's Brewpub, Paul Welch. The NCIS database reported he'd been arrested three times in his life, the first for breaking and entering when he was nineteen years old. Since it was his first offense, he'd been placed on probation, but within the year he'd been caught driving a stolen car, earning him three years in prison. There he'd behaved himself and was released after serving half his sentence.

Welch kept a clean record for nine years, but on his thirtieth birthday, he was pulled over for driving under the influence. The judge gave him probation again, something he wouldn't have been granted today when even a first offense got you a minimum of forty-eight hours behind bars.

For the last thirty-four years, he'd kept his nose clean, which allowed him to pass Uber's comprehensive background check. Barnwell saw nothing that would suggest a leap from drunken joyrider to killer.

Welch had circled the block the night of the murder, but if she was right about the elapsed time shown on the videos, couldn't have stopped. She resolved to drive the route herself to make sure. But had he dropped someone off? She pulled up the two sequences, now enhanced by the digital forensics team, watching the gray Kia pass one way and come back the other. She saw no sign of a passenger. No other vehicles appeared in the security footage, but as she'd told Jeffrey two days before, that didn't preclude someone using back streets to approach from another direction.

"Find anything?" She looked up as Jeffrey slid into his chair, a mug of coffee in hand.

Lydia told him what she'd learned about Welch, and he scooted closer to her so they could converse over the hubbub of the surrounding detectives. "So we have this guy who got drunk in a saloon, filled Sullivan's ear, then came looking for him. Why?"

"Could he have revealed a secret that allowed Marty to put the squeeze on him?" she asked.

"Sounds like it," he said. "I've been thinking about Marty's boss. If you're right, Marty discovered Coppola was defrauding his customers by charging them for a higher grade of materials than what he installed. Did he use that against him, starting his own business while slacking off on the roofing projects?"

Lydia held up both index fingers. "We're missing something. Marty worked with Al Kuczienski, who is a close friend. Perhaps his only friend. But he said he didn't understand why Coppola let him get away with so much. That's difficult to believe." She recalled his sudden reluctance to speak during their interview.

"Good point. We need to circle back and see if he's hiding something." She wrote it down, taking it as an assignment, while he continued the review. "Finally, we have Daniel Sedlak. Did all this begin when Sullivan broke into his funeral home looking for evidence he'd defrauded his mother? Or is that a coincidence?"

"I don't believe in coincidences," she said.

"Nor do I." He sat in silence finishing his coffee while he thought. "Let's go back to the assistant DA, lay out all we know, and ask her to authorize warrants for the bank records of both Coppola and Sedlak. We need to uncover where Sullivan got the rest of the cash."

"Why don't you handle that, since you and Dawkins get along so well?" This elicited a snort and shake of his head from Jeffrey. "Meanwhile, I'll visit Paul Welch. He knows we're looking for him. Let's find him before he leaves town."

"Take a uniformed officer with you. He has a record and may be dangerous."

The advice was unneeded, but she accepted it. "And one more thing," he said. "Daniel Sedlak insisted he didn't want us checking his alibi with his wife. Which means..."

"That we need to do so," she finished for him.

THE UNIFORM DIVISION assigned officer Jerold Mullins to accompany her to Sharps Hill. She was less than delighted. Months before, the officer had challenged Barnwell on her first case, a body found in a ditch along a state road in the west part of the county. She accepted his assignment without comment, however, reasoning that some backup was better than none.

As he drove, she explained what they were after. "I don't know what we'll find. Welch has a record, but he's never been violent. He may be harmless, but he could also be armed and dangerous."

"You want me to go the door first?" he asked.

"No, thank you. Hang in the background. Your uniform might intimidate him. I just want to question him. He may have done nothing wrong."

Mullins gave a slight shrug as though to say, have it your way, and drove the rest of the route without comment. The address was a small one-story home with a detached garage, set back only twenty feet from Foundry Street. It was a brick structure with a peaked roof and a covered porch that ran the length of the front.

"Nice neighborhood," Mullins said. Barnwell didn't respond to his sarcasm.

She mounted the front steps, spotting a worn red leather sofa tucked behind the brick half wall, which was lined with potted geraniums wilting in the heat. A picture window looked out on the street, and the wooden door had a small portal at eye level. Barnwell rang the doorbell and a miniature version of Big Ben tolled within the house.

No one came to the door, and she heard no footsteps. She rang again, then knocked. No sound came from inside. Stepping toward the picture window, she peered into the living room. A faded white divan faced the window, with a chair on the wall to the right. Above the sofa was a printed photograph of Pittsburgh's Point Park, marking the confluence of the Allegheny and Monongahela rivers to form the Ohio. To the left, she saw the back of a television set. From this angle, she had a straight view into the kitchen.

The detective stepped off the porch and stared at the house as though it would tell her something. "You looking for Welch?" She turned to find an older man inching toward her on a walker. "You're too late," he said. "He packed his car two nights ago and lit out."

"Do you know where he went?"

"No idea. He's the guy you're looking for, right? The man on the TV?" He glanced over his shoulder to make certain he wasn't being observed. In a softer voice, he said, "I called your tip line."

"And I returned your call," she said.

"I know. I didn't want to get involved. Sorry."

This was an old story. Everyone wanted the police to do more to protect them, but when asked to help, they shied away, afraid to take responsibility. She pumped the man for more information, but he expressed ignorance. All he knew of Welch was that he was retired—from what, he didn't know—and that he had an Uber sticker on his car. He kept to himself, neither bothering anyone nor taking part in neighborhood activities. He had no pets, and if he had relatives, none came to see him.

"He was gone a lot at night. I'd see him leave, but I turn in early, so I don't know when he came back. I'll tell you one thing."

She thanked him, knocked on a few more doors, but learned nothing more. Paul Welch had seen his pictures on the evening news, packed his Kia, and fled.

AFTER FORTY-FIVE MINUTES with the assistant DA, Lyle Jeffrey felt he'd belted one out of PNC Park. The detective laid out the cases against Walter Coppola and Daniel Sedlak and reminded her the victim had deposited large sums of cash into his account. "We've proved he was blackmailing Petarsky, but we haven't identified the source of the rest of the money. We need to see the bank records of the other two."

He was prepared for a lengthy cross-examination, for Melissa Dawkins had not attained her position by being impetuous. To his astonishment, she said, "Done. I know how important it is to find the perpetrator before he covers his tracks. Is there anything else I can do for you?"

He rose to leave, saying she'd done enough, but she stopped him. "I'm sure you've checked the civil division to see if anyone's filed lawsuits against either of them."

Detective Pat Corrigan was investigating Coppola's use of substandard roofing materials, but Jeffrey had neglected to look into Sedlak. Rather than kicking himself, he said, "That's my next stop."

Leaving his vehicle at the courthouse, he walked the two blocks east on 4th Avenue and entered the City-County Building on Grant Street. Nora, the longest serving clerk, was helping a citizen file a lawsuit. He waited, suspecting it was time well spent. As soon as she'd accepted the man's paperwork, she motioned Jeffrey to the counter. "And how's my favorite detective today?"

"I'll bet you say that to all the guys."

She held up a scolding finger. "And women."

He raised his hands in surrender. "Just a slip of the

tongue. I have a female partner, and she's running rings around me. Makes me feel old."

He told her what he was after and her fingers danced across the keyboard. This is something he could have done himself, but she was better at it, searching for any actions involving the funeral home, Sedlak, and other members of his family. She struck oil almost immediately, giving him a case number and sending him to one of the public computers to read it.

Two years before, Bryan and Evelyn Odell had sued Sedlak Family Funeral Homes, Inc. in small claims court, alleging the mortuary had failed to honor a cremation contract issued to Evelyn's late mother. The case had been dismissed. The file didn't list the reason.

Jeffrey wrote the couple's name and contact information, returned to his vehicle, and called the number. When Mrs. Odell answered, he explained that he'd found their lawsuit and wanted to know the details. "I can't believe someone's finally looking into this," she said. "We've been after justice for two years and can't get anyone to listen."

He asked her to explain what had happened. "I'd rather you spoke to my husband. He remembers all the ins and outs. I got so frustrated..."

She didn't finish the sentence. "He's an electrician. I'll text him and see if he can find time." Before he emerged from the tunnel, she returned the call. Both of them would meet him over his lunch hour.

Before returning to headquarters, Lydia had Mullins circle the neighborhood where Marty Sullivan had been murdered. He did so three times while she recorded the trips on the stopwatch function of her phone. Even with the patrol officer making the circuit above the speed limit, the trip took at least eight-five seconds. The rest were closer to a hundred. There was no way Welch could have stopped, even to let someone else out of the passenger seat.

Why would he have fled? He wasn't wanted for anything. Either he had a hand in the murder, which now seemed doubtful, or he had information about the killer. She could think of no other explanation. She issued a four-state alert to law enforcement agencies, providing the photos taken at the bar, a description provided by the bartender and Welch's neighbor, and the license, make, and model of his car.

She hit the restroom and returned to her desk, taking deep drinks from her water bottle while she made notes on a pad. *The roofer, the drinker, the undertaker ...* Petarsky seemed to be in the clear. Sedlak and Coppola had reason to silence the victim, but she and Jeffrey couldn't shake their alibis, so neither may have had the opportunity.

And means? They'd found no trace of a .22 caliber handgun. She renewed her frustration with the Pennsylvania legislature for not allowing firearms registration, even prohibiting it. *So much for law'n order.*

Her personal cell phone rang, the screen bearing the name Anna Molnar. "Hey," she said, "what's up?"

"You're handling the murder of that young man in Etna, aren't you?" When Lydia acknowledged as much, her neighbor said, "Are you on Nextdoor?" The site served as a community bulletin board with occasional forays into political screeds. "Someone's posted a complaint against him, saying he didn't complete a home renovation job," Anna continued. "Two others say the same thing."

Lydia asked her to send a link, but Anna didn't know

how. "Is Tommy around?" she asked, knowing that the youngster had somehow mastered the intricacies of cell phones and computers, even though he had neither.

Minutes later, her phone dinged, and she tapped on the link to find a thread labeled, "Don't hire this contractor." She read the first entry.

I hired a young man named Martin Sullivan to redo my guest bathroom. The price was well below what a more established firm offered, and since a neighbor had recommended him, we paid him a third upfront. For weeks, he promised our project was next on his list, but he never returned. He won't answer my calls. I guess I got taken, but my advice is not to do business with him.

This was followed by posts advising the woman she should call the police, another telling her you get what you pay for, and a few expressing sympathy for her plight. She responded to the first by saying she had notified the police department in Braddock, but got no action.

Below this, she found another post:

We've had the same experience. Marty was supposed to replace our back deck "as soon as the weather warmed up." It's been three months now, and it's plenty warm. He got us for $4,000. I haven't reported it, because I keep hoping he'll honor his commitment. He said he has to get permits through the city, but when I called two days ago, they told me he has submitted no plans.

Finally, a post from another member of the site asking if this was the same Martin Sullivan who'd been murdered in Etna five days before. "If so," the writer said, "you may be out your money, because the paper said he had no survivors."

She called Braddock police, a small agency in a rundown borough east of Pittsburgh, within miles of Etna.

The officer who answered the phone said the chief was out on a call, but would get back to her when he returned. Barnwell knew the department was understaffed and doubted she would learn much.

The person who'd posted the original complaint went by the name Victoria C. Lydia saw no way to identify her based on the paucity of her information. The follow-up post had been written by a Jess Cooper of O'Hara Township. She reached his home. His wife said he was at work, but supplied his cell phone number. "We really got taken."

Cooper answered her call almost immediately, shouting his last name rather than a greeting over the sound of equipment in the background. When she explained why she was calling, he said, "Let me call you back. I gotta get away from this racket."

Lydia waited—she thought patience should be in the job description of every law officer—but he returned the call within minutes. He explained he worked in a dry cleaning establishment and had to step outside to speak to her. It took no prompting for him to recount what had happened. In early April, he'd contacted Sullivan to look at the aging deck at the back of their home. He'd been recommended by a neighbor, for whom Marty had done a similar job the previous fall.

"I saw what he'd done for Barney," Cooper said. "It was solid work. That's why it took me so long to raise a ruckus. I thought he was reliable, and I knew he worked alone. The price was way below what I could have gotten elsewhere. I figured he was busy, and the time it was taking him was the trade-off for saving a few thousand bucks. Silly me."

As he'd stated in his post, Cooper said he'd paid Sullivan $4,000 up front. "Part of that was for materials," he said.

Lydia thought she saw where this was going. "He wanted it in cash, didn't he?"

"Well..." The man drew out his response. "Yeah, I was paying him under the table. That's why he could give me such a good price." He paused for a moment. "Is that a problem? Am I in trouble? I didn't ask if he was doing it to avoid taxes. I guess I didn't want to know."

Barnwell assured him she wasn't interested in that aspect of the transaction. "You know he's dead?"

"Yeah. I'd heard about the man being shot last week, but I didn't connect it to Sullivan until a person online pointed it out. What do you think? Did he rip someone else off and get killed for it?"

That was a possibility, she told herself after she'd thanked him. If so, they could add a half dozen additional suspects to their list.

More to the point, Barnwell now knew the source of the remaining cash Sullivan had deposited.

Bryan Odell sat next to his wife in the front window of Panera's, half a tuna salad sandwich before each of them. "Evie's father died when he was only sixty-one. It was a complete surprise. He hadn't been sick or anything. His heart just gave out on him. Went to work in the morning and never came back. We were in a panic," he said. "He'd left no instructions."

"I guess he never thought he might die," she said. "Not at that age, anyway." She looked up at her husband, willing him to continue.

"So we went to Sedlak and arranged for his cremation. We paid — I can't remember, but it was quite a chunk. It all went smooth, though, so we were happy with the way they handled things. But after the service, a member of the family, a woman…"

"Delores?" Jeffrey prompted when he seemed to hunt for the name.

"That's it. She mentioned they have these plans where you can arrange for your funeral or cremation in advance, pay up front, and when it's your time, all the arrangements are paid for. Gwen—that was Evie's mom—she said she wanted to do that for herself. 'I don't want to put you kids through this again.'"

Bryan stared at the sandwich he had yet to touch, seemed to think about it, and took a bite. "They do a nice job here," he said as he wiped his mouth. Jeffrey nodded. If the price of the story was listening to a restaurant review, he'd take it.

"So she paid a thousand dollars and signed some papers. They gave her a fistful of documents. This was while we were still dealing with her dad's arrangements. Insurance stuff, changing his social security benefits. She didn't understand most of it."

"Bryan offered to handle this for her," Evelyn said.

"She was an independent woman," he continued. "Lived on her own until her last breath."

"So what happened to the agreement with the funeral home we don't know," she said.

Like watching a tennis match, Jeffrey let them pass the ball back and forth, telling the story with little need for his intervention. Bryan ripped open a bag of chips and popped a couple into his mouth. "When she passed, I went through her things looking for the agreement, but couldn't find it. I called the funeral home, assuming they'd honor it. We got the runaround."

"That's putting it mildly," she said. "The owner, Daniel, denied any knowledge of a contract. We tried looking for her bank records, canceled checks, anything, but Mom didn't hang on to stuff like that after three years."

"Meanwhile," her husband said, "the clock was ticking. They had Mom's body, but wouldn't cremate her until we agreed to pay them. We insisted they honor the agreement she'd made years before, but they wouldn't budge. We arranged for another funeral home to collect her body."

Evelyn, who hadn't touched her sandwich, pulled a tissue from her purse and dabbed at her eyes. She nudged her husband to continue the story for her.

"We had her service, said our goodbyes, and were prepared to let the whole thing slide," he said. "Evie was in mourning. I was working and trying to juggle the paper-work. We'd decided to take our lumps and move on."

"But then?" Jeffrey said when the man seemed to run out of road.

"Sedlak sent us a bill for over $700 for services they claimed they'd performed on her body. I boiled over and took those bastards to court. Fat lot of good that did us."

He described the process. They couldn't afford an attorney, so represented themselves—*pro se*, in legal parlance—filing a small claims suit in magisterial district court. Having taken this course in the past against clients who refused to pay him, Odell knew that winning and collecting were two separate things. "We didn't get that far," he said. "I hadn't expected Sedlak to contest it. That's what happens, you know. These people know that even if you win, you'll spend more money trying to collect, and you're not always success-ful. I thought they'd just wait us out."

He took the last bite of the sandwich as he shook his head. "This high-powered attorney shows up, claims we got confused in all the turmoil following her dad's death, that Gwen had listened to the pitch for pre-planning but only agreed to consider it. Keep in mind, fifteen years had passed, her bank had changed hands, so we didn't have a scrap of paper to show they were lying."

"So you lost," Jeffrey said.

"Not only did we lose, but Sedlak threatened to sue us for the $700 they said we owed."

"And did you—?"

"No," he said. "I told them to go ahead. 'Take us to court,' I said. 'Prove you so much as touched the body.' We'd paid the new funeral home, so we knew they'd done nothing to it—to her."

Sedlak had taken no action against them. The unpaid bill had not shown up on their credit report. The Odells had come away with a minor victory, although they'd lost the battle.

Jeffrey knew better than to provide legal advice, but he wanted to leave the couple with something. "We're investigating a case quite similar to this, also involving Sedlak," he said. "It reminds me of an incident a few years ago in which a company had breached the trust of an unwary consumer. He also lost in court, but as I recall, he presented his situation to the attorney general's office. They opened an investigation and closed the business down."

"Do you think we should do that?"

"I'm not saying that," Jeffrey said, the picture of innocence. "I'm just recalling what these people did." Even as he spoke the words, however, the detective wondered if the state would take any action on a case over a decade old.

ON THIS, the first day of summer, the sun blazed, unbroken by a single cloud, and the electronic sign on a bank read nine-four degrees. Despite the rain of a few days before, every stretch of lawn was the color of hay. This was like being back in Texas, Lydia thought, far too early for temperatures to reach these heights. Those who doubted the reality of climate change had only to step outside their air-conditioned homes.

After checking to make certain Daniel Sedlak was at the funeral home, Barnwell drove to affluent Fox Chapel where the spacious lawns were green. She could only imagine how much green they spent to keep them that way.

She parked in the driveway, pressed the button on the Ring camera, and when asked, displayed her ID and identified herself. "Daniel's not here," a woman's voice responded.

"I know. I'm here to see Mrs. Sedlak."

She got no response, but a minute later, the door opened and a slight woman with dark eyebrows and blond, nearly white hair answered. "What's this about?" she said.

"Are you Mrs. Sedlak?"

"Wendy, yes." She stood in the doorway wearing a pained expression, as though Barnwell were a canvasser for the local Democratic Party.

"May I come in?" she said. "I have a few questions. This won't take long."

"I'm not sure I should talk to you without..." She looked over her shoulder as if someone could help her, then relented, stepping aside without a word, leading her into the dining room and taking a seat at the foot of the table.

Barnwell took a seat alongside her and pointed her body cam toward her. "I'm recording this," she explained. Wendy recoiled from the device like it might bite her. "One week ago tonight, were you at home?"

"I'm always at home, unless we're on vacation."

"Your husband was with you?"

"Yes." But she made it sound more like a question than a statement. Was she hiding something?

"In the early hours of the morning—Thursday morning, this would have been—a police officer called the house, asking to speak to your husband. You answered. Do you recall that?"

Wendy Sedlak nodded her head without answering.

"What did she tell you?"

"That there'd been a break-in at the funeral home and Daniel should come in."

"And how did you respond?"

She'd looked down before speaking. "I said I'd tell him." She rubbed the fingernails of each hand against each other, oblivious to the damage they might do to her flamingo pink polish.

"And did you?"

"Of course."

"He was awake?" When she didn't answer, Barnwell said, "When the phone rang, it must have awakened him, too."

The woman looked up and gave her a guileless look. "We sleep in separate rooms." And before Lydia could pursue the question, she added, "He snores. It's better that way."

"So you went into his room and ...?"

"I told him a police officer had called the house, that there'd been a break-in at the funeral home, and he should go in and make certain nothing was taken."

Barnwell didn't need to parse the sentence. "He wasn't

home." Wendy blinked twice and cleared her throat. "I didn't…"

"You told him a police officer had called the house, meaning he wasn't there at the time."

"I'd need to—"

"This is important, Mrs. Sedlak. If you tell me something that isn't true, and I learn you're concealing evidence of a crime, you can be charged. Your husband was not home, was he?"

"No." Her voice almost faded away as she choked on the word. "Please don't tell him…"

"Where was he?"

She emitted a long sigh and buried her mouth in her knuckles. "I don't know. Honestly. He says he plays poker with some friends, but he comes home late."

"And you don't believe he's playing cards."

"I—I'm not sure."

Lydia pulled out her card and wrote her personal cell phone number on the back. "If you think of anything else, call me. If you need help, call. Any time. Day or night."

Wendy Sedlak nodded but folded the card lengthwise in a shaking fist.

BARNWELL LEFT, buoyed by what she'd learned. Sedlak's wife had just destroyed his alibi for the night of the murder. She was tempted to return to headquarters, but knew Jeffrey was conducting another interview. She stopped for a late lunch, poking at a chicken Caesar salad as she thought about the case.

A message from Ross Sutton interrupted her. "Got the receipts from Home Depot." She'd asked him to discover what materials Sullivan had purchased from the big box store, and he'd come through. She called him on her cell, since what he had to say didn't belong on the police frequency.

"I've posted the report to the file," he said.

"Thanks, but I'm halfway across the county. Can you give me the highlights?"

Sutton gave one of his drawn-out sighs, letting her know how put-upon he was. "Nothing out of the ordinary. A couple of toilets, tiles, a handful of other plumbing supplies." Marty was not a licensed plumber and should not have taken the job without one.

"A large quantity of lumber," Sutton continued, "shingles…"

"Shingles," she said.

"And roofing felt, a quantity of nails, screws…"

"How many shingles? Just a few, or was this a pallet?"

Sutton read off the dates, quantities, and prices. She thanked him and ended the call. Little jobs, Coppola had said. Nothing that competed with his work.

Jeffrey had asked her to question Kuczienski, an assignment that took on new urgency. She could wait for his return, but her route would take her through Etna. She texted the roofer, requesting another half-hour of his time. "Boss sez 2 hot 2 wrk," he wrote. "Meet @ house @ 2."

Why was he responding in a decade-old language? With voice-to-text on modern cell phones, one could speak into the device and entire sentences rolled out, though the results were occasionally laughable. This gave her time to finish her salad while she planned her questions. As she rolled to a stop before his home, the question of his texted response answered itself as he closed the cover of a flip-phone.

"We're meeting out here again?" she asked as he dropped his leg off an adjoining chair and rose to his feet.

"Naw, Shari took the baby to her mom's. She has AC. C'mon in."

He held the door open for her, and she entered a room covered with the paraphernalia of babydom: a stack of onesies on one end of a sofa, a bouncer before the fireplace, and a straw basket filled with plushies atop the ottoman whose fabric showed stains of what she took to be spilled formula.

Kuczienski directed her to the other end of the sofa and asked if she wanted a beer. "Yes, I do, but no, I won't," she said.

He shrugged and wandered into the kitchen, returning with a cold one in his hand. "What's on your mind?" he asked as he squatted on the edge of a recliner.

She set the camera before him and explained why she was making a recording. She could barely hear him over the roar of a window fan, so raised her voice, hoping his words would overcome the racket. If not, Ross Sutton might be able to filter out the noise.

"When we spoke three days ago, you told me Marty had been neglecting his work and was paying more attention to the side jobs he pursued on weekends. Something was going on between them, you suggested, but you didn't know what. Are you sure about that?"

He stared at the foam flooding the rim of his beer can. "Al?" she said.

Kuczienski raised his head, glanced at her penetrating stare, and looked away. "I didn't *know* anything, you understand. Marty told me something one day, but I didn't pursue it."

He nodded toward the stack of baby clothes and a box

of disposable diapers in a corner of the room. "I need this job, understand?"

"I do. So what did he tell you?"

"He pointed to a stack of shingles one day. 'You see these Grade 3s?' he says. I didn't say anything. 'They're paying for Grade 4s.' I asked if he was sure, and he said he was."

"Did he tell you how he knew?"

"No, and I didn't quiz him. What did he mean to do about it? 'Nothing,' he says. 'I just thought you should know who we're working for.' I said it didn't surprise me." A pained expression came over his face, like an errant child pleading to be understood. "I'm under no illusions, understand? But I have a family to support. I keep my head down, do my job, come home at night, and mind my own business."

She jotted down a few notes, not that she needed to. The act gave her time to think. "These side jobs of his. Did any of them involve roofing projects?"

Kuczienski took a long mouthful of beer, wiping his mouth on his arm. Was he deciding how much to tell her? "At least one," he said.

"He took a job that competed with his boss?"

"He took the job *from* Coppola." She said nothing, nodding her head to encourage him. "I don't know how he found out, but he learned one of his neighbors had requested a quote from Coppola. Marty went to him and said he could do it for less, but that he'd only be able to work it on weekends. The guy must have agreed, because the next thing I knew, he had us working this job on his own. And using Grade 4 shingles." He laughed to himself and took another sip from the can, crushing it in his hand as he finished.

"So you worked the job with him."

"Yeah. First and last time."

"There were others?"

He stared at the mangled metal as though it were a Magic 8-Ball. "Must have been," he said, "because he asked me to work on another project. I begged off."

"Did you explain why?"

"Naw, I just said I needed to spend weekends with my wife and kid." He rose, took the can into the kitchen, and returned with another. "When he first pulled me in, I didn't know he'd stolen the contract from the boss. When I found out, I almost walked away. If Coppola had found out, we both would have been in trouble."

"Did Marty seem concerned?"

"I asked him that. He said the boss had given him permission."

"But you didn't believe him."

"No. I overheard a conversation between Marty and the guy who owned the house. He complimented him on the job and thanked him for saving him money. Marty shushed him. 'This is between you and me,' he said."

"Was he aware you'd overheard the conversation?" she asked.

He considered before answering, the fan seeming to raise its decibel level to fill the void. "I think so, but I guess he trusted me not to say anything." He looked around the living room, letting the sound of the fan fill the void. "I just realized ..."

"Marty was using you."

He covered his chin with his knuckles and looked at the thin green rug, whose stains attested to the presence of an infant tossing a milk bottle aside. "I guess so."

When the two detectives gathered at headquarters late in the afternoon, another surprise awaited them. Pat Corrigan, the detective Jeffrey had investigating accusations of fraud against the roofing contractor, interrupted them, holding a sheaf of papers in his left hand. "You have me looking into this Coppola character, but you also mentioned the funeral home director. Something tugged at my memory, and about an hour ago, I remembered what it was. I called the attorney generals's office. They confirmed it for me."

He took a seat and deposited a small stack of paper on Jeffrey's desk. "I uploaded this to the server, but it's short enough to print out."

Lydia reached for the paper, but paid more attention to his words. "Three years ago, the AG received a complaint from a Braddock resident that Sedlak had cheated them out of $1,000. They claimed that years before, their father had purchased a cremation contract from Sedlak, but when he died, they couldn't find the paperwork. Sedlak denied ever having made the deal. Without proof, they went to the AG, but—"

"Let me guess," he said. "Because there was no record of the transaction, they couldn't prove fraud."

The detective nodded. "So the family paid him again?"

"Yeah. They paid twice, but then thought better of it and filed a complaint."

"Braddock, you said?"

"Yeah. A Black family."

"Easy target," Lydia said.

"Uh-huh. The rich getting richer by preying on the poor."

She thanked the detective, telling him he'd done a great job.

"If you don't mind my saying so," he began, looking down at Lydia. She raised her brows, inviting him to say whatever he was thinking. "You're the one doing a good job. I heard Inspector Morris last week calling you a star."

"He did?"

"Yeah. It's not his way to compliment us to our faces. But someone said something ..."

"Disparaging?" she offered. "That girl detective?"

"Something like that." She filled in the word he was unwilling to share. "Morris cut him down. I thought you should know."

"Thanks, Pat. I appreciate it."

"Feeling good?" Jeffrey asked.

"Never better." But in his wake, she focused not on Inspector Morrison's defense of her, but about his need to do so. When, she wondered, would the old guys stop talking trash about her and get with the program?

She put it aside. Between the two of them, they'd learned enough to bring two suspects in for questioning. Coppola had been charging roofing customers for more expensive material than he was giving them. Marty got on to him and stole projects from him. Was he aware of it? "And where was Marty getting his inside information?" Lydia asked. "Someone asks Coppola for a bid, and Marty undercuts him. He was playing a dangerous game."

"He had Coppola in the palm of his hand and knew it," Jeffrey responded. "Did he remove the threat by removing Marty?"

And then there was Sedlak, who'd been taking advantage of older customers during moments of mourning, making contracts for funeral services but withholding the paperwork. Neither detective doubted this was why Marty Sullivan had broken into the funeral home, an event that could have led to his murder. Sedlak's wife had now destroyed his alibi.

"We should have their bank records in the morning," Jeffrey said. "Then we'll know whether he was shaking them down. Even without that, we have enough to call Sedlak in for a formal interview. Until then…"

"We wait," she said.

As she entered the parkway, she called Calvin to see if he wanted her to pick up dinner. "No," he said, "I've seen to it. Just get here as soon as you can."

"Why? What's up?"

"Come on home. You'll see."

She took the Carnegie exit and wound through the business district until she reached Boquet Street. Another vehicle was parked before the house, but cars lined the road every night, and she gave the matter no thought.

As she entered, the smell of pizza enveloped her. Good for him, she thought, certain he'd brought a small veggie for her. She tossed her bag on the sofa, called out a greeting, and walked into her kitchen to find Calvin grinning like a fool, sitting across from a man whose back was turned toward her. She didn't need to see his face to recognize him.

"Chief," she said, "what are you doing here?"

"Mayfield has been telling me about your little mystery," Karol Novak said. "I have a few free days to look into it, if you'll let me."

"Will I," she said.

CHAPTER NINE

LYDIA ARRIVED at headquarters the following morning with a sense of anticipation. She and Calvin had spent two hours briefing Karol Novak about the Frank Alberti case. Their former boss was six months into a retirement he'd delayed for over a year. He and his wife Barbara were leaving in two weeks to take their granddaughter, Jennifer, on a trip to France to practice her French. "I hope she's as good as we think she is," he said. "Otherwise, we'll be lost when we leave Paris for the countryside."

Lydia recommended Simone's, an authentic French restaurant in Rouen and a list of must-see places in Normandy. It had been a decade since she'd visited, but as she spoke, the smells and tastes of northwest France came back to her. She wished she were accompanying the trio.

Between now and his departure, Novak would try to reconstruct what had happened three decades before. As he took notes, Lydia recounted everything she'd learned about the murder of Frank Alberti since finding the yellow purse in the attic.

Alberti had been slain in a motel room he'd rented in

Ross Township. He'd brought no luggage, leading them to believe he'd arranged to meet someone. He'd previously had an extra-marital affair with a woman named Jane Quinlan. Police questioned her, but couldn't shake her alibi. A woman named Jane had written a letter to Alberti's house. Lydia was sure his wife had intercepted it, placed it in an expensive handbag, and hidden it in the attic.

"An anonymous caller turned the cops on to Jane Quinlan," she said, ending the sentence on a high note as though to continue.

"You think the victim's wife—"

"Emilia Alberti," she supplied.

"—tried to frame her husband's girlfriend?" Novak asked.

"And hid the letter to give herself deniability," she answered. His summation clarified what had been in the back of her mind for two days.

Novak tugged at loose skin on his neck that was threatening to become a waddle. "Why would she have held onto it?"

"Who knows why people do the things they do?" Calvin said.

Novak jotted down another line on his writing pad. He'd been a compulsive note taker ever since the two of them had worked for him. Only as she was leaving the Boyleston police force had she discovered why. He'd suffered a head injury during an amateur soccer match, impairing his short-term memory and forcing his retirement from the Pittsburgh Police Bureau.

"Let's see what I can uncover," he said. "I'll start with this Quinlan woman."

With someone now handling the mystery of the yellow purse, Lydia enjoyed a solid night's sleep, and entered the bullpen, hoping they'd make major progress on Marty Sullivan's killing. They would search Sedlak's office and home for the murder weapon while they grilled him at headquarters. Only after they charged him or crossed him off their list would they bring in Walter Coppola.

She opened her computer to find an alert from digital forensics detective Ross Sutton. "You've read it," Jeffrey said as he carried his omnipresent coffee mug to the desk alongside her.

"No large cash withdrawals from either Coppola or Sedlak," she answered. "I'm not surprised. We know Marty shook down Dr. Petarsky, but the rest were advance payments on building projects he never started."

"I wonder what he was thinking?" he said. "Taking money for work he wasn't prepared to do was bound to catch up to him."

"Perhaps he intended to follow through. The hospital was pressing him for his mother's medical bills. He didn't have the money, and the only way to get it was to sell his house." She recalled how he'd left his mother's room undisturbed, almost as a shrine. "He was unwilling to do that. He secured advance payments to pay his mother's bills and planned to complete the jobs during the summer."

"Maybe," he admitted, but both of them had seen the dark side of Marty's behavior. Perhaps he was just ripping people off.

MINUTES BEFORE NINE, two teams of officers descended on Sedlak's residence and funeral home. They served search warrants seeking any firearms on the premises. Sergeant Jeffrey had tried adding business records to the order, but the assistant DA had limited the warrant to the hunt for the murder weapon.

Sedlak arrived at headquarters a few minutes past ten, his attorney in tow. Unlike his contentious demeanor of three days before, he seemed subdued, aware of the searches underway. Did he also know they were investigating his deceptive business practices? Had his wife told him she'd undermined his alibi? Whatever the reason, he was docile as he followed them to the interview room, accepting the single uncomfortable chair while his lawyer got to pad his behind.

Jeffrey led the attack, recounting Marty Sullivan's midnight invasion of the funeral home. "When we questioned you the day following the incident, you claimed you'd never met the intruder. Do you still say that?"

"I said I didn't recall meeting him."

"You told us you could think of no reason he'd broken in. Is that still your story?"

"If I don't recall meeting him, why would I know what he was doing there?" His attorney placed a restraining hand on his arm. "No," Sedlak said.

Jeffrey removed a document encased in plastic from his folder. "We showed you this document at your home on Sunday. It's a cremation contract signed by Grace Sullivan and by Delores, your sister. You told us you didn't believe she'd paid the $1,350. We've examined her bank accounts and know that she had. You promised to review your records. Have you done so?"

"Yes," he said, turning toward his attorney. "It appears a mistake was made at our end."

Barnwell noted his lapse into passive voice. Things happened. Errors occurred. Mistakes were made.

"You have a pattern of such 'mistakes,'" Jeffrey said.

"We spoke to the Odell couple who told us a similar story. We know there were others. When a spouse or a child is arranging care for a loved one at your mortuary, you suggest they take out a contract either for themselves or for another relative. You take their money, but you also take advantage of their bereavement by retaining the agreement, hoping that when their time comes, their relatives will have forgotten about it."

The lawyer spoke. "That's a serious charge. You'll have to prove it."

"The attorney general has opened an investigation. I'll let her handle it." Sedlak pursed his lips, his eyes studying the dark surface of the table. "As for this," Jeffrey said, holding up the contract, "our forensics team has proved it's an original document. After casing your funeral home in advance, Sullivan broke in a week ago last night, and entered your office. He was out to prove you'd bilked him and his late mother out of over a thousand dollars. He'd already confronted you, but you sent him away."

Sedlak said nothing.

"We've interviewed others..."

"All right," Sedlak said, falling for the bluff. "Yes, when Mrs. Sullivan died, her son came to see Delores. He was sure his mother had made an agreement with us, but he couldn't find the paperwork. She told him we had no record of such an agreement. He asked to speak to me. I told him the same thing."

"But you knew it wasn't true."

"My client should answer no more questions," the attorney said. "You haven't charged him with anything. We're here voluntarily. If you have nothing more—"

Lydia overrode him. "You also swore you were home the night of Sullivan's murder. Do you still maintain that?"

His attorney reached for his arm, but Sedlak forged ahead. "I was sleeping in my bed. My wife will confirm that."

She and Jeffrey had discussed how to handle this. "Your wife took Officer Ingram's call. She then called your cell phone. Why would she do that if you were in the adjoining bedroom? You weren't at home. Where were you?"

"My client has nothing more to say," the attorney said.

"When you arrived at the mortuary, you immediately entered your office, checked the file drawers, and assured us nothing was amiss. That wasn't true, was it? You'd discovered this contract was missing." She recalled his palsied hands as he spoke to her. "You knew who had broken in and why. That night, you drove to Sullivan's home and demanded he return it. You'd brought the handgun you keep in your desk."

"I've never been to his house, and I've never harmed anyone."

"What happened? Did he try to grab the gun? Was that why your first shot went wild? Did you threaten to kill him unless he returned the contract? Did he refuse? Is that when you fired three shots, two into his skull?"

"I did no such thing."

The attorney rose. "That's it. Charge him, or we're leaving."

"We'll be in touch," Jeffrey said, gathering his papers. He announced to the recording that the interview was concluded at 10:48 a.m.

"What do you think?" Jeffrey said after they'd left.

"He's guilty of something," she said. "I'm just not sure what."

"You believe him?"

She sighed and ran her hand through her blond curls. "I don't know what to think. He was so firm in his denial, almost as though he were offended at the suggestion. I guess we'll soon find out."

They had neither Sedlak's prints nor DNA, so they couldn't prove he'd ever entered Sullivan's house. The search warrant would either come up with a match to the murder weapon or leave them empty-handed. Without physical evidence, they'd have no case. At least, she told herself, they'd unmasked someone who promised to help those in need, but only helped himself.

Moments later, the team at the funeral home reported they'd recovered a vintage Smith & Wesson Sigma and a spare .40 cartridge from Sedlak's locked desk drawer. They'd found no other weapons. It took the officers at his home another thirty minutes, but they found nothing.

This didn't clear him, of course. Sedlak could have removed the weapon, hidden it away somewhere, or tossed it in a river. There was still the matter of where he was on the night Sullivan was murdered and why he'd lied about it.

As though in response, Lydia's office phone rang. "Look," Sedlak said, "I need to tell you something, but I insist you be discreet." *The supplicant insists.*

"Meaning?"

"It's about where I was that night. I'll tell you on the condition you don't share this with my wife."

"I can't promise anything, Mr. Sedlak, but if you have an alibi that we can substantiate, we have no case and no reason to reveal it to anyone."

He said nothing for several seconds as she listened to

him wheeze as though he were asthmatic. "The thing is, I have a friend. Wendy thinks I play cards with him and two others every Wednesday night, but..."

When he paused again, she said, "I get the picture. What is this man's name?"

"Do I have to drag him into it?"

Some people can be so thickheaded. "Unless I confirm this, it's just another one of your stories. It changes nothing."

"All right," he said, "but he'll want you to be equally circumspect." *A grand way of saying the man didn't want his name dragged into this mess.*

"You're both married?"

"No, but he has a position to consider. He'll be quite angry, but..."

After some additional jousting, Daniel Sedlak provided the name of an influential state senator.

***

Karol Novak spent the morning searching for the real estate agency from which Jane Quinlan had mailed her letter to Frank Alberti. Six decades had passed, and he doubted anyone who'd worked with her would still be alive, but it was worth trying. He soon learned the agency had been sold to a larger one in the early eighties when the owner passed away. His widow was also gone.

Novak next visited the courthouse, going through death records. He didn't find Jane Quinlan, but in the civil registry he learned that a Jane Warren had married Jess Quinlan in 1956. She had just turned eighteen. Three years later, Corporal Quinlan was shot and killed during the US invasion of Panama, leaving Jane to raise a one-year-old son named Timothy on her own. In 1966, Jane

Quinlan wed Max Arnholdt, a naturalized citizen born in Germany. He died in 2002, making his wife a widow once more.

What had become of her? He found nothing further in the public records. If she had remained in Pennsylvania, she was still alive, for there was no death record, but she might also have retired to Florida or some other sunny clime.

Novak wasn't one to give up. He searched for Timothy Quinlan and learned he'd taken his stepfather's name months following his mother's marriage. Novak had endured no end of teasing over his Slovakian given name. He could imagine the youngster starting first grade with a new surname. Had that caused him confusion or resentment?

He found a man by that name listed as manager of a store in the Giant Eagle supermarket chain. The corporate office in O'Hara Township accepted his explanation—a retired chef of police working with a detective from the Allegheny County Police Department—and informed him Arnholdt had retired on his 65th birthday, two months before. After some prodding, they provided the man's home telephone number.

Arnholdt's wife answered and turned the phone over to him. Novak explained who he was. "I'm trying to locate your mother. Is she still with us?"

"A police matter?" he said.

"Yes, but she's not suspected of anything. This concerns someone she knew years ago."

"The man who was murdered," Arnholdt said.

"Yes," Novak replied, hiding his amazement that he'd heard the story.

"She answered all your questions back then." Before Novak could explain that they'd discovered a letter she'd written years before, he said, "She loves visitors, though. I'm sure she'll be happy to tell you what she knows."

He gave Novak the name and address of a retirement home in Ross Township and said he'd call to prepare her for the visit.

BARNWELL OFFERED to write up their report of Sedlak's interview, so Jeffrey drew the short straw. State Senator Wayne Loomis kept his district office in Monroeville. "Can't we handle this by phone?" he asked, but the detective wanted to sit across from him when he posed his questions, reading his facial expressions and body language.

The office was at the end of a strip mall. Jeffrey arrived to find the front door unlocked but no one at their desks. "Come in," a man's voice called from somewhere in back. He emerged from his office in shirtsleeves and his tie undone. "I sent the staff home," he said. "This is a private matter. I don't want our conversation overheard."

Or even to know a police officer was speaking to him, Jeffrey guessed. "Dan told me what you're after. I could have saved you the trouble. I can't tell you anything I wouldn't have said when you called."

Jeffrey didn't apologize. "Can we sit down?"

"My office," he said, turning and leading the way. Loomis took a seat behind his desk, which was framed by a profusion of photographs of the senator with governors, senators, members of Congress, and sports and entertainment figures. He'd been in the state senate for years and chaired its appropriations committee, which held the commonwealth's purse strings. Loomis was a power and wanted everyone who came here to recognize it.

As Jeffrey positioned his body camera before the man, he said, "You don't have to record this, do you?"

"I do," he said. He was not about to be cowed by the senator's attitude of self-importance. "Where were you on the night of June 15th and who was with you?"

"I expect you to handle this with the utmost discretion." That word again.

"I'm investigating a murder."

"Still, I demand—"

"And if things are as Daniel Sedlak claims, there's no need for us to reveal any part of this conversation. He hasn't been charged, and if he's done nothing, we have no reason to release any details of our investigation." He leaned forward, looking the man in the eye. "I require your cooperation."

With a tortured sigh, his resistance gave way. "We've been friends since college. We get together once a week to have a few drinks and reminisce. There's nothing unseemly about that."

"On the night of Wednesday, June 15th—"

"Daniel came to my house, as he always does. He arrived about nine o'clock and was about to leave when his wife called."

"He was getting dressed?" Jeffrey asked, remembering Barnwell's description of his appearance when he arrived at the mortuary.

Loomis fumbled for a moment, began to speak but caught himself, then said, "He'd taken off his coat and tie when he arrived. Just to relax while we talked."

"You live alone?"

"Dina and I separated some years ago. We're still married, but we only see each other socially."

"Can you provide any evidence you're telling me the truth? I can't rely on your story."

Loomis took in a deep breath and spread his arms to encompass the photographs, awards, and other recognitions surrounding him. "Do you think a man in my position would make this up? Two men alone. Imagine how my enemies would misinterpret something like this."

Jeffrey returned his glare. "So I have to take your word for it."

"No, you *have* my word on it. There's a difference."

"Because if we find you've not been honest with me, it's a felony, and it will become public."

He leaned back in his chair and, in a small, weary voice, said, "I've told you the truth."

Jeffrey could have probed to make the man admit what the two of them were doing together, but that was none of his business.

LYDIA TOOK lunch at her desk as she keyed in a report of their interview with Sedlak. A call from someone in the entry area interrupted her. He asked if she was the officer looking for Paul Welch. When she confirmed it, he said, "I think I can help you." She buzzed him into the reception room, then double-timed her way downstairs, amazed that, for the second time in a week, a person had come to headquarters without being ordered to do so. Usually, they had to drag information out of potential witnesses.

The man seated in one of the green chairs had skin the color of a brown egg. He was in his mid-fifties, slender, with a clean-shaven head. "Tyrus Walker," he said as he extended his hand. Lydia took it and noted it was slightly clammy. Was it the temperature outside or was he frightened? Perhaps a little of both.

"You have information about the man we're trying to find?" she said.

"Yeah. He just called himself Paul, but the news says his last name is Welch."

"How do you know him?"

"I don't, really, but he used to come into the bar where I work. He'd have a few beers and then start talking. His mouth got real loose, if you know what I mean."

Barnwell decided this was not a conversation to be had in the entryway. She led him upstairs into the interview room they'd vacated an hour before, directing him to the comfortable chair. Walker took in the camera overhead, and his eyes darted around the bare walls. "This is just a place to meet," she said. "I'm not interrogating you."

When he blinked, she added, "I've hidden the thumbscrews."

He looked at her in confusion, then returned her smile and seemed to relax. He told her he was a carpenter who worked weekends as a bartender in O'Hara Township. This was close to Welch's Sharp's Hill neighborhood. "He used to come in Friday nights. Not every week, but most. He'd sit at the bar and start downing drafts. Iron City, mostly."

As Welch drank, he said, he'd strike up a conversation with anyone within range. "Some folks found him entertaining, I guess. Others tried to ignore him. He never bothered the ladies. He only talked to men."

"What did he talk about?" she asked.

"That's the thing. It's why I came here rather than calling you to the bar. I don't want to get into any trouble there. The tips are good. I'm not sure how Stew—that's the owner—how he'd like me talking about customers."

"I appreciate it," she said. "Few people volunteer information." Particularly, she thought, people of color.

"He used to talk about his war experience. Said he'd done two tours in Vietnam. He'd brag about the number of Vietcong he'd killed. I paid little attention. Just drunk talk. I hear a lot of it."

"I'm sure you do."

"But one day, he said to this guy, 'You ever killed anyone?' And the fellow he was talking to—you could tell he wasn't into it—said he hadn't. And so Paul starts bragging about how many he'd killed in Nam. I'd heard all this before. But then he says, 'That wasn't my first, though.'"

Lydia leaned forward, not wanting to miss any nuance in Walker's tale.

"When the guy didn't respond, he said, 'You don't believe me?' Like he was trying to start a fight, you know? And the man says, 'Oh, I believe you. I'm sure you did.' Like he was trying to end the conversation. He was fishing in his pocket for some bills, like he just wanted to get out of there.

"Paul grabs his arm. I'm about to intervene. We don't want any fights there. The cops don't like having to come to our place to break things up. On Southside, they're closing bars that can't control their customers."

Barnwell knew this all too well. Pittsburgh Police had even tried to shut down a convenience store in Downtown that served as a magnet for druggies.

"But before I could, he says, 'I was once a hit man.' He was slurring his words now, and the other guy was trying to get away, but he kept at him. 'I got paid to take out a guy. One bullet to the head. Bang. Just like that.'"

Walker looked at her as though that ended the story. "What happened then?" she said.

"The other guy got up and left. Threw a ten on the

counter and shot out the front door without another word. Paul—Welch, is it?—he's reeling by then. He can barely sit on the barstool. I call Stew over because I'm afraid of what he might do. I tell him we got to get rid of him, that he's talking about killing people. Stew cuts him off. Says he's bothering other patrons and has had too much to drink. Time for him to go."

"And he left?" Barnwell said.

"Yeah. He gives him a look like he wants to fight him, but Stew's a big guy. Used to be a boxer. No one's going to mess with him. So the guy gets up and leaves. I say, 'Hey, you need to pay up.' He tells me to go fuck myself, and Stew says just to let him go, but not to allow him in again."

"Has he ever returned?"

"Nope. I'm guessing he sobered up and realized he'd said too much. Didn't want to show his face there."

Barnwell asked when this had taken place. Early spring, Walker replied. She asked about the other customer. Walker said he hadn't returned either. "I guess he got scared off. He'd only come in a few times before and always paid in cash." That left Barnwell with no way to track him down.

She had one more question. "Did you believe him about being a hit man?"

Walker gulped, his eyes widened, and his skull danced on his thin frame like a bobblehead. "I don't know, but I'm not about to find out. He seemed like a mean mother."

<hr>

JANE ARNHOLDT SAT in a recliner with her back to her window. Despite the backlighting, Novak noticed pixie-like features, and her white hair blooming in the sunlight added an angelic halo. She had once been beautiful, and given her age, still was. She held the photocopy in her hands, veined but steady, studied it for a moment, then removed her reading glasses, allowing them to dangle from a chain around her neck. "Where did you get this, after all these years?"

"A woman found it hidden in a purse in her attic. She's a police officer and asked me to find out more about it."

"Ah," she said, folding her hands on her lap. "This was a long time ago. It was silly of me to have written it. I think I knew he'd been using me, but I still had hope. Maybe he'd read it and feel sorry for me." She seemed to consider this. "Why would I want someone who only pitied me?"

"How did you meet?" Novak asked.

She looked out at the parched grass. "We need rain," she said.

"Yes." He recognized she was stalling for time and gave her all she needed.

With a sigh, she returned her attention to him. "He came into the real estate office where I worked. I was the secretary. Administrative assistant, they call it today, as though they're ashamed of what they're doing. I took pride in the job and did it well."

The woman looked at him for reassurance and didn't resume until he'd nodded. "He said he was looking for a small house, that he and his wife were divorcing. Since most of his business travel was between here and Cleveland, he wanted something in the North Hills, closer to the turnpike. I assigned him to one of our agents. She showed him around for a few weeks, but then said he'd decided not to buy, but to rent."

Jane paused for a moment, as if gathering her courage to reveal the more intimate parts of the story. "He returned to the office a few weeks later and asked me out to lunch. I said

I didn't go out with married men. He again told me he and his wife were getting a divorce."

"A smooth talker?" Novak suggested.

Her face lit up, a small smile caressing her lips. "He was a salesman, and the best ones know how to sell themselves. Isn't that what they say? And here I was, a young widow raising a child on my own. He sold me a bill of goods."

"How long were you together?"

"About six months." She told him their affair had lasted from the fall of 1962 to March 1963. "He'd come by every other week, bring groceries and always a gift for Timmy. He loved him, and I thought..."

Novak leaned toward her and covered her hand with his own. "Mrs. Arnholdt, I've been a cop all my adult life. I've heard dozens of versions of this story. He took advantage of your loneliness. It happens all the time."

She clutched his hand in silent gratitude. "Then he stopped coming. I didn't know why. We hadn't quarreled. I thought we were getting along great. One night, he was there. I made him breakfast in the morning, and he gave me a big hug when he left. That's the last I heard from him."

"So you wrote your letter," Novak prompted.

The woman launched into a lengthy defense of her decision, explaining that without a work telephone number or address, she had no other way of reaching him. "I had his name and knew he lived in South Side, so I looked him up in the white pages. You could do that back then."

She covered her hand with her mouth and shook her head. "It was a Saturday. I waited until everyone else had left, typed the letter, and put it in a billing envelope. By making it seem official, I hoped his wife wouldn't suspect anything."

"You know he was still living with her?" Novak said.

"Yes, she was being difficult about ending the marriage. She'd threatened to ruin him financially and darken his reputation. In those days, getting a divorce in Pennsylvania was no simple matter." She blew out a puff of air. "Too easy now, if you ask me. Anyway, he'd told me just to hold on, that he was working through it."

"And you never heard from him again?"

"Never. He didn't call, didn't come by the house, and never responded to my letter. Now, I know why." She looked out the window again, a faraway look in her eye. "You say his wife discovered it? If I hadn't sent it, I wonder..."

"Mrs. Arnholdt—"

"You can call me Jane. Everyone else does."

"Jane, you say the last you heard from him was in March 1963. When did you write the letter?"

"Toward the end of the month. I remember because Timmy's birthday was coming up, and Frank always brought him presents."

"Did you have any further contact with him after that date?"

"No. I never heard from him again."

"Did you try to reach him?"

"It's like I said. I wrote the letter, and that was that. When he didn't reply, I knew it was over. Why do you ask?"

Alberti had been murdered in a nearby motel room on April 13th, but he didn't answer her question. "Did anyone else know about your relationship?"

"My next-door neighbor, Sarah Miller, saw him coming and going and asked about him."

"Someone at your office?"

"Oh, no," she said, drawing back as though he'd

suggested she'd paraded around in her underwear. "That would have been the end of my job."

Novak considered the information. Someone had lured Alberti to the motel room and then killed him. If Jane had played no role in it and no one else knew about the affair, there was only one explanation.

"How did you learn he'd been murdered?" he asked.

"It was the week of Timmy's birthday, and I'd taken him to Erie to see his grandparents—his father's mom and dad. They loved him, and I thought it would take his mind off Frank's absence. When we got back Sunday evening, the police were waiting for us. They separated us—Timmy was scared—and put me through the wringer. Even after they confirmed I was out of town at the time of the murder, they went through all my bank accounts, thinking I'd paid someone to kill him. It was terrible. And..." she began.

Novak waited. "That's when they learned about it at the real estate office. They fired me. It was weeks before I found another job."

She bit her lip, recalling the turmoil that had followed Alberti's slaying.

"And how did you feel when you learned what had happened to him?"

She shook her head, her white hair billowing as though caught by a gentle breeze. "I was heartsick. I didn't know why anyone would do such a thing to him."

The woman seemed to ponder the question. "Do you think...?"

"That's what I'm trying to find out, Jane." He thanked her for her help, bent and kissed her on the forehead, and left.

Lydia heard Jeffrey out about his meeting with Senator Loomis. "We have no way to confirm it. It's just his word. But as he points out, he wouldn't put his reputation on the line unless it were true." Which left one fewer suspect in the murder of Marty Sullivan.

"Meanwhile," she said, "I had a most interesting walk-in." She related what the weekend bartender had told her about Paul Welch.

"Remember what Seth Goodman, the other bartender, overheard at Julio's? Welch is drinking heavily. He engages Sullivan in conversation. Marty doesn't pay attention at first, then his attitude shifts and he moves them to a quieter table. He listens to Welch's rambling, steals a look in his wallet, picks up the tab, and leaves. Two weeks later, Welch comes into the bar and asks Goodman to identify his drinking partner. Goodman names Sullivan. A few nights later, he's murdered."

"We know Marty was shaking down people with secrets," Jeffrey said. "That may be what happened here. I'll reissue the APB, adding that Welch may be armed and dangerous."

"Until then?" she said.

"It's time to bring in Coppola." Seeing a frown pass over her face, he said, "You disagree?"

"No. It's just that..." She tried to turn her thoughts into words. "Something bothers me. I can't put my finger on it."

He waited while she thought. "Maybe it will come to me. Meanwhile, you're right. Marty held a sword over his boss. It's time we raised the roof."

CHAPTER TEN

LYDIA AWOKE at four in the morning, knowing what had bothered her the previous day. She often got her best insights as she slept, her subconscious processing information she'd received days, sometimes weeks, earlier. This could be both a blessing and a curse since once the idea came to her, she couldn't put it to bed, let alone herself.

She arose and entered the bathroom, closing the door, but not bothering to be surreptitious. Nothing disturbed Calvin when he was conked out. In the kitchen, she prepared a mug of herbal tea, pulled her notebook toward her, and wrote her conclusion at the top of the page. She then went through the list of suspects, even those who could prove their whereabouts on the night of Sullivan's murder. If her theory was correct, only the veterinarian, Dr. Sid Petarsky, had an opportunity, but his home security videos ruled him out. No other suspect met the requirement.

She took Howie for a walk, even though Tommy would do so later. Should she share her conclusion with Jeffrey, tell him everything they'd thought about the case to that point was mistaken? They'd summoned Coppola to headquarters in a few hours. She would wait until they'd questioned the roofing contractor.

"You're up early." Calvin kissed her on the neck, giving her shoulder a light squeeze before taking a seat at the counter. "Working overtime?"

As she brewed his coffee, she shared her conclusion. "Makes sense," he said, "but where does that leave you?"

Lydia had no answer, but as she stirred their eggs over low heat, it presented her with another question. "I'm trying to understand what happened to Marty. He was an only child, abandoned by his father, and raised by a single mother to whom he was devoted. He was an introvert, forming few close bonds with anyone, dropping out of his one extracurricular activity so he could work to support his mother. From what others have told me, he was a gentle soul, gaining the trust of his employer and caring for Grace after her diagnosis."

"A model citizen," Calvin said.

She finished the eggs and microwaved two slices of bacon for him, the combination of salty, sweet, and smoky flavors wafting through the kitchen. She opened a window to clear the odor and put a single slice of smoked salmon on her plate.

"When his mother died, he snapped," she continued. "He went after everyone he felt had wronged his mother, cheated himself, or shortchanged others. He sought retribution, with no regard to personal consequences. It got away from him. What caused such a massive change?"

"We've seen it before," he said. "Anger is a great motivator, but it's not a good friend."

"What made him snap?" she said. "Who can explain such a profound change?"

"Ask the girlfriend. What's her name?"

"Dora. She's another example. They were close for years, yet when his behavior made her pull away, he showed no emotion."

"Perhaps she can tell you something," Calvin said. "Women understand men better than we do."

"Where did you come up with that?" she asked. "Does it work in reverse?"

His laugh was like the blast of a foghorn. "No."

"I love you," she said. He smiled and nodded, but didn't return the sentiment. She fixed her blue eyes on him, waiting for something that never came.

"Thanks for listening, anyway," her voice an ice cube tossed into an empty glass. She left her breakfast untouched and headed toward the cafe where Dora Macklin worked.

Traffic was a hopeless tangle, as on most weekday mornings, but as she crossed the bridge to Butler Street, she found it at a standstill. A broken water main on a side street had turned 40th Street into a river. Pittsburgh's infrastructure was so old pipes were always bursting. Not a month went by without a fire in an aging structure, claiming at least one life. A year before, a bridge over Fern Hollow had collapsed, taking a city bus with it. Three years before that, a sinkhole in Downtown swallowed another bus. It was a miracle no one was killed during either of these events, though some had suffered serious injuries. As a relative newcomer, she found Pittsburgh's historic charm, from nineteenth-century buildings to brick streets, also a liability.

She was tempted to give up on meeting with Sullivan's former girlfriend, but she made her way around the impasse and, fifteen minutes later, pulled to the curb before the cafe, whose red, white, and green facade boasted its ethnic heritage.

Since Lydia had never met Dora, she asked at the

counter and was told she wasn't there today. "She's taken a few days off," the young woman said. "It's not a great time."

"Is she in mourning?" Lydia asked.

"I don't know. She's not here, that's for sure."

Barnwell looked out over the tables, through which a single server darted with a harried expression on her face. "Do you know when she'll be back?"

"No idea, but it better be soon, or the boss will give her plenty to mourn about."

She'd come all this was for nothing. Her questions about what had turned Marty Sullivan from a responsible citizen to a blackmailer and thief would have to wait. She considered taking a seat at the counter and ordering breakfast, but one look told her she'd be late for the interview with Coppola. She'd pick up Danish at a coffee shop somewhere, provided, of course, she didn't run into any more sinkholes, broken water mains, or fire trucks.

As HAD Daniel Sedlak the day before, Walter Coppola arrived with an attorney. Thiis, however, was his business lawyer, unaccustomed to criminal cases. "Do you mind telling us what this is all about?" she asked. "You've questioned Walter twice. He's told you all he knows."

"We've found a few discrepancies between what he's told us and what we've learned from others," Jeffrey said. "We're here to clear them up."

"You haven't charged him?"

Jeffrey assured her they had not. Satisfied, the attorney told him to answer their questions to the best of his recollection and folded her hands as Lydia began the recording. They led him through the time he'd first met Martin Sullivan, how he'd started as a part-time laborer and grown into someone on whom Coppola depended. "He was a very reliable guy. Hard working," he said.

When Jeffrey asked why, when they'd first asked if he had any friends, Coppola had failed to mention Kuczienski, he repeated he'd been unaware they were personal friends. "Marty was a private person," he said. "He never mentioned being close to anyone, other than his mother, of course. I guess you'd call him a mama's boy. There's nothing wrong with that. She'd raised him on her own. He'd always been good to her, but when she got sick, he decided it was his turn to take care of her."

It was the same story everyone else had given her. Her curiosity aroused again, Barnwell asked, "How did her death affect him?"

Coppola held out both hands, palms up. "He was devastated. He was never a great talker, but he said even less in the days and weeks after her funeral. I tried asking him how he was doing. He'd kind of shrug, say all right, and go about his business."

Before she could ask another question, he said, "I know how he felt. My wife is going through a bad patch right now. If I were to lose her..."

"I'm sorry to hear that," she said. Coppola muttered quiet thanks as tears clouded his eyes. "Is that why you tried to help Marty?"

His look showed he hadn't followed her. "You said you'd thrown some side jobs his way."

"Oh, yeah. I knew he was having money problems. Medical bills insurance didn't cover. Whenever someone brought little projects to us, I referred them to him."

"But not roofing jobs?" she said.

"No. Other stuff. Maintenance work. A bit of bathroom remodeling."

Jeffrey stared at him, tapping his pen against his notebook. "Nothing major. You're sure about this?" He raised his eyebrows and drummed the fingers of his left hand on the table.

Coppola hesitated, as though realizing he was walking into a trap.

"We've learned that's not quite the case, Walter. He did some large roofing jobs that could have gone to you."

"Did he?" Coppola widened his eyes and threw up both hands. "I didn't know that. If he'd asked my permission, I wouldn't have given it."

"You referred some of these projects to him."

"Not roofing," he said. "That was my business. I wouldn't have farmed that out."

"He underbid you on some contracts."

"Are you sure about this? If so, I'm disappointed in him. He should have told me."

"Walter, if you bid on a project and the customer hires someone else, don't you look into it to find out who got the business?"

"Not necessarily. I move on. There's plenty of work to go around. Pittsburgh is falling apart."

"He was using members of your own crew on weekends. He stole projects from you, employed your workers, yet you knew nothing about it. Why?"

"I knew he used some others, Kuczienski, for example."

"Who you claim you didn't know was his friend?"

He gave the slightest of shrugs. "I liked the kid. I trusted him. If he took work from us, I guess I trusted him too much."

"How did he undercut you? When you gave someone a

proposal, how did Marty learn about it? Where was he getting his information?"

Coppola heaved a sigh of defeat. "Maria suspected someone had been breaking into the office overnight. I found nothing missing, but she made me change the locks."

Barnwell leaned across the table and lowered her voice as though sharing a confidence. "Didn't you make the connection between an intruder and someone underbidding you?"

His shoulders sagged. "Guessed it, but couldn't prove it. I was never sure."

She insisted he had to know Sullivan was working roofing jobs, but Coppola didn't budge. "Here's what we've learned," she said. "Marty discovered you were using substandard materials on many of your jobs, charging customers for a higher grade of shingle than you installed and pocketing the difference."

Coppola protested, but Lydia shoved two photos under his nose, the contract she'd found while sitting in the back seat of his truck and the label on the stack of shingles. "One of our detectives has uncovered several other examples. Marty found out you were cheating customers and held it over you."

He said nothing, starting at his hands. The attorney asked for a moment with her client. "You may, but we're not ready to charge him with that. We want to know where he was during the early hours one week ago."

"I told you I was home," he said. "Haven't you checked it by now? Ask my son. He was there. My wife—" Coppola broke off and sat in silence. He rubbed tears away with his sleeves. "Truth is, my wife is dying," he said. "I don't like to talk about it. She doesn't want others to know, so I—our children—we say as little as possible. We've called in hospice and moved her home. It's a matter of days. Hours, maybe."

The detectives sat in stunned silence.

"I'm losing her, and thanks to you folks, I'll probably lose my business. I have nothing left. But," he said, his voice tightening, "I did not kill Marty Sullivan. Yes, he had me by the balls. I struggled over how to get him off my back. But the thought of killing him never crossed my mind. I would never do such a thing, and I did not. We were at home that night. We never go anywhere. Ask my son."

Section 15.59 of the Pennsylvania code requires law enforcement agencies to retain records of parking violations for one year, complaints involving domestic pets for two, and motor vehicle accidents for five. They must hold investigative reports on homicides, however, for seventy-five years.

Novak knew this well. He'd served for years as Pittsburgh's chief of detectives, then headed the police force of a small borough for nearly three. He recognized the difficulty of finding old records. The department had moved twice since Alberti's death, first to a wing of the old municipal building and then to its present home on Municipal Drive.

He'd called in advance to let the records officer know what he was after. By the time he arrived Friday morning, she had stacked the musty files on a table in a windowless carrell. Leafing through the original investigation with uniformed officers buzzing around him, he found the newspaper reporter had it about right. On the night of April 13th, 1963, Andrew Ferris, a delivery driver from Erie, heard what sounded like a gunshot. He was watching the

Pirates game on television and, aware that the person in the adjoining room was viewing a cop show at full blast, paid no attention. Then he heard an engine rev and back out of the driveway, screeching its tires. When he opened the door to investigate, he spotted a car he took to be a Ford Fairlane dart into traffic, "right into the path of a delivery truck. The driver had to brake so suddenly he turned into the curb," he told the investigating officer.

"Since that's my business, it pissed me off. I checked on the driver first. He was angry, but okay. Then I recalled the noise I'd heard and thought I'd better investigate. Two doors down, I found a door open and a body lying on the floor in a pool of blood. I didn't have to enter to know he was dead, but I checked for a pulse anyway, then ran down to the front office to call the police."

Today, the man would have reached for his cell phone and dialed 9-1-1, but Novak guessed this cheap motel didn't even provide phones in the rooms.

He read through the report of the first officer on the scene, satisfied that he had secured the room and called for backup. Together they'd called in detectives experienced in handling crime scenes—this was before the county had established the office of medical examiner and professional-ized it. Likewise, it would be two years before voters elected a licensed physician as coroner. From what Novak could tell, however, his predecessor had done an acceptable job, retrieving a .38 caliber bullet that had torn through the man's chest, rupturing his aorta before wedging itself in the wall behind him.

The victim's driver's license identified him as Francis Alberti of Carnegie. They contacted his wife, Emilia, who didn't believe what they told her. She insisted he was at a Pirates game at Forbes Field. What business did he have in

Ross Township? Police wondered the same thing, since the victim had no luggage with him. Only when they told her the make and model of the car parked at the door of the motel room did she accept her husband had been murdered.

The following morning, they received an anonymous tip claiming Alberti had been seeing a local woman, Jane Quinlan, who was angry he'd broken up with her. They located and questioned her.

Novak read through the transcript. Anna had been distraught during the interview, interrupting herself at several points to regain her composure. As the older version of herself had told him the day before, she claimed she was in Erie, celebrating her son's birthday with his grandparents on the night of the murder. The couple confirmed her story.

He turned to the transcript of an interview they'd conducted with Emilia Alberti, the victim's widow. She, too, had an alibi for the evening, playing gin rummy with three friends who often got together at her home.

"Were you aware your husband was having an affair?" a detective asked.

"Frank? No. Where did you get that idea?"

"We've spoken to the woman. She admits they began seeing each other last fall."

The transcriptionist had noted a long pause at this point. "I don't believe it."

"He told her you were divorcing."

"You're making that up. We were perfectly happy together."

"You've never heard of Jane Quinlan?"

"No, never."

"He's never mentioned a woman named Jane? Any other woman?"

"Never. This is a complete surprise. You're sure about

this?" The woman became angry, asking how her husband could have done this to her. She maintained she was unaware of the affair.

But thanks to the letter she'd concealed in the handbag, Novak knew she'd been lying, a denial that suggested Barnwell's instincts were correct.

A uniformed figure stopped at the entrance to the cubicle. "What's your interest in this old case?" he asked. Before Novak could answer, he said, "Follow me to the conference room. We need to talk."

COPPOLA PROVIDED his son's business and mobile phone numbers. Jeffrey tried the first, waiting six rings, and left a message on his voicemail. He called the mobile number with the same result. On a hunch, he redialed it. "Who is this?" a voice demanded.

Jeffrey identified himself. "Sorry," the voice said. "I get so much spam, I don't answer unless I know the person."

Barnwell listened while Jeffrey asked him to identify himself. "Wally Coppola," he said. "You calling about the man who worked for Dad who got himself shot? I never met the guy."

"I have a more specific question," Jeffrey said. "Where was your father one week ago last night and the early hours of Friday morning?"

"Dad? He must have told you that. We were all at the house. Mom is dying. We'd just brought her home from the hospital. Sylvie and I keep running back and forth from Ligonier. It's rough on her. She's about to have our second." He gave a rueful laugh. "It's weird, you know. One generation dies, while another is born. It would be something if both happened on the same—No, I don't want to go there."

"And your father was with you the entire night?" Jeffrey repeated the dates.

"He never left her side. We'd brought her home from the hospital that afternoon. We thought she wouldn't make it until morning, but she's still holding on. I have an older brother and sister. They're both coming in tonight. I think she's waiting for them."

Jeffrey thanked him, expressed condolences, and ended the call. "Is there any point in checking with the hospital?" he asked.

"No," Barnwell said. "It's about what I figured."

"You knew he was in the clear?"

"I assumed it," she said. "You see—"

Her radio sounded an alert. She listened for a moment and told the dispatcher she was on her way. "They've found Paul Welch," she told Jeffrey. "He's barricaded himself in a house in South Park. The SWAT team is trying to talk him out."

She left without explaining why she'd already decided Coppola was in the clear, leaving Jeffrey to wonder where they were now.

* * *

THE OFFICER INTRODUCED himself as Norman Rollins. Novak reached for his ID, but he waved it away. "You may not remember me, but I was in your class at the police academy years ago."

Novak squinted and said, "Of course I do," though he did not.

In response to his question, Novak explained he was

looking into the case as a favor to a county detective. "It started off as a personal matter, but it's become more than that." Rollins said nothing, waiting for more. "Why do you ask?" Novak said.

"My dad worked this. He didn't get many unsolved murders. Bar shootings, domestics—he usually knew who had done what to whom and why."

"And how," Novak added.

"Yeah. But he never solved this one. He kept working it as long as he was on the force, but could never prove who killed this man, Alberti. After he retired, I kept at it. I pull out the file each year, hoping I can find something he missed. I never have."

"I spoke to Jane Quinlan yesterday," Novak said. "Jane Arnholdt now. She's quite sharp. Her story matches what she told your father back in '63."

"I've spoken both to her and her son. They tell the same story. When Dad interviewed the kid's grandparents, Jane's former in-laws, he believed they were telling the truth. The kid watched TV at their house Saturday night. He recalled every detail of the programs he watched. This was way before DVRs, and Dad questioned him before friends could coach him. He checked her bank records, thinking she might have paid someone to kill him, but he found nothing. I'm convinced she had nothing to do with it."

"But," Novak said, sensing there was more.

"We got onto her through a phoned tip. Ross Township didn't record calls back then, but the duty officer said the caller sounded like a woman. Whoever it was spoke just above a whisper, speaking in a low register to make herself sound like a man."

"And his theory was..."

"He questioned Alberti's wife. She claimed to know

nothing about it. Her alibi also checked out. And when he told her about the other woman, she expressed surprise." Rollins suppressed a chuckle, telegraphing his cynicism.

"Your dad didn't believe her," Novak said.

"No, but he couldn't prove anything. He looked into her finances. She sold his car after we turned it over to her, deposited the check in her bank account, then withdrew it a month later. Since she was spending quite a lot in the months following her husband's death, Dad could never trace the money. She inherited the house, of course, and Alberti had a $25,000 life insurance policy. That doesn't sound like much, but it's ten times that in today's dollars."

"A quarter of a million bucks. That's worth killing for."

"Particularly when your husband is having an affair," Rollins said, "but she denied any knowledge of it, and he couldn't prove otherwise."

"She must have been a convincing actress," Novak said. He opened his own file folder, extracted a photocopy of the letter Lydia had unearthed in her attic, and explained its provenance.

"Christ!" Rollins said, as the implications of the find settled over him. Together, he and Novak pieced together the timeline. Jane Quinlan had written the letter toward the end of March. Two weeks later, her husband had taken a motel room for the night, bringing no luggage. A gunman had burst into the room, shot him once, and driven away.

"Emilia Alberti hired someone to kill him," Novak said. "Whoever it was lured her husband to that motel while she went out with her friends to play cards."

"It seems likely," Rollins replied, "but how do we prove it after all these years?"

"If that murder were to take place now, county police

would lead the investigation. Let's turn this back to Detective Barnwell and see what she can make of it."

Route 88 is a heavily traveled highway from Pittsburgh's southern suburbs into Washington County. The standoff forced South Hills police to reroute the heavy traffic onto country roads. Barnwell flashed her ID, and an officer let her through the roadblock. Just past the light rail tracks, another uniformed local officer halted her unmarked Dodge Charger at the outer perimeter and instructed her to walk the rest of the way. "We don't know what he's got in there."

She advanced on foot from to within sight of a two-story, wooden structure with a first-floor porch and second-floor balcony transversing the front. A flagpole jutting from just below the roof displayed a large Confederate flag which flapped in the breeze like a child sticking its tongue out.

Sergeant Hillman, who commanded the unit, stood behind the command vehicle alongside a slender man in his mid-forties sporting a long, red beard flecked with gray and a T-shirt bearing the legend "Live Free or Die."

"This is Caleb Rossiter," Hillman said. "He owns the house. Welch showed up Monday night, looking for a place to hide."

"Does he have arms inside?" Barnwell asked.

"He don't, but I do," Rossiter said. He ticked off an impressive inventory with which he concluded, "That's all I remember. There may be more." He said he knew Welch through a group called Mingo Creek Irregulars. Only later would her research show the name was linked to the Whiskey Rebellion that had occurred during George Washington's administration. Between this organization and the flag, Rossiter was continuing to wage two conflicts others thought had been settled.

He explained that Welch had shown up at his door for a place to stay. "You knew we were looking for him," she said.

"Not then. I do now. Anyways, he didn't do nothin'. I asked him, and he said so. That's enough for me. Don't know why you folks are after him. A man can't live his life without government interfering."

"We want to ask him a few questions about a man who died. We haven't charged him with anything."

He sniffled as though suffering from a cold and ran his arm across his nose. "Then why'd you put out an alert on him?"

Barnwell didn't answer. It was pointless to debate with a person whose mind, such as it was, was made up. "He threw you out of the house?" she said.

"Someone ratted on us, and the locals showed up. When he wouldn't come out, they told me to leave and called you folks in. I don't know why you're doing this. He ain't done nothin'."

"Have you tried talking to him?" she asked the sergeant.

"We're reduced to using the bullhorn, but he's not answering. He's turned off his cell phone, and the house has no land line."

"We're off the grid," Rossiter said. She wished they could get rid of the man.

"May I try?" she asked.

The SWAT commander eyed her up and down. "Let's give it a few minutes."

Barnwell could have insisted, but since he was in charge of this operation, she didn't argue. A voice boomed over the bullhorn. "Welch, come out with your hands up. We don't want to see anyone hurt."

There was no sound from within the house. The sergeant told Rossiter he could go. "Where to?" he said.

"Just stay out of the way," Hillman replied. He looked at Barnwell as the man wandered off and shook his head. "Damned militia types."

He invited her inside the command vehicle as another officer launched a drone. As she sat before the console, Lydia flashed back to two summers before, when Patrolman David Kimrey, her estranged boyfriend, had intervened in a domestic dispute. Contrary to all his training, he'd advanced on a home where a veteran of the Afghanistan conflict, suffering from PTSD, had barricaded himself in his house. Once officers had distracted the man long enough to remove his wife and children, Kimrey had approached, unarmed, extending his arms to show he meant no harm. The gunman took him down with one well-aimed shot.

Lydia had blamed herself for Kimrey's actions. The night before, he'd come by her apartment, begging to resume their relationship. She'd turned him away, refusing even his request for a parting hug. When he went down in the street hours later, she'd assume he was trying to prove himself to her.

Chief Novak tried to reassure her, explaining that Kimrey's deteriorating performance had forced him to place the officer on a work plan. "If he was trying to prove something to anyone, it was to us," he told her, referring both to himself and to Calvin Mayfield, then deputy chief.

It all came back to her, and despite the summer heat and clinging humidity, she shivered. "You all right?" Hillman said.

"Yes. I'm just thinking about the last stand-off I

witnessed. It didn't end well." She thought about what Kimrey might have done rather than placing himself in harm's way. "Is there anyone he's close to?" When an armed suspect barricades himself, SWAT teams often call in a friend or relative to reason with him.

"He's divorced. Both his ex-wife and daughter say they want nothing to do with him."

As Lydia watched the monitor, the drone detected a figure retreating from a window into the shadows. "I don't see him holding a weapon," she said. The technician rolled the video back and paused it. As she'd suggested, Welch was empty-handed.

An hour passed. Sergeant Hillman didn't seem to be in any rush. On this June day, the sun wouldn't set until after nine, so it was safest to wait him out as long as he could. If Welch didn't surrender, armed and shielded officers would burst into the house and end the standoff—one way or the other.

The bullhorn blared at fifteen-minute intervals, but it drew no response. Footage from the drone caught occasional glimpses of the man prowling inside. Rather than a fierce opponent, Welch seemed like a caged animal, avoiding windows and retreating into shadows whenever the airborne camera glimpsed him.

Another county vehicle arrived, and SWAT officers backed a small robot off the lift gate. They attached a throw phone to an arm and sent it off. "Paul, don't panic," Hillman said over the bullhorn. "I'm dropping a phone into the living room via a side window. I'd like you to pick it up and speak to me."

The robot made the delivery and backed away. Welch neither opened fire nor responded. Hillman made another plea, explaining how to use the device, which didn't need him to do anything but speak into it. Barnwell began to pity the man, convinced he hadn't committed the murder. "May I try?" she asked.

Perhaps feeling they had nothing to lose, Hillman relented. Holding the microphone to her mouth and speaking in a calm voice, she said, "Mr. Welch, my name is Lydia Barnwell. I'm a county detective. I'm the one who's been trying to reach you. Would you pick up the phone and speak with me? No one's going to harm you. We want to end this peacefully."

There was no answer. "I'm investigating the murder of Martin Sullivan. You met him a few days before he was killed. I'm trying to learn what he said to you? Please talk to me." No response.

"Paul, I know he was blackmailing others. Did he do the same to you? Is that why you tried to find him?" Again, no answer.

"This is getting us nowhere," Hillman said. "You're making things worse."

Lydia held the bullhorn down and looked off to one side as she weighed whether to play a card. "Paul, I don't believe you had anything to do with his murder. I've looked inside Sullivan's house. I know someone else was there."

A pause. Then a weak voice sounded over the phone. "I never got in."

"I know," she said, using the same muted tone as she moved from the bullhorn to the phone. "I need to learn why you tried to track him down. I have an idea, but I need you to confirm it."

When all she heard was heavy breathing, she used a voice of reason, as though speaking to a child. "You haven't threatened anyone, Paul. You haven't hurt a soul. Please come out so we don't have to come in after you. I don't want to see anyone hurt."

No answer. "Please," she said. "Help me end this."

The front door opened a crack. Two hands extended, a foot easing open the door, the man on the front steps blinking in the direct light of the afternoon sun.

Officers in bulletproof gear advanced on Welch, who knelt on the porch without being asked to. They dragged him to his feet and pulled his arms behind him, slapping plastic handcuffs around his wrists. He offered no resistance.

"How did you manage that?" Hillman said.

"I told him the truth."

"You're serious? You think he didn't commit the murder?"

"Not Marty Sullivan's, anyway. He couldn't have."

She didn't explain how she knew this, nor had she outlined her reasoning to Jeffrey.

CHAPTER ELEVEN

PAUL WELCH WAS BOOKED and spent his night in the county jail, charged with failing to follow instructions of law officers while they decided what additional charges to bring. Barnwell would interview him at ten in the morning. Between now and then, Novak had invited her to breakfast at his home in Boyleston.

As much as she respected Karol Novak, she loved his wife. Barbara had served as her sounding board during her last days living with David Kimrey. When the chief promoted her from patrol officer to detective, Kimrey resented being left behind. His performance suffered; at home, he became insufferable, wearing his resentment like a shroud. Barbara had listened as Lydia explained the problem, never advising her what to do. She'd asked probing questions that led her to take the step.

Now, as Barbara served a spinach frittata and home-made bread, Novak reviewed what he'd learned from the Ross Township sergeant the day before. "Emilia Alberti lied when she was questioned about her husband's relationship with Jane Quinlan," he told her, "and the person who phoned in a tip naming her was a woman disguising her voice. That doesn't prove Emilia hired someone to kill her husband, but it throws a new light on the case."

Lydia thought as much and said so. "I've taken this as far as I can as a civilian," he said. "It's a criminal matter now, so I'm throwing it back in your lap."

She thanked him for his help, though she didn't know what to do with these revelations at the moment.

"How's Calvin doing?" he asked.

She was surprised he hadn't asked him himself. "Fighting the same battles you were," she said. "Lentz continues to act as though Boyleston is absorbing the other two departments rather than partnering with them in a regional force. He'll be glad when the transition is complete."

"That won't change Lentz," Novak warned. "He'll continue to throw his weight around. Tell Calvin I wish him well, and if there's anything I can do to help..."

The conversation turned to their impending trip to France with their granddaughter. Barbara told how far she'd come in mastering the language. "She's only twelve, but speaks like a native." Her maiden name was Fournier and had been raised in a French-Canadian family. Her grandparents spoke only French. When she said Jen had mastered the accent, Lydia believed her.

She glanced at her watch. Jeffrey would arrive at headquarters in a quarter hour and expect her to help plan their interview with Welch. As much as she hated to do so, Lydia thanked them and left. They were the closest thing to family she had.

THE DETECTIVES HUDDLED for half an hour, then rode together to the county jail on 2nd Street in Pittsburgh, a modern office building flanked by two imposing brick structures containing the cells from which prisoners could glimpse the Monongahela River through small, barred windows.

They took over an interview room. A guard shuffled Welch in, his legs and arms both bound, and helped him lower himself into a chair after unshackling his wrists. As the video from Julio's had shown, his thin frame was dwarfed by a bulging belly that presented an unhealthy appearance. Without a cap obscuring his head, she could make out his features, heavy jowls with bushy black eyebrows, what appeared to be a broken nose, and sparse gray hair with remnants of what had once been reddish brown. He looked from one to the other and settled on Barnwell. "Why did you bring me here?"

"You barricaded yourself in a home in South Park and refused to come out. You tied up dozens of officers for six hours."

"I didn't hurt no one."

He might be charged with nothing more than the bare minimum with which they'd booked him, but she was not about to speculate. "We've been trying to speak to you about Marty Sullivan," she said. "You encountered him at a bar in Sharpsburg a few days before he was murdered. The two of you talked for over half an hour. Days later, you returned and asked the bartender how to find him. You remember that?"

He stared at her for a moment as though deciding what to say, then nodded his head. She asked him to confirm it aloud for the record, which he did. "Do you recall meeting with Sullivan?"

"Okay. Yeah."

"What was the subject of your conversation?"

Welch gave the slightest of shrugs. "I don't remember. I'd had a few beers."

"Come on, Paul. Whatever you discussed was enough to make you return to the bar to locate him. What was so important?"

"He seemed like a nice guy. I wanted to get to know him better."

"Hmph." Barnwell barked out a response to show her contempt. "Marty was extorting things from people, from money to favors. What hold did he have on you?"

Welch gave a derisive snort. "He didn't have nothing on me."

"Yes, he did," Jeffrey said. "That's why you returned to Julio's. You wanted to find him so you could shut him up."

"Not me. It wasn't me that killed him." He turned back to Barnwell. "You said so yourself, that you know I didn't do it."

"That's what I thought, but you're not playing straight with me, Paul. That makes me wonder if I had it wrong."

She turned her back to Jeffrey, while Welch kneaded his hands in agitation. "It wasn't me."

"Paul," Jeffrey said, "Another witness tells us you said you'd once killed a man."

"I never said that."

"You bragged about your supposed experience in Vietnam. We know you never served there, by the way. You claimed you'd once shot someone in the head. 'I got paid to do it.' That's what you told him."

Welch looked to either side of the room, trying to find a way out. "I never said no such thing."

"Would you like us to bring him in?" Jeffrey said.

"Bring who in?" He looked up at them, his eyes blinking like a turn signal. "I didn't tell him that."

Jeffrey glanced at Barnwell, who agreed to his unstated suggestion with a nod of her head. "We're taking a break," he said. "Meanwhile, consider your situation."

THEY WENT INTO AN ADJOINING ROOM, Jeffrey asking a guard to bring him a cup of coffee. "How do we stop his stonewalling?" she asked as they watched Welch fidgeting on the monitor.

Jeffrey had something else on his mind. "What's this about telling him you knew he didn't kill Sullivan?"

"I wanted to get him out of there without bloodshed."

"Okay," he said, "smart move." There was no law against cops lying to someone during an interrogation.

She considered whether to share the conclusion she'd reached. She wasn't always adept at reading people. When she'd first met Lyle Jeffrey, she'd thought he was hitting on her, only to learn he was trying to recruit her from the small borough to the county's police force. But give her a series of facts, and she could arrange them in patterns others couldn't see. This was one such case. She knew she was right.

"But he didn't," she said.

"What? How do you know that?"

"You were in Sullivan's house. Remember what you saw. Nothing on the first floor had been disturbed. Not a thing was out of place. On the second floor, his mother's bedroom hadn't been touched. Anyone entering stirred up a cloud of dust like in an old western. In Marty's room, there was no sign of a struggle."

Jeffrey grunted and nodded his head.

"How did the killer get in? By knocking? Did Sullivan open the door, then back up the stairs without a fight? No. Whoever it was came in on their own, crept up the stairs, and entered Marty's bedroom unimpeded. It had to be someone he knew, perhaps even trusted. Petarsky had a key, but his alibi seems solid. Coppola and Sedlak didn't have access. Neither did Welch."

Jeffrey drank his coffee while he pictured the scene he'd found when he first entered the victim's house. "Assuming you're right—"

"I am."

"Where does that leave us?"

Lydia took a pull on her water bottle. She closed her eyes, rerunning a scene through her mind. "Welch didn't enter the house, but he was there."

She told him what she remembered—and what she'd just reconstructed—and the two formulated a plan.

THEY'D TAKEN Welch's fingerprints when booking him the night before. The medical examiner's office found no match with the unidentified set found in the victim's bedroom. While this didn't prove Welch hadn't entered the house, it bolstered Barnwell's argument. They knew from the two security videos, however, he'd been in the neighborhood. Both wished they were at headquarters where they could review the recordings, but there was no time for that now.

"It took you long enough," Welch said when they returned and resumed the interrogation.

"Why does it matter?" Jeffrey shot back. "Would you be more comfortable in your cell?"

He wiped his hand over his face. "No, the other guy in there is dangerous."

"Paul," she said, "there's something we haven't told you. We have security camera video taken the night of the murder."

She let it sit there for a moment while she watched his reaction. He drew in a deep breath and the corners of his mouth turned down even further. "We have your car circling the block and passing in front of Sullivan's front door. We know you were there."

He managed a small smile of triumph. "Then you know I didn't go inside. That's what you said yesterday, that you know I couldn't have done it."

"We only have video from the front," Jeffrey said. "Once you found the right house, you could have gone in the back."

"Well, I didn't. I went there to talk to him, but I decided not to. I drove by and left."

"Which brings us back to why you had to see him," Lydia said. "At Julio's, the two of you started speaking at the bar. Marty moved you to a table in a far corner of the room. He bought you more beer, even picking up the tab, which was unlike him. He got you drunk enough to tell him something. Something so important it put you in jeopardy. Then he contacted you. What did he want?"

When he didn't answer, she said, "We have you on tape, Paul. You've dug yourself a hole. If you want us to dig you out, hand us a shovel. What was he after?"

Welch scanned the ceiling tiles as though looking for inspiration. "Money," he said. "Thousands of dollar. Money I didn't have, not that I would have given it to him."

"How did he approach you?"

"He called me. I don't know how he got my information, but he knew my name, address, and phone number. I'm surprised he didn't have my social security number."

Recalling the video at the bar of Sullivan drawing the man's wallet toward him as he staggered to the bathroom, Lydia suspected he might have.

"I was supposed to leave ten thousand dollars in cash in a bunch of shingles at a construction site, hidden in an envelope behind a label."

"But you didn't."

"No, I decided to talk to him, try to reason with him, you know?"

Jeffrey took a breath as though to ask the next question, but Barnwell cut in. "What did he have on you, Paul?"

The slightest of hesitations. "Something I did a long time ago."

"You killed someone."

"No. I never did that."

"You've told others you were a hit man. You even described killing a man. We know you did so."

She kept at him for several minutes, hinting at details she did not have. As she badgered him, Welch seemed to retreat into himself, his resistance washing away like the tide engulfing a sand castle. He cupped his hands and leaned his forehead on them. "Yeah," he said in a muffled voice. "It's been long enough, I guess."

The detectives looked at each other. The commonwealth has no statute of limitations on homicide, but they weren't obligated to tell him so. "Who was it?" she said.

"A guy. I don't know why she wanted him dead, but she did." Lydia's pulse quickened. Had she been expecting this?

"He had a nice car. She promised to sell it and give me the money after I'd taken care of him."

"Who was he?" she said, aware of the tremor in her voice.

"I don't recall his name. She told me he'd be in a room at this motel. She gave me his description and the make of his car. I parked in the lot and waited for him."

"In Ross Township?" she said.

"Yeah. How did you know?"

She ignored the question. Let him think she'd known all along. "When did this happen, Paul?"

"I dunno. '62 maybe? No, it was after Christmas that year. It had to be winter of '63."

Over the next fifteen minutes, they pieced the story together. At first, they had to drag it out of him, but as he warmed to the task, he reveled in recounting it, just as he'd done to at least two other people. Only when he'd finished did Lydia turn toward her partner, allowing him to finish what they'd come for. "Paul, you insist you didn't go into Sullivan's house the night he was murdered."

"I didn't."

"Why not?"

In a tone that suggested they should already know this, he said, "'Cause someone went in ahead of me."

***

"I don't believe in coincidences." That's what she'd told Jeffrey three days before when referring to Sullivan's break-in at the mortuary the day before his death. Jeffrey had agreed with her. Still, here they were, having solved a six decades old murder based on a letter she'd found in a handbag. What if she'd never cleaned the attic? What if Anna hadn't found the concealed compartment?

Yet, as she thought about it, she realized the two events weren't directly connected. They'd questioned Paul Welch in connection with another slaying, one she was now convinced he hadn't committed. She and Jeffrey had been determined to know why he'd tried to find Sullivan two days before he died. Only by hammering him and allowing him to think the statute of limitations had expired did Welch admit to what he'd done.

What would they have done with this knowledge? Gone back through unsolved cases, armed with Welch's description of the murder and the approximate date when he carried it out. It wouldn't have taken them long to tie him to Frank Alberti's slaying and, through his testimony, Emilia's role in it.

It would have come out, she told herself, even without her discovering the incriminating letter.

While admitting to that murder, Welch denied involvement in Marty Sullivan's death. But he'd been on the scene. He admitted driving past but said he hadn't gone in because he saw someone else enter the house.

Sitting with a half-eaten tuna salad sandwich before her, she logged into the computer system, opened the folder containing evidence from the Sullivan murder, and clicked on the first of the two videos from security cameras in the neighborhood. She watched as the gray sedan cruised up Francone Street, the driver's face concealed in the shadows.

It was the second sequence that she recalled, taken from a house a few doors down from Sullivan's. A lone figure passed before the camera dressed in jeans or slacks, a loose fitting long sleeve shirt, and a baseball cap. Eight seconds later, the gray Kia crawled past. She paused the video. She couldn't see the man's face, for his head was turned toward the homes across the street, as though looking for addresses.

She resumed the video. The car moved on, and a teenaged trio walked past. Then a figure emerged from a home opposite the camera. He held a cell phone and spoke into it in what appeared to be agitation. This was the man who'd called 9-1-1 to report shots being fired.

Lydia scrubbed the image back ninety seconds and reviewed the sequence. She called Jeffrey in and allowed him to watch as she bit into the sandwich.

"You see what I do?" she said, her mouth full.

"Yeah."

"Those kids," she said. "We need to find them."

Jeffrey commandeered two uniformed men and began a door-to-door search of the neighborhood to locate the three teenagers. Lydia returned to the home of the next-door neighbor, Margaret O'Dowd. Unlike the first time she'd interviewed her, the woman answered the door immediately and welcomed her like an old friend.

"Have you found who killed him yet?" she asked. "We're still on pins and needles here. What if he returns and breaks into one of our homes?"

"We're making progress," she said, glad to be able to tell her the truth.

Maggie offered her iced tea, but remembering her last encounter with the sugar bomb, Lydia raised her water bottle in silent denial. "What I need is your help."

She moved the woman into her dining room and opened her tablet computer. "Please watch this video and identify anyone you see."

"Let me get my glasses."

Barnwell waited while she puttered around in the kitchen. "I can never find them, and I can't see them when I'm not wearing them."

"Do you want me to search?"

"No," she said. "Oh, here they are." She returned to the table. "Now then..."

She made no comment as the gray vehicle moved past. Maybe automobiles weren't her thing. Then again, in the feeble light, one passenger car looked much like another. "Do you recognize that person?" Lydia asked as the solitary figure walked by.

"Can you show me again?" Lydia scrubbed the video back with her finger. "How did you do that?" Maggie asked.

Lydia explained the process, exhibiting a patience she did not feel. "Recognize anyone?"

"No," she said. "I'm sorry. It's not a very clear picture, is it?"

Hiding her disappointment, Lydia let the video run. "These three boys," she said. "Do you know them?"

"Not by name," she said, "but I see them all the time. They shouldn't be out after dark, should they?"

"No," she said. "You're sure it's them? You couldn't identify the other person."

"It's the way the taller boy puts his arm around the other. He does that sometimes. I think these two might be brothers."

"Do they live in the neighborhood?"

"They must, because they—the brothers, at least— bounce a ball as they go by the house. It's annoying when I have the windows open."

Lydia closed the cover on the tablet, disappointed she'd learned so little. She closed her eyes for a moment, recalling their talk eight days before. The woman had launched into a long conversation about Grace Sullivan and the nocturnal visits of the veterinarian. Before she could continue to question her, however, the ACPD detective had arrived to help her search Martin Sullivan's house.

"You told me about Grace's visitors," she said, "but I didn't have time to ask you much about Marty. Did many people come to see him?"

Maggie considered the question, her white hair billowing like a cumulus cloud in the cross-breeze moving through the open windows. "No," she said. "He had no friends over. Not that Grace's health made it an inviting place."

"How about after she passed away?"

She thought again. "No. He just came and went." Lydia held her pen over her notebook, trying to think of what to ask next. "Apart from this girl, of course."

"What girl, Maggie?"

"I don't recall her name. Dorothy?"

"Dora? Dora Macklin?"

"That's it. I don't know her to speak to. She lives nearby, I think, but I don't know where. I don't get out like I used to."

Lydia asked how often the woman had seen her with Marty. "She started coming over after Grace's memorial service. Only in the early evening. I don't think ever she spent the night." She shook her head, perishing the thought.

"You hadn't seen her there before? She didn't visit the house until Grace was gone. That's your recollection?"

"Yes. And not right away. It was a few weeks after. I'd seen them together before that, walking through the neighborhood."

"When did you last see her?"

Again, she considered her answer before she spoke. "Memorial Day weekend. I remember because they cooked out on the back porch. Whatever he was making smelled delicious."

Lydia smiled, thanked her, and left. Maggie hadn't been able to identify the figure in the video, but she had given her quite enough.

JERRY MULLINS WORKED at a big box hardware store where he stocked shelves and loaded heavy appliances onto trucks. Barnwell showed her ID to the store manager, who asked if he was in some sort of trouble and, once reassured, directed her to the loading dock. It was late afternoon, and Mullins was unloading the truck with worn-out appliances they'd removed from homes and apartments. He was as sweaty now as when he'd appeared at headquarters a week before.

She asked him to take a break and reread the notes she'd taken as he sought permission from his supervisor. He led her into the break room, offered her a soda, and grabbed one for himself when she declined. He upended the bottle and drank it down in two loud swallows. "Sorry about that," he said. "It's fu—It's hot out there."

"Frigging hot," she said.

"Yeah. That, too."

They shared a chuckle. "When you came into head-quarters last week to tell me about Marty's strange behavior at the funeral parlor—"

"Was I right about that?" he interrupted.

"You were. It was vital information. I told your boss just now you're helping us with this investigation."

"I am?" he said, crinkling his face in surprise. "Okay."

"During our conversation," she continued, reading from her notes, "you said, 'He has this girlfriend, Dora.' You also told me you hadn't seen her in a while."

"Right."

"'She's his one friend, or was.' Why did you correct yourself?"

"Did I?"

"From 'is' to 'was.'"

"Because he's dead."

"And that's all you meant by that?" He shrugged, and she said, "You think they were still together?"

"As far as I know. We all knew each other. I would have heard if they'd broken up."

FINDING three teenage boys with the freedom to be abroad well after midnight should have posted no problem, Jeffrey thought. Given the late hour, they probably lived in the neighborhood. All he and the two uniformed officers had to do was go house-to-house, carrying the grainy photograph taken from the video. Someone would know them.

Had it been a weekday, it might have been that simple, but on this, the first Saturday of summer, few people were home. Whether they were spending the day at a local park or had fled to Lake Erie, a majority of houses stood empty. Only older folks had stayed put, sweltering in the heat that had nudged into the nineties.

The officers moved up one street and down another, sweating in their uniforms, but no one recognized the trio. An hour into their search, Barnwell radioed the information

Maggie O'Dowd had supplied. "She thinks two of those boys are brothers."

"Their school," Jeffrey said as he wiped the perspiration from his face.

One of the two officers, familiar with the area, "That means either Shaler Area High or North Catholic."

Jeffrey looked up the public high school on his tablet and found emails listed for the principal and vice principal. He wrote both, hoping one of them was in town and within reach. The vice principal was the first to respond, providing her cell phone number.

"Brothers out after hours?" she repeated when he'd explained himself. "Seven or eight come to mind. Do you have a photo?"

He sent it while keeping her on the phone. "It's hard to tell. They look a bit like the Delaney boys. If so, the one with them is probably Jimmy Derraugh. The brothers are good kids, but Jimmy's a bit of a troublemaker. I trust you not to repeat that."

He promised and took down the addresses of both families. They lived two doors from each other, three blocks from the Sullivan house. He approached the Delaney residence first and, as they had on their first pass through the street, found no one home. They skipped the next house and knocked at the home of Jimmy Derraugh. There was no answer. Jeffrey was about to give up when a man's voice from above said, "Who is it?"

"Police," he responded, though that should have been obvious from the two officers fighting for the shade beneath a scrawny maple tree in the front yard.

Following a substantial pause, the voice called, "What do you want?"

"If you could come down," Jeffrey said, unwilling to call

out the name of a juvenile for anyone else on the street to hear, "I'd rather speak to you in private."

Another pause, then a resigned, "All right." Through the screen door, he heard heavy footsteps, then a man appeared behind the mesh, a pair of shorts rimming his overflowing belly that didn't quite cover a sleeveless t-shirt. "I was trying to take a nap."

"Sorry to disturb you," he said. "I'm looking for Jimmy Derraugh. Is he home?"

"What's he done now?" the man said.

"Nothing that I know of. He was out with a couple of friends a few nights ago."

"That would have been the Delaney boys. Always looking for trouble, that pair."

"Well, I don't think they were doing anything wrong that night. Not that we know of, anyway. I need to find out if they recognized anyone while they were out."

The man nodded, as though satisfied. "Do you know where they are now?" the detective asked.

"At the pool over in Etna, I should think. What time is it? They should be along pretty quick."

The officers made the trip to Etna's community pool in eight minutes. Jeffrey pulled his cruiser to the entrance, a position from which anyone entering or exiting would have to pass. Leaving one officer in charge, he asked the attendant if she'd seen either of the boys. She explained she was a college student who didn't know any locals.

He walked into the pool area, an incongruous figure in slacks, a long sleeve shirt, and oxfords amid children and adults wearing as little as they could get away with. He questioned the lifeguard, who gave him the same answer as the young woman at the entrance.

Then he stopped an attractive girl who looked to be

about the same age as the three boys. "Yeah, I know 'em," she said. "See that kid who just came out of the tube? That's Danny."

He thanked her and intercepted the boy as he was pulling himself out of the water, ready to remount one of the blue slides. "Danny Delaney?" he asked.

The kid frowned and took a step back, throwing him off balance. "Yeah?" he said, as Jeffrey reached out to steady him.

"Where's your brother and Jimmy? I need to ask you a few questions. Nothing you've done wrong," he added, seeing the boy's panicked expression. "It's about something you may have seen."

The boy called out for his brother, whose name was Mike, and their friend. The three converged on Jeffrey, Jimmy looking about him nervously. "Is there somewhere we can sit and talk?" the detective said. "I want to show you a video."

That piqued their interest. "At one of the picnic tables," Danny said, "if you can get us back in afterwards."

"I'll use the full force of the law," he answered with a smile. "C'mon. This'll just take a minute."

The three followed him, curious now. Jeffrey grabbed the tablet from his cruiser, found a shaded spot at the end of a table, and ran the video clip. "This was taken a week ago yesterday. You were out walking late at night, right?"

Two of nodded their heads. "Did you take any notice of this gray car as it passed?" None had. "Do you recognize this person?"

"Sure," Danny said. "Everyone knows her."

Lydia wasn't certain she'd find Al Kuczienski at home on a Saturday afternoon. She took him for a baseball fan and wondered if he'd gone to a Pirates game. Were they playing in town? No sooner was that thought out of her head that she considered a more sarcastic question: Were they even playing?

She pulled up to find not only Kuczienski on his front porch, but his wife beside him and the baby on his lap. After introducing herself to Shari and declining his offer of a beer, she apologized for returning and told him she had one more question. She recalled someone comparing Jeffrey to Columbo. She couldn't recall who, but there was always just one more thing.

"Do we need to do this privately?" he asked.

She was momentarily confused, then realized he might not have told his wife about Marty discovering Coppola's shingles sham or his undercutting the boss on roofing projects. "No, this is fine." She looked down at her notepad. "This concerns his girlfriend."

"Dora?" Shari asked. "Has something happened to her?"

"Not that I know of." She turned back to Al. "You were the one who first told me about her. You called her 'a girl he's going with.' Do you remember saying that?"

"Yeah, and you said they'd broken up. First I'd heard of it."

"They did?" Shari said.

"You know her?"

"We both do. I've known Dora since grade school. Who says they'd broken up?"

"I guess I have it wrong. They were still together when he was murdered?"

"Yeah." Her voice went up half an octave, and she

tossed her head as she said this, giving Lydia a look that was almost defiant.

"You're sure about this?"

"I don't know who's been telling you stories…"

Al stopped bouncing his son and touched his wife's arm with a free hand. "She's just trying to get things straight."

"I don't like the idea someone's spreading shit about her and Marty. She loved him. They were a pair. It's not right someone should talk trash on her, not after what she's going through."

"Losing him," Lydia said.

"That and … You know."

"I don't," Lydia said.

She proceeded to tell her.

THE THREE BOYS told Jeffrey a neighbor had brought them to the pool, but had since departed. They asked if they could hitch a ride with him. It was against regulations. The county wasn't running a taxi service, but he agreed. Along the way, Danny, who sat up front, quizzed him about all the electronic gear above and below the dash. "Come down to Greentree sometime," he said. "I'll show you around headquarters."

"You'd do that?" said a voice from the back.

"Of course. All three of you. Let's set a date, and I'll pick you up."

If just one of the three became interested enough to become a cop, he'd count the day an even greater success. Better yet, if they just went straight.

He would have loved to know what kind of parenting— or grand-parenting, in Jimmy's case—allowed the trio to be out on the street in the early hours of a Friday morning, but that would await another time. If it came at all.

He dropped them off, shook hands with each of them, and called Barnwell on his radio. Without going into details, he told her he'd found the three boys who'd walked past the murder house moments before shots were fired. "And they identified her. It's—"

"Dora Macklin," she interrupted. "And I think I've uncovered the motive."

CHAPTER TWELVE

CALVIN AWOKE BEFORE SHE DID, banging around in the basement as he pulled fishing gear together. She followed the racket and found Tommy Molnar sitting in the kitchen, an oversized police academy cap so low on his forehead it almost blocked his eyes. Howie sat at his feet alongside Ginger, Tommy's dog. "They're going with you?" she said.

"Sure, Miss Barnwell." She had suggested he call her Lydia, but the word stuck in his throat. Anna had trained him well. "Chief lets them sit beside each other in the bow. They love when the wind blows through their hair."

"Grab me a picture, will you?" she said as Calvin emerged from the basement.

He leaned over and planted a kiss on her lips. Nothing passionate. His failure to return her endearment two days before still hung over her, and she didn't acknowledge his gesture now. "Big day ahead for you."

"Majorly." Lydia watched the two of them leave, the white boy looking up at the Black man. A sob caught in her throat. For reasons she couldn't explain, the pair of them together, with the dogs trailing them, made her both euphoric and wistful. She wished she had a family like this. For that matter, she wished she'd had a family.

The moment passed. She and Jeffrey had strategized until late in the evening, he wolfing down a pepperoni pizza while Lydia contented herself with a Caesar salad. What they had was circumstantial evidence. The teenagers had identified Dora Macklin as the person they'd passed, but they hadn't seen her go into the house. Paul Welch had seen a woman enter the house, but she was facing away from him. He couldn't identify her.

Dora had lied to Jeffrey about her relationship with Marty Sullivan. They had not broken off months before, as she'd claimed, but been together as recently as a week before his murder. That had been their breaking point, and Shari Kuczienski had revealed what caused the split, providing Barnwell with a motive.

They called in Lieutenant Glen Carpenter, who had just been appointed chief of detectives, and gave him all they knew. He found their case convincing, but told them what they already knew: it would not yet stand up in court. They needed something more solid. He suggested a two-pronged strategy, one to which the assistant DA agreed when they reached her on her cell phone, pulling her away from a Downtown dinner date with her wife.

At eight the following morning, Carpenter served Macklin with a search warrant for her apartment and an order requiring her to report to headquarters for questioning. Barnwell and Jeffrey were waiting when the squad car delivered her. She was dressed in jeans—the same pair she'd worn the night of the murder?—and a blue cotton, off-the-shoulder pullover.

Macklin made no attempt to hide her anxiety. She

fidgeted as she took the chair across from the two detectives and chewed at a fingernail. Dora had deep circles under her eyes, and her complexion was wan. She'd run a brush through her dark hair, but it still looked like a ball of tangled yarn.

Jeffrey opened with the required warning: "Dora Jean Macklin, I'm charging you with making false statements to police and impeding an investigation. We may press other charges as our investigation continues. You have the right to remain silent. Anything you say can and will be used against you in a court of law. You have the right to speak to an attorney and to have an attorney present during any questioning."

"What false statements," she said. "Why am I here? I should be at Mass."

Lydia, who was not a churchgoer, replied, "We all should."

Jeffrey said nothing, grateful she had not asked for a lawyer. He allowed the silence to flow between them like spilled molasses as she raised her fingernails to her teeth again. Finally, he broke the silence. "I think you know why you're here."

"No, I don't." Her voice quavered, and her eyes darted between the pair.

"When I questioned you after Marty's murder, you told me you'd broken up months before and hadn't seen each other since." When she returned his statement with a blank stare, he said, "Do you remember that?"

"I don't recall the date. It could have been later."

"How much later?"

"I don't know."

"Weeks? Days?"

"It was before that. I don't remember exactly when."

"How about the night he died?" Jeffrey persisted.

"No," she said, biting down on the word like a strip of jerky.

He leaned back, eyeing her without speaking. Lydia took her cue. "A witness saw you entering Marty's house at about 12:20 Friday morning, minutes before he was shot."

"No," she said. "No, I never went there."

Lydia reached into her file folder and slid a still shot taken from the video across the table. "We even have you on a security camera one minute before you entered the house." She watched as Dora's eyes blinked, telegraphing her distress.

"Turning a key in the lock to gain entry," the detective continued. "We matched the key on your ring just now."

"I—He never asked for it back, but that doesn't mean I was there that night. It must have been someone else."

"Three other witnesses passed you on Ballard Street just before you entered. This is not good, Dora."

More blinking. Her eyes turning away. A deep breath. "Why are you in my place?" Her tone defiant as she went on offense. "You're going through my private things. I have rights. This is America."

"How are you feeling, by the way?" Barnwell asked. "Have you recovered?"

The belligerence went out of her like an accordion, squeezing out its last note. "What do you mean?"

"It takes a lot out of a woman, not just physically, but emotionally. You must be exhausted. Do you need to take a break?"

Dora returned her stare for a moment, then looked down, tears rimming her eyes.

"Do you want to tell us what happened?" Lydia asked.

"Nothing," she said, her voice choking. "I was sleeping. I'd just returned from the doctor, and…"

"That was last week," Lydia said. "You had the abortion after Marty's death, not before. What happened the night he died?"

She raised her arm to wipe her face. Lydia shoved a box of tissues before her. She grabbed a handful but clutched them in her hand. "I can't afford an attorney. I've spent every dollar I had—"

"Are you asking for one?"

"Yes. I don't like the questions you're asking."

Lydia tried to conceal her frustration over having to halt the parade before Santa arrived. "You can apply for a public defender at your arraignment."

Her face contorted in confusion. "You can't keep me. I need to go home."

"You're under arrest, Dora. We're transferring you to the county jail where you'll spend the night."

She buried her head in her folded arms as she blubbered.

***

BARNWELL AND JEFFREY sat across a conference table in the DA's office, documents spread before them. Melissa Dawkins, a pair of half-frame reading glasses balanced on the tip of her nose, faced them, glancing at her watch. Dora Macklin was to be arraigned on a minor charge in a court-room one floor above ninety minutes from now. The detectives had come in advance, both to prepare the attorney for the hearing and to divulge what more they'd learned from the search of her apartment. "We found Dora's fingerprints in Marty's room," Barnwell said, "plus her DNA on his nightstand."

"But if she was seeing him up the time of his death, that's not conclusive," Dawkins said.

"Agreed," she said, "but there's more." Lydia had listed all the evidence they'd gathered and worked through it to show Dawkins they'd overlooked nothing. "We turned up two items that seal the deal. The first is Dora's cell phone, in which her calendar shows a meeting with the victim three days before his murder. 'Tell Marty the news,' it reads.

"She placed five calls to him over the next two days, none of which he answered. Meanwhile, she searched for family planning clinics and called two of them. She sent Marty a text the day before his death asking him for $650 to cover the cost of terminating her pregnancy. He never responded."

"And you haven't found his phone?"

"We did," she said. "It was lying in an old backpack in the back of her closet, hidden behind a clothes hamper."

"I wish you'd led with that," the attorney said.

Jeffrey broke in. "She's saving the best for last."

"Give," Dawkins said.

"We also found a handgun, a Beretta 71. The magazine holds eight .22 long rifle caliber bullets. Only five remained. The crime lab tested it last night."

"And?" Dawkins prompted, checking her watch.

"They matched all three to the bullet recovered from the wall behind the victim's bed. The grip had been wiped clean, but Dora's were prints on the trigger."

The prosecutor allowed herself a rare smile and rose to dismiss them. "That gives me only an hour to up the charge before her arraignment."

"What we'd prefer," Jeffrey said, "is to keep the minor

charges for the moment. Once the judge assigns a public defender, we can resume the interrogation."

"Counsel's first act will be to ask for her release on bail," she said.

"She can't make it," Jeffrey replied. "She's broke and has no assets to pledge as collateral. Dora's not a flight risk; she has nowhere to go."

Dawkins argued with them for another minute, but Jeffrey won the day. He wanted to question Dora Macklin without her knowing what they had on her. If they could break her, they'd strengthen the case, perhaps even tie it in a bow.

Dora shuffled into the jail's interview room, looking even more disheveled than when they'd first spoken to her. She wore no makeup, and while Lydia didn't think she had the day before, her face was more ashen. If she had combed her hair with her hand, it had done little good, and her eyes seemed to have retreated into her skull. Being caged with a handful of recidivists—women who'd been through the system before and were adept at terrorizing neophytes—was not conducive to a sound night's sleep.

Barnwell felt a twinge of sympathy for her. She knew what had led her to commit the crime. But murder was, after all, murder.

Jeffrey led the charge. "When we broke off yesterday, we were correcting your version of events. You told us you were asleep when Marty was murdered because you'd returned from your medical procedure. But you went to the clinic after he died, not before."

She averted her eyes, staring at the tabletop, giving no

sign of emotion. "You entered Sullivan's house at around
12:20. We have you on video near his house. Three
witnesses saw you on the street. Another saw you enter the
house moments before a neighbor heard three shots fired."

He paused for a moment to let this sink in. "We've
placed you there, Dora. What happened between the two of
you?" No response. "Did you argue?" Nothing.

"Since you won't tell us, let us tell you. When you
learned you were pregnant, you met with Marty and told
him the news. He didn't react as you'd thought he would.
He wanted nothing to do with a baby. You left hurt, angry.
You'd thought you were a couple, that he would marry you,
and you'd live happily ever after. Marty, you, and your
child. A happy family living in a house you owned."

Through all this, she gave no sign she was listening,
hugging herself—perhaps she had no nails left to chew—and
rocking back and forth without making eye contact with the
detectives or her court-appointed attorney.

"You thought this over for a few days, trying to reach
him by phone to change his mind. But he wouldn't take
your calls. You didn't have the resources to raise a child on
your own. You'd seen too many unwed mothers struggling
to make it. So you got an abortion."

"I'm sure it was nothing you wanted to do," Barnwell
said, not having to feign an understanding tone. "This
wasn't your choice. But once you'd made it, you faced
another problem. How were you to pay for it? You have
no savings. You live hand-to-mouth, relying on tips.
Missing work for a few days would deepen your financial
situation. So you did the sensible thing. You asked for his
help."

For the first time, Dora looked up at her. If she'd had
tears left, Lydia thought, she would have shed them. But all

she had was a baleful look, her red-rimmed eyes beseeching the detective to understand.

"And he wouldn't give it," Lydia said, her voice dripping with contempt. "It was your problem, as far as he was concerned, not his. He had all this money coming in, and you knew it. You're not blind. But he cast you adrift, you and the life he had created but now rejected." She scoffed and shook her head.

"We were planning to marry," she said.

The attorney placed a hand on her arm. "Remember what I said," she told her. "You don't have to say a thing. Just remain silent."

Barnwell was familiar with the game. The lawyer hadn't objected to their questions because she wanted to know how much they'd discovered. She'd told Dora not to respond. It was time to spring the trap.

"We have everything," she said. "Your phone tells us every time you called. We've read your text messages, growing more distraught as you plead with him. We also found his phone in your closet, the one you took after you killed him."

Dora broke eye contact as she spoke, looking down at the table again. It held nothing to read, no solution to her dilemma. Lydia threw out her trump card. "We have the weapon, Dora. It has your fingerprint on the trigger. We've matched the slugs to one we recovered from Marty's room."

In the ensuring silence, Jeffrey said, "We're charging you with murder."

She covered her face with her hand, swaying from side to side in her chair to the point Lydia feared she'd fall over. "I didn't mean to," she said.

The public defender interrupted. "My client has nothing more to say. She's not telling you any more."

But Dora overrode her, raising her voice in a plea for understanding. "I'd called and texted him. I tried to visit him on the job, but I couldn't find where he worked that day. He'd promised to marry me. 'Just give me some time,' he said. To get over his mother, he meant. Now he refused. I could have lived with that if it weren't for being pregnant. I needed him to help me."

"So you took the gun to threaten him," Lydia said.

"Yeah," she said, her face brightening. "That's all I meant to do. I didn't want to hurt him. Just to make him do the right thing. You understand."

"You let yourself in with your key. You didn't knock or ring the bell."

"He wouldn't have let me in. I needed to surprise him. He was in his room, but hadn't undressed. He told me he'd been watching a Pirates game that'd gone extra innings." She sniffed, drawing mucus into her throat, swallowed it down, and coughed.

"He must have heard the door open," Lydia said. "Was he hiding from you?"

Dora gulped and nodded. "I think he heard me and ran up the stairs, because the hall light went out as I opened the door." She trembled as a chill came over her. The detective waited, knowing she'd continue her story to justify what she'd done.

"I asked him nicely. 'You know I can't afford this,' I said. 'Please help me. I won't ask anything more of you.' His lips curled up in a sneer. He laughed at me, something he'd never done before. It was hateful, more like a snarl. It wasn't like him. He was usually so..."

"Thoughtful?" Lydia offered, as she hunted for the way to put it.

"Kind," she corrected. "That's when I pulled the gun

out of my waistband, just to frighten him, you understand? He laughed again and said I didn't have the guts to use it. He reached out to grab it, but it went off."

Once more, Barnwell noted how a witness could shift from active to passive voice. Things just happened.

"He looked shocked. He fell back and groaned, asked me what he thought I was doing, and dabbed at his head. Then he started screaming at me. He called me a bitch and threatened to call the police. That's when the gun went off again."

"Dora, you made him turn around and kneel against the bed."

"Did I?" She twisted her mouth in puzzlement. "Maybe I was trying to show him I was serious. I never meant to hurt him."

In the silence that followed, her face took on a mournful expression. Her plaintive voice was directed only to Lydia. "Men shouldn't be allowed to do whatever they want and walk away. You know that."

Barnwell did, but that didn't justify murder. She left it to Jeffrey to announce the charge and end the interview.

"WHAT A GREAT IDEA," she said. Calvin had left her a text telling her to meet him at a restaurant in the city. Many local had stopped going "dawn-tawn," as they referred to it. Too much crime, they said. You can get shot down there. In truth, the area was no less violent than other parts of the city, but facts didn't matter. Since the last department store had closed, there was no reason for most people to come into the commercial district unless they were attending a concert or a play. And some wouldn't do even that, making the same tired argument that it was just too dangerous.

He'd chosen a steakhouse, but assured her they had lighter dishes on the menu. It offered curbside valet service, but there was no way a civilian was going to get behind the wheel of a police vehicle, marked or unmarked, so she parked at the courthouse and walked the six blocks.

The manager greeted her at the door liker she knew her. "Ms. Barnwell," she said. "Mr. Mayfield already has your table. Please follow me."

As she walked past the bar area and into the spacious dining room, others looked up from their tables as though they knew why she was there. It was an odd sensation, like being a model on the runway. She smiled as she passed them, couples and families, white, Black, and mixed, and took the seat the manager held out for her while Calvin rose and smiled, kissing her on the cheek.

The manager handed them menus. It took a moment for Lydia to notice the heading. "Welcome, Allegheny County's Finest."

"You do this for everyone?" Lydia said.

The manager smiled, her blonde hair shining through the backlighting from an overhead lamp. "Only our VIPs," she said. "Enjoy your evening."

"Wow!" Lydia said. "How much is this costing you?"

Calvin's face lit up. "We're celebrating a special occasion."

"Because I've solved my case." When he didn't answer, she said. "What else?"

He hid behind the menu. "It's all done."

"What?"

"The three councils have agreed to the merger. The

South Hills Regional Police Force opens for business on September 1st."

"Have they selected a chief?"

"You're looking at him."

"All I see is the back of your menu."

The sommelier introduced himself, and Calvin asked for a bottle of pinot noir. "I'm told it goes with both steak and seafood," he said.

"Not all, but…" He suggested several options, to which Calvin responded with questions. He withdrew, then returned with two samples. Their back-and-forth was beyond Lydia, but Calvin settled on a light-bodied wine from an Oregon vineyard, Christom. "The winemaker named it after both his sons," the sommelier said.

She didn't care. She decided she'd double her intake and have two glasses. He brought the wine to the table along with a plate of bacon wrapped sea scallops. "Something for both of us," said her carnivorous companion. She tried them and decided to violate her normal aversion to red meat.

True to form, Calvin ordered the New York strip steak, while she went for the twin lobster tails. "I hope you'll try some of this," she said. "I'll never finish."

But she did. They ate in silence, neither talking about the events of the day, for it wasn't table talk. She smiled at him between bites. Although she remained annoyed with his inability to commit, he was thoughtful to celebrate both their successes. As she thought about Dora Macklin languishing in a nearby cell, however, the enjoyment drained out of her. The woman had made a terrible mistake. Unforgivable. Yet she'd been driven to it by a man she loved and who she thought loved her. Lydia's breath caught in her throat as she looked across at the man she loved, shoveling food into his face. Was she in the same position?

She shook it off and returned to the question that had led her to seek out Dora days before: what had made Marty undergo such a radical change? In the end, he'd loved only his mother. A mama's boy. A twisted soul. Had Dora thought he would transfer his devotion to her after Grace died? How wrong she had been. She'd trusted him, and he had betrayed her. Now both had paid the price.

"What?" she said. Calvin had spoken to her, and she'd missed it.

"Tommy suggested something to me while we were fishing yesterday morning."

"Are you taking him camping?"

"No. Well, maybe. That's an idea. But he said something I've been thinking about for a while. He put it into focus."

"And?"

"He said, 'When are you going to marry her?'"

Lydia laughed. "That kid!"

He folded his hands as though in prayer. "He said, 'I can tell you love her. Why don't you ask her?'" His deep brown eyes bored into hers. "So will you?"

"You're asking me to marry you?"

"I just did. It's a serious commitment. I mean..." He paused, fumbling for the right words. "Marriage is forever, and you can have your pick."

"Stop it," she said. "Yes."

"You will?"

"I just said so, didn't I?"

He reached in his pocket, withdrew a small box, and knelt at her feet. Everyone in the restaurant seemed to turn their way. "Oh, stop," she said, stifling a giggle. The manager held up a camera. Lights flashed.

After solving two murders in as many weeks, Lydia felt the department owed her something. A vacation for changing the color on the Baltimore Board from red to green. A week in Antigua would do. If not that, a weekend in the Carolina mountains. Either could serve as their honeymoon. Failing this, how about a night at the Youngstown Holiday Inn Express?

Tax supported trips were not the provenance of police officers, however. County officials attending conferences? That was a different matter. They could fly to Vegas, take in shows, gorge themselves on crab legs, and run up liquor bills on taxpayers' dimes, at least until an enterprising reporter discovered their overindulgence. Not that there were many of them around anymore.

Instead, she was rewarded with a week on the night shift, standing by in case something happened. Which it would.

As if in response, the radio crackled with news of a police chase. Someone had pulled a woman out of her car in Shadyside and made away with it. Pittsburgh police were in pursuit of a late model white Mercedes. She listened as they pursued the vehicle up Fifth Avenue, past the hospitals in Oakland and onto I-376. The driver peeled off onto Boulevard of the Allies, and looped north on 579 with an increasing number of patrol cars in pursuit.

Months later, she couldn't explain why she'd headed across the Fort Pitt Bridge, listening as the chase unfolded. This was a Pittsburgh police matter. ACPD had no role in it. Something, perhaps a premonition, impelled her toward the scene. As she listened, the car veered off the interstate onto Route 28, then south on 31st street, recrossing the river through the Strip District.

The carjacker was leading them in a circle, weaving in and out of nighttime traffic. If this didn't stop, she thought, someone would die.

He careened up Polish Hill and into the Hill District. *He's heading home.* Again, she'd be unable to explain how she knew this. She just did.

As the car raced down Wylie Avenue, officers laid a spike strip east of Kirkpatrick. The driver blew through them, popping all his tires, and turned south. At Reed Street, just above Kennard Playground, he encountered a roadblock. He reversed up the hill, nearly hitting a patrol officer approaching from behind. As Lydia arrived on the scene, she heard a hail of gunfire. The car jumped the intersection with Rose Street and backed into a brick wall, dislodging part of it.

Lydia emerged from her cruiser and trotted up Kirkpatrick toward the wrecked vehicle, which was now surrounded by police with guns drawn. They ordered the driver out of the car, but heard no response. A police officer approached from behind, shielding his upper body on a pile of collapsed brickwork as he shined his light into the side window. The driver's head rested on the steering wheel, blood splattering onto the collapsed air bag like a cry for help.

As the officer jerked open the door, the body of a teenaged boy slid to the left. His seatbelt kept him from falling out. An absurd thought came to her: at least he'd remember to buckle up. As she viewed the scene from a distance of thirty feet, she recognized his face. She stepped forward and confirmed her impression. Theo Mosely, whose attorney had beaten his carjacking charge three weeks before, had stolen one too many cars.

Behind her, she heard a wail. "What have you done?" A Black woman advanced on the officers, a neighbor with his arm around her as she staggered forward, an accusing finger held before her. "You killed my boy," she shouted.

Others, alerted by the sound of squealing tires and gunshots, moved in behind her. A man took up the cry. "You murdered him."

More police arrived, moving the crowd back, but Lydia could feel the anger swelling around her. This threatened to get out of hand. And because this was an officer-involved shooting, ACPD would take over. "I'm a county detective," she shouted. "I witnessed what happened. We'll conduct a full and fair investigation."

"You lie!" someone shouted.

She approached the crowd. "You have my word."

They would have brushed a male officer aside, but there was something about this woman standing her ground that quieted the throng. They didn't leave, but watched in sullen silence as crime scene investigators arrived, accompanied by the county officer stationed at the jail who would lead the probe. Under his direction, Lydia began taking statements. She made a show of questioning the young policeman who'd fired the shots and now sat on his haunches, trembling as he struggled to control his shock at having killed another human being, this one a teenager.

It took her two hours to complete her work. The medical examiner's team carried the body away. A wrecker hauled the car. The crowd disbursed, muttering like distant thunder.

Lydia returned to her vehicle, got behind the wheel, and

buried her head in her hands. Despite an effort to keep her composure, tears welled in her eyes and overflowed. *What an incredible waste.* If the jury had convicted Theo Moseley, he'd still be alive. His mother would be dejected but not bereft. And there was a chance—slight, but conceivable—that incarceration would have done him some good, throwing him enough of a scare to redirect his path once he was released.

She had solved two murders, but someone had landed on her square and sent her back to Go. The game would never end. No matter how close her piece might move along the board, she'd never get to the home square.

Every day would bring a new competition with a new opponent. Neither she nor her fellow officers would ever win.

ACKNOWLEDGMENTS

The story is a work of fiction. Unless otherwise indicated, all the names, characters, events, and incidents in this book are the product of my imagination. While many locations referenced in this story exist, they are used in a fictitious manner, and none of the people or events depicted in these settings are real. Any resemblance to actual persons, living or dead, or actual events is purely coincidental.

I am indebted to Allegheny County Police Superintendent Christopher Kearns and his deputy, Lieutenant Venerando Costa, for giving me a tour of ACPD headquarters and answering dozens of my questions. They were generous with their time, and their expertise has helped me make this novel more realistic.

Superintendent Kearns has held every position in the department, from patrol officer up through the ranks to his current position. Like many law enforcement officers, his is a family business, with siblings and some of his children serving for law enforcement agencies.

I admire his dedication and the work of every member of the ACPD.

I am also grateful to Mandy Tinkey, Laboratory Director of the Allegheny County Medical Examiner, who provided the same courtesy to me while I was writing the previous story in this series, The Dead of Winter.

Special thanks to our older daughter, Kristen Dunder,

who, besides finding some typos, provided the current law on Currency Transaction Reports to the federal government.

Any mistakes or liberties I have taken with law enforcement or forensic practices are my own.

ABOUT THE AUTHOR

James H Lewis has published nine novels, seven in the
mystery genre, a family drama, and a historical novel set in
World War II Canada. His short stories have been
published by Mystery Tribune and in anthologies. He is a
former journalist whose work has appeared in the Washington Post, on ABC News, PBS, and the Eurovision News
Exchange. Lewis lives in Pittsburgh, PA and is a member of
Mystery Writers of America, PennWriters, and The
Author's Guild. Follow him at jameshlewis.com.

facebook.com/JamesLewisAuthor

bsky.app/profile/jameshlewis-author.bsky.social

instagram.com/jameshlewis_author

amazon.com/~/e/B07JMWL8NF

threads.net/@jameshlewis_author

linkedin.com/in/pittjimlewis

bookbub.com/authors/james-h-lewis

ALSO BY JAMES H LEWIS

THE LYDIA BARNWELL NOVELS

The Dead of Winter

THE CHIEF NOVAK NOVELS

Novak's Mission

Novak's Quest

Novak's Verdict

THE WORLD WAR II NOVEL

The Quadrant Conspiracy: The Plot to Kill FDR

THE ALAN RUDBERG NOVELS

Sins of Omission

Breaking News